One

The immense boat plowed through the water, bringing the men who would change the Maidens from virgins to women.

Aria knelt on the beach, waiting. Her head bent and her hands folded across her chest, she tried to focus on the upcoming ceremony—the physical ritual that would change her life as well as her body.

Would it hurt? She trembled, and her thighs weakened, threatening to crumple her to the sand.

"Focus." Her whispered command was inaudible above the ocean's waves. "Focus your mind before you are thought a fool."

With a firm mental shove, she set her fear aside and concentrated on her surroundings, looking for comfort or distraction. Diversion came in the form of a scarlet curl. A lock of hair dangled in front of her face, blown free from the pins that bound its companions in the traditional upswept style. Gently, she tossed her head, hoping to move it to a less obtrusive area.

Another loosened to join it.

The oars of the boat sounded like thunder as the men approached in the dimming light. Aria did not need to look up to know the two moons, the dark Grey Warrior and the Silver Maiden, rose in the sky behind her. Only once a season did the spheres rise side by side and make their way across the sky.

It was why they gathered tonight, the Warriors and the Maidens.

The wooden vessel rushed onto the sand, plowing to a stop and scattering everything in its path. Her breath caught, and the blood raced through her veins. Tonight she would cross the barrier from maid to woman, and in the morning, she would take her new position as an Apprentice to the Elders. She glanced up through her eyelashes just in time to see the Givers—Warrior priests who rarely left their Keep—walk down a wooden ramp and off the boat. None spoke as they lined up along the sands, their black cloaks billowing in the breeze as the cool light of the moons washed over them. They bowed their heads in homage to the Maidens. Their right hands rested on their sword hilts.

She was not ready. The urge to flee rose on a wave, threatening to overwhelm her, but thoughts of the Elders kept her in check. They had given her a home, companionship, and a purpose. She could not disappoint them now. Steeling her resolve, she vowed to do what was necessary. She would hold fast to her promises. Lowering her gaze, she waited.

Which Giver would take her on the journey? She had heard stories. Some women described it as an invasion— an act to be endured. Others said it was wondrous, and the physical union of two bodies was akin to Trancing. Which was true? Either or both?

She would know soon enough.

The choosing began as, one by one, each Maiden on the beach entered Trancer consciousness. Delving into the mind of her closest sister, she ascertained her needs and focused on her desires. What did her sister want in a lover? Which Giver was appropriate? Then, answers found, the Trancer let the Goddess guide her through the waves of Fate until she found the Warrior who met those needs. As their final charge, the Trancer called the name of the appropriate Giver for all to hear.

It was a test of skill, ability, and of each Maiden's deservedness to serve as an Apprentice. That was how it was done.

How it had always been done.

A bead of sweat slid from the base of Aria's neck to the small of her back as her closest friend, Iliana, rose and entered Trancer consciousness. Her breath erratic and her skin pale, Aria tensed at her friend's mental touch. Iliana was delving her mind, walking through her psyche, and finding her true desires. Desires unknown even to Aria.

Instinctively, Aria fought to hide her thoughts, but found them pushed wide open as Iliana continued her search.

Then, her mind grew silent. Iliana was gone and seeking the Warrior priest who would belong to Aria for the night. She called out the name of Aria's Giver.

Talon.

She was his Given, and because of his pride, he'd failed to protect her...

Talon stood and walked over to the hearth to let the Healer have the room she requested.

"Be patient, my brother," Lore said. "The Healer is well trained, and Aria is stronger than you think."

Talon tried to take comfort from the words, but failed. "I should have been here."

"Then what? Could you take on an entire Reaper army?"

"No, of course not." Talon's rising voice was subdued with a scathing look from the Healer. "But I could have saved her from this tragedy. I could have kept her safe," he finished with a whisper.

"This is odd." Both men turned at the Healer's comment. Still partially covered, Aria lay in exhausted sleep as the Healer tended her.

Talon strode over to the bed, fear racing through him. "What is it? What is wrong?"

The Healer continued to clean the blood from Aria's body. "Other than some scrapes, she does not have any serious wounds. I did not find any earlier but thought it due to the speed of my exam."

"Where did all the blood come from? Is it not hers?" Glancing at the soiled sheets on the floor, he feared the answer.

The Healer did not reply but continued washing, silently assessing her patient. Dipping the rag into the now red water, she pulled the blanket aside and began washing the blood from Aria's thighs. Talon did not turn away, dreading what the Healer might say but needing to know.

Finally, she stopped, placed the rag back in the bowl and left it. Standing, she covered Aria with Talon's cloak.

"Well?" Talon asked.

"It is hers."

His instincts for revenge and protection rising to the surface, Talon bristled. A question weighed heavy on his lips but had to be asked. "Was she violated?"

"No." The Healer's smile was a mixture of both sorrow and relief. "She bore a child."

To my critique partners:
Alexis, Amy, Cathy, Gina, & Nikki.
You made me a better writer.
To Gary, Glennis, Patrick, & Heather—Love You!
To my parents, who always believed in me.
And to my editor, Linda,
for giving a new author a chance.
Thank you.

Other Books by Sharron McClellan
THE SEEKER
(Coming in 2004)

The Given

***

Sharron McClellan

ImaJinn
Books

THE GIVEN
Published by ImaJinn Books, a division of ImaJinn

ISBN: 1-893896-88-9

10 9 8 7 6 5 4 3 2 1

Books are available at quantity discounts when used to promote products or services. For information please write to: Marketing Division, ImaJinn Books, P.O. Box 545, Canon City, CO 81215-0545, or call toll free 1-877-625-3592.

Cover design by Patricia Lazarus

ImaJinn Books, a division of ImaJinn
P.O. Box 545, Canon City, CO 81212-0545
Toll Free: 1-877-625-3592
http://www.imajinnbooks.com

Aria glanced up as his name sounded over the sands, but her chosen Warrior did not acknowledge the call. Which one was he? They all looked so much alike. Well-trained fighters, they all bore the muscles and scars that came from their favored profession. Most were tall, almost frighteningly so. Like the *kota* trees that grew alone in the dunes, they appeared invincible and enduring. As if nothing could fell them.

The still-warm sands shifted as Iliana sank down, spent from the necessary mind trance.

Aria closed her eyes. Time to prove her ability as a Trancer. Letting the outward sounds fade, she cleared her mind and forced her thoughts into the gray realm that lay between the physical world and the spiritual world of the Trancer. As if in a dream, she rose to her feet. Within moments, she passed through the colorless void and into the netherworld of Iliana's mind. Thoughts, like currents, flowed over Aria. Blues and green. White, as smooth as down and brighter than the sun, captured her attention. It was not what she sought.

She turned her search towards desire, and a deep, rich red emerged. Like a drop of scented oil, it hung heavy with unexpressed passion, naming all Iliana ever wanted in a lover. All she ever desired.

Swiftly, Aria left Iliana's thoughts and dove into the currents of life, flowing over them, through them, and embracing their brilliant colors. She called to the Goddess, the deity who gave them all breath, to help her in her search. The answer came in the form of a claret flame—a twin to the red drop that was her friend's desire. *Ah, Iliana's Giver.* She touched his mind, but his inborn mental shielding allowed only a cursory glance. It was enough. She called his name.

What seemed like moments later, she knelt back in the sand, as tired and mentally exhausted as her best friend. It was over. Were her words true? Did she even speak? As the memory faded, she saw Iliana smile. She must have said something. Aria relaxed. Tucking her robe under her knees, she forced her labored breathing to slow.

The High Mother sang, ending the ceremony. The song spoke of faith, tradition, and the blessings of the Goddess. The Maidens rose, and the Givers walked towards them, ready to do their duty. Her legs still shaky, Aria stumbled over the hem of her robe. A hand—warm, callused and powerfully male—caught her elbow, steadying her. She turned her gaze upwards too see her rescuer. He was impossibly tall with hair as dark as katah' fur. The deep strands looked as silky as the predator's coat. Her fingers itched to run through it and take pleasure in its texture alone—if she dared to loosen it from the ceremonial cloth ties that bound it behind him.

He smiled, and she knew. It was Talon. Her Giver.

"Do not look so surprised." His voice, deep and masculine, flowed over her like warmed stroking oils.

"I am not surprised," Aria answered truthfully. "I am merely pleased you are agreeable to my eye."

Talon chuckled. "As you are to mine." He clasped her hand in his. "Let us go to your chamber."

"So soon?" Her panic rose despite her intentions and Giver's air of assurance and strength. "You are ready?"

He chuckled again. "Not so soon. We have all night."

All night? What did he have planned? She attempted to hide her shock and ignorance by ducking her head and pushing her wayward curls back from her brow.

He stopped her with a gentle hand, his fingers drawing the locks forward again. "Leave them. Please."

She nodded, unable to speak.

He brought her hand to his mouth, kissed the palm, and then nipped a slender fingertip.

A low growl emerged from her throat, surprising Aria.

"See, you are more prepared than you thought. Come, show me your room."

She pulled her hand away. "A moment, please?"

Talon gave a single nod and crossed his arms over his broad chest, waiting.

Aria took a deep breath and lowered her gaze. So many emotions coursed through her—apprehension, fear, excitement and, yes, even desire. She dared a glance at Talon. Wide shouldered and proud as he stood waiting for her, his stance was fierce. His strength, pride, and beauty made her want to pet him, but she knew it would cost her.

Had Iliana chosen true?

She banished the thought. *Of course.* He was her Giver.

Her lack of trust would be most displeasing to the mothers and a slap to Iliana.

She met his eyes. They were dark, like looking in a mirror at night. "This way, Talon." She liked the way his name sounded on her lips, and the corners of her mouth crept upward.

Holding her head high, she walked towards the Tower with his hand in hers, prepared to make the Elders proud and to follow the ceremony that tradition dictated she must.

***

He fills the room, Aria thought with awe as Talon entered her chamber and closed the door behind him. She walked to the fireplace, turning when the tip of his sword rapped against a vase of *isi* flowers, spinning them off a low wooden table. With a Warrior's speed, he caught the vase before it hit the floor and placed it back in its original position. He shot her a look of sheepish apology and cautiously passed by a setting of bread and wine.

His obvious care showed a thoughtfulness she did not expect from a man trained in the art of war. It pleased her.

Still, she trembled as the unknown loomed before her.

"Are you frightened?" Talon asked, coming up behind her as she watched the firelight dance on the stone walls.

"A little. I have heard stories of what this night will be like."

His breath caressed the back of her neck, disturbing the escaped locks of hair. "All of them true, no doubt."

Her skin prickled at the intimacy of the gesture. She turned to face him. "True?"

"Yes, for the person who lived the story, it is always true." He tilted her chin up with a sun-darkened hand. "Your experience will be your own. As true for you, as theirs was for them."

"What will my story be?" Aria asked, curious as to his thoughts. Talon's eyes were kind, and they crinkled when he smiled at her. But his imposing size made her wonder if he would be as gentle as she would wish.

He reached around Aria and gathered her into his arms. "Whatever you want it to be," he whispered in her ear. Letting his hands glide up her back, he buried his fingers in her hair.

Aria sighed as he massaged her scalp and released her hair from the pins, letting it tumble past her shoulders and down to her waist. "It is brighter than fire." He pressed the curls to his lips and grazed her skin with his palm.

He released her hair, and Aria sighed again, but this time with disappointment. His touch was pleasurable. Intimate. Iliana had chosen well.

He smiled at her reaction and walked over to pour two glasses of wine. Motioning her over to his side, he handed her a goblet.

"Sip," he commanded, his deep voice soft in its demands.

Aria raised the glass to her lips and let the tart liquid flow over her tongue.

"It will help you relax." He took a drink from his chalice.

"I am relaxed," Aria lied, hoping the firelight hid the blush she knew crept up her neck.

Talon chuckled, and she knew her lie had failed.

She took another gulp of wine. It burned in her stomach. She broke a piece of bread from one of the loaves and offered it to him. Talon took the bread, but did not eat. Instead, he broke a smaller piece off and pressed it to Aria's lips. "Here. Eat before the wine takes you away."

Shyly, Aria opened her mouth and let him feed her like a cub. She tasted the salt on his skin as she plucked a piece away with her teeth and tongue. Her lips tingled at the feel of his hand on her jaw, his fingertips on her mouth.

His scent of musk and leather slid over her skin, overwhelming her. Her lids grew heavy. She wanted more of his touch. More of this moment. She wanted him. A surge of desire rolled from her stomach to the juncture between her thighs where it pulsed with an intriguing heaviness.

"Talon."

He answered her whispered plea with the taste of more bread on her tongue. Bit by bit, he fed her until the bread disappeared. Then, he brushed the crumbs away from her lips with a callused thumb. She experienced a pang of disappointment that there was no more.

"Now I know you will be present in all respects," Talon

murmured.

Aria nodded as if she knew of what he spoke, but she did not. She knew nothing. She knew of the sensations but not how to assuage them. Did he feel the same?

My Goddess, what do I do? She faced the fire, letting the warmth of the bright flames soothe her restless spirit. She wondered if Iliana felt so impatient, so unsure, so alive, and so greedy. Or was it only herself?

Talon stood behind her, his great size as tangible as if he touched her.

But he did not. He waited.

For what? For her? Passion rolled through her again, urging her to act, to complete that which it wanted. Naiveté pleaded caution. "Would you like me to touch you?" she asked, wanting to be forward but not sure how.

Talon turned her around to face him. "If you want to, my little one."

Little one? "My name is Aria. I may be inexperienced, but I am not a child."

Talon pulled her close, resting his rough cheek on top of her head. "It is an endearment, not an insult, but I will do as you wish." Suddenly, he swept her off the floor and into his arms. "Now, do you still want to touch me?"

"Do you want me to?" Aria wrapped her arms around his neck, praying he would not drop her. "Is it proper?"

Talon shook his head at the comment "How did you get to be so innocent? Others are eager when the ritual is upon them. Sometimes frighteningly so." His lips quirked into a smile. "Why so innocent, my Aria?"

She blushed. Her name sounded sensual on his lips. Rich as wine. "I have come to the Tower only recently. I do not know the ways of which you speak."

"Where did you live before?"

"In the Laini settlement."

Talon nodded. "Ah, the mountains. I hear they are given to superstition and follow the old ways—the ways before the Goddess brought us wisdom and understanding."

Aria bristled at the comment, but she could not deny it. "It is true. When my family found out about my mental abilities, they sent me away. They do not suffer Trancers to live among them."

It surprised her to see compassion in his eyes at her comment.

"So, you never knew about the ways between a man and a woman?"

"As I told you, I have heard stories, but no more than that. I want to please you, but I am unsure of what to do. Fearful."

"Name your fear, and I will conquer it."

He would kill fear for her? A smile lit upon her lips. "That I will disappoint you and, therefore, disappoint the Elders."

Talon placed a soft kiss on Aria's lips. She was so sweet. Her eyes were the color of the first leaves, and her skin was as soft as the petal of a flower. She was also frightened. She shivered at his touch. "You could never disappoint me."

At his reassurance, her body relaxed in his arms. "Can you kiss me back?" he asked.

"If you would like."

"I would. Very much." He bent his head down again and hid a grin as her lips reached for his, answering his request. His other Givens had been kissed before, and some more than that. But not this one. No, she was untried in all ways.

Their lips met, skimmed each other's flesh with the tenderest of touches.

Now, he did smile as she pulled away, breathless and fearless all at once. She was wonderfully brave, trying to appear calm when he knew her body trembled at the thought of their upcoming union.

He touched her lips with his again, gently forcing them apart, not giving her time to react in fear. Slowly, he tasted her. It was a heady feeling. She tasted like wine and bread. Like new honey. Like a Maiden who had never been kissed. She stiffened at the gentle intrusion before she melted into him.

Soon, he would melt into her. He hardened at the thought, straining against the clothes that confined him.

"Aria?" He spoke her name against her lips.

"Umm," she answered, her eyes lidded.

"It is time."

Her eyes shot open. "Time? I thought we would eat

first." She wiggled loose from his arms and ran to the table. "See, here is fruit and more bread."

He closed the distance between them. "No more food."

"How about wine?"

"Certainly no more wine. I want us both to have our wits about us for what is about to happen."

"We may get hungry."

He sat down in one of the heavy wooden chairs and pulled Aria onto his lap. "We shall feast on each other."

"We could get thirsty."

"I will quench your thirst." Talon nuzzled her, biting the soft spot where slender neck met pale shoulder.

"But—"

"But what?" Talon kissed her ear.

"If you get thirsty it could interrupt your concentration."

"The only thing interrupting my concentration is you," Talon replied. She shifted abruptly as if wanting to leave, and compassion overwhelmed him. She was frightened, but tradition gave neither of them a choice. There was just one way to alleviate her worries now—push past them and continue with the ceremony. "Now, let us see how I can interrupt your concentration." He stood up, taking her with him.

Swiftly, surely, Talon carried Aria over to the bed and laid her on top of the silken covers. The firelight flickered over her, burnishing her skin.

"I am afraid," she whispered.

"I know, but your fear will leave soon enough. Trust me in this." Unbuckling his sword, he set the scabbard aside, unsheathed the blade, and placed it on the bed above Aria's head with its razor-sharp edge facing them. Leaning over her, one hand on each side of her body, he gazed into her eyes. Neither moved as Talon spoke. "I am the Giver. Do you accept what I have to give?" The ancient words hung like a heartbeat between them.

"I am the Given. I accept." Her quiet voice filled the room.

Talon breathed a sigh of relief, glad to see Aria was stronger than her fear. Straddling her, a knee on each side of her thighs, he reached down and untied her robe, letting the pale cloth fall away from her body. "Open your eyes, Aria," he commanded, his voice husky with promise. "See how pleased I am with what you are offering me."

Aria peeked through her lashes, and Talon chuckled to see her eyes widen further when she saw the evidence of his desire, straining against his leather breeches.

"Now, I will feast." The hunger in his tone spoke of neither bread nor fruit but of Aria. "See, your breasts are ripe and waiting for me." He leaned down to suckle upon a pink nipple.

Aria moaned at the sensations that radiated from where Talon kissed her with his lips and teeth. Her stomach twisted into a knot, and the area between her thighs constricted with each sensual tug. "What are you doing?" she managed to ask with a little gasp.

"I am tasting you. You did worry I would be hungry." He placed a hand under her waist and lifted her closer to his mouth.

Aria whimpered with pleasure as he continued to ravish her, captivating her with one sensation after another as he made a path from one turgid nipple to the other. It was exquisitely uncomfortable, and she wanted more.

"Magnificent," he murmured, pulling away from her heated flesh. "You are magnificent."

Aria's answer was another little moan, of both pleasure and chagrin, as Talon's free hand pushed her robe off her shoulders, pinning her arms by her side and leaving her exposed. Warmth made its way from her toes to the top of her head, and she knew she blushed. "Are you sure this is part of the ritual?" she stammered.

"Anything I can do to pleasure you is part of the ritual. Do you enjoy what I am doing?"

Aria nodded. "But I feel odd. Hot and nervous all at once."

Talon chuckled. "Then I am doing it right." Still straddling her, he sat up and pulled his rough shirt over his head, throwing it to the floor. Pulling Aria up to him, he slid her robe off, freeing her arms and laying bare her body, before he lowered her back onto the bed. His broad chest shadowed her from the firelight as he slid down her body, skin gliding over skin, and laved her bellybutton with his tongue.

Aria bolted upright. "This cannot be right."

Talon glided back up her body, now damp with heat and his tender ministrations, and kissed her, urging her back, "Does it feel good? Does it feel right?" His hands stroked her from shoulder to waist.

She pressed against him, her body urging her to finish what her mind doubted. "Umm, yes, but I have never heard the others discussing such matters."

Talon's brow furrowed at the comment. "Forget what the others have said. The Given ceremony is different for everyone. I will not hurt you, and nothing we do is wrong as long as it is pleasurable."

Aria wanted to believe him. She brushed a single strand of hair away from his face and saw something unexpected, concern and caring. Did he care that she enjoy this experience? It was not a prerequisite that she did. Only that she get through it and begin her new life as a woman within the group. Some enjoyed the ritual. Others simply endured it. It did not make a difference when the results were the same.

She saw it mattered to her Giver. Anxiety lifted like a weight from her heart. She took his hand in hers and kissed the palm, noting its scars from previous Given ceremonies. "I am ready."

He nibbled on her neck. "No, not yet, but you will be." His hands, experienced in pleasure, roved over her body, learning every inch. His mouth followed not far behind, tasting and licking and nibbling, until Aria found herself begging Talon to finish what he had started. Her skin was as sensitive as the air before a storm, and her insides were wound tight. She was sure she was dying, and only Talon kept her from crossing over to the other side.

"Now you are ready," he whispered. Moving to stand at the end of the bed, he pushed his leather breeches down his legs and to the floor, kicking them aside. When he straightened, Aria's eyes widened at the sight of his erection pressed hard against his abdomen. Coming back to bed, he nudged her thighs apart with his knee and settled against her. He stared into her eyes. "I am the Giver. Do you accept what I give to you, freely and with no reservations?"

Aria nodded, frantic that Talon do something, anything, to make her complete—even if it meant causing her pain. "I am the Given. I accept with no reservations and more than freely. I am begging you to give to me what you must." Her nails dug into his back as he reached down with one hand and placed himself at her entrance. She glanced downward. "Will it hurt? You are so..." She hesitated, unwilling to offend her lover. "...large."

Talon smiled, his teeth white in the dimming firelight. "You will feel a pressure, but no pain. Then, once you are used to me, you will feel pleasure. I promise you."

She nodded acceptance.

Talon gritted his teeth and pushed against Aria, the thin membrane that proclaimed her Maiden's status blocking his path.

He pushed harder, and she squeezed her eyes shut. Her breath came in little pants. "Do I hurt you?" he asked. His promise to cause her no harm pained him, but he meant to keep his word. He was ready to die from lack of fulfillment, but if she were not ready then he would withdraw and continue to prepare her.

"No," Aria replied with truth in her voice. "Just pressure, as you promised. It is the anticipation that makes me tremble."

"Then let's end the wait, for both of us." He kissed her forehead. "Open your eyes, Aria. I want to see your soul when the change occurs. I want to see you change from maiden to woman."

Aria opened her eyes.

Talon kissed her brow again. "No pain. I promise."

She leaned up and kissed his mouth. "I trust you."

"I will guard that trust." Reaching down between them with one hand, he found the button of flesh he knew would bring her ecstasy. Slowly, firmly, he stroked it with his thumb.

"Talon," Aria cried. "What is happening?"

She bucked against him and cried out. Her eyes locked with his, caught up in passion. Her slim legs wrapped around his hips.

"Aria," Talon cried hoarsely. Reaching for the Warriors' blade that rested on the bed above them, he gripped it, letting the razor edge slice his palms open. Blood for blood, as he simultaneously broke through the barrier that hid his Given's depths.

Aria's cries sounded, and convulsions gripped his member as he slowly pressed his full length into her. He let go of his blade, the burning wounds in his palms keeping him focused. Gritting his teeth, he pulled away before he let himself sink back into her. He continued the rhythm, holding his own pleasure at bay until Aria's cries became wilder, and she tightened around him again. He watched her, loving her eagerness, her lack of guile.

She arched her back, and he knew she was oblivious to anything but the pleasure that coursed through her body. Passion and innocence in one woman, she was everything he wanted but had never had until now.

Her fingernails raked his sides. It was time for his suffering to end. In a maelstrom of light and pleasure, he spilled himself into her with a cry, hearing his Given call his name as she reached her release.

Carefully, he settled his weight onto Aria as she still convulsed around him. Her cries grew breathy and weaker until she gave a great sigh, and her body went limp. Holding her to his chest, he rolled over onto his side, taking her with him.

Unwinding the strips of cloth that bound his hair, he coiled them around his hands before he pulled her closer. His dark hair fell over his shoulder to mingle with her red curls. His chest tightened as she snuggled against him, and the desire to protect her crashed over him. He stroked her hair, comforting and protecting her, cherishing his Given with every murmur, as she fell asleep in his arms.

***

Aria woke to find the morning light streaming through the windows and her back pressed against Talon's chest. She wiggled with pleasure, enjoying the warmth of his body. He rewarded her with a sleepy murmur as his well-muscled arm pulled her closer.

She brought his hand to her lips for a kiss. Uncurling his fingers, she unwound the cloth from his hands and traced the hairline cut he had received during the ritual.

The ritual. Now she knew of the pleasure that could occur between a man and a woman. Languidly, she stretched, mentally scoffing at the previous dreams and fears her Giver had put to rest.

She turned over and gazed at Talon. He was as

impressive in the morning as he had been in the deep of night's passion. She reached out and traced a scar that ran from the corner of his eye to below his jaw. She had not noticed it yesterday. Today, it showed white against his tan skin. *A Warriors' mark.* Later, she would ask him to tell her the story of the battle, but for now, she wanted to indulge. Feeling coy, she kissed him. His lips were warm upon hers. "Wake up," she murmured.

He replied with a grumpy, "No."

She pressed her lips against his again, prolonging the moment until he awakened and returned the kiss. He tasted like wine and musk. Like sex and love. Hard and ready, he pressed against her stomach.

"Aria." Her name was husky on his lips, a plea for her to welcome him into her body.

She answered by throwing her leg over his and guiding him into her welcoming depths.

Her breath hissed from between her lips as he filled her. "Talon, please," she begged. "I am eager for you."

The only reply was a low chuckle as he supported the small of her back with his hand and rocked against her.

Aria thought she would die as Talon sensuously assaulted her body. Her heart raced, and her soul flew as passion devoured her like a wild animal took its prey. Would it never end? Her thoughts expanded, and the forces of Trancing began building inside her with each stroke. Each breath, each touch, assailed her thoughts. Pressure in her mind, as well as her body, clamored for release.

Like a dam collapsing with the weight of the water behind it, her passion shattered both her mind shield and Talon's. Their thoughts meshed, and Aria clung to him as his sensations overwhelmed her.

Shock. Shock and alarm at her intrusion. Talon's split-second of fear raced through Aria, and she felt her heart would stop.

It did not. Instead, Talon's shock changed. Transformed to interest and a burning curiosity of the forbidden. A desire to know more. To know her.

It was all the encouragement Aria needed, and she flowed into him, past thoughts and past reality, until she was so deep inside him that she lost herself.

A flash of blades. His first kiss. Searing pain. Honor

duty, shame, and laughter. It was all there, a lifetime of experience and emotion, overpowering her and filling her. She took it in like a starving child takes a loaf of bread. She lived his wants, desires, and needs.

And he lived hers. He felt the pain when her family abandoned her. He tasted her fear of her gift, heard her cries when she wept alone at night. He felt it all, lived it, and with a Warrior's strength, bound her emotional wounds with his soul.

He healed her and was healed.

For a brief moment, a heartbeat in an infinite number of heartbeats, they were the same. There was no beginning and there was no end as they joined and release took them, binding their souls.

It was less than paradise and more than life, and Aria knew neither of them would ever be the same.

Then, the emotional bond slipped, dissolving like smoke in the wind.

Talon rolled away, physically separating himself from Aria, but not before she felt one last emotion.

Shame.

Talon felt shame and dishonor for what they had done.

She wanted to cry. She did not. She could not, because there was no shame in her heart. What had happened was right. She felt it in her bones.

The morning shadows moved across the floor, as they lay apart, absorbing what happened.

"What should we do now?" Talon raised himself up on his elbows, his squared jaw rigid with barely restrained anger. Aria knew it was not directed at her, but at himself.

She shook her head. "I am not sure. I have heard of a true joining spoken of only in whispers. I have never heard of it happening."

Trancers were not supposed to delve into their lover's psyche, and an experienced Trancer would not have done so, even inadvertently. But she was inexperienced. She was a novice, and that was why the Elders chose the Warriors to serve as Givers. A Warrior's mental shielding was inborn and kept out Trancers or anyone who would know their thoughts.

Yet, somehow, she had managed to break through Talon's shield.

And he had let her.

"We must forget we joined." Talon sat up, his head in his hands. "We must pretend it never happened."

Aria took a deep breath. "It is too late," she whispered. Honor demanded that she show him the proof. Rising to her knees next to him, she raised her eyes to his and watched for his reaction.

It was immediate. "Your eyes. What happened to your eyes?"

"Have you heard the stories?"

"Of course, but they are stories."

"No, they are true." She did not need a mirror to see that her once pale green eyes had darkened and were now the color of the heart of the forest. "If a Trancer binds her soul with another, her eyes go through the change, reflecting the depth of the union. Green becomes deep forest and blue becomes night."

Talon touched her cheek, tracing it with a fingertip. His look spoke of disbelief. "If we are truly bound, if I have a piece of your soul, do you have a piece of mine?"

"Yes."

He withdrew his hand, and she saw the impact of her words strike home as his eyes clouded with wariness. "Do you know everything about me? Where I came from? Who I am?"

"No, only images, pieces really, of your life," she said, knowing any explanation would be awkward and unclear but also knowing she had to try. "Mostly, I felt you as you did me. Your emotions. The things—" She hesitated, struggling to make herself clear. "The places in your soul that make you a good man."

Her heart fell at seeing his eyes cloud further.

"You had no right. Could you not stop this binding?"

"Not once started." Aria bit her lower lip at the anger in his accusation. "It was not my intention to join with you, but it is done."

"Perhaps, but how can I accept it?" Swinging his legs over the edge of the bed, he bent to retrieve his clothes. Standing, he turned his back to her and dressed in silence.

"Talon?"

"Yes." He yanked his tunic over his head.

"I did not ask your acceptance. I ask for forgiveness."

She fought to keep her voice from breaking.

"I am not angry with you. I am angry with myself for my own lack of strength. I should have stopped you, but I did not." He faced her, his eyes bright with pain. "I welcomed you. I faltered in my duty."

Aria flinched at the cruel judgment he passed upon himself. "No. I refuse to believe there is fault in this, Talon. How can I when I carry you here?" She laid a hand on her breast. "To say there is fault is like cutting out a piece of my heart."

"You are young, and youth can be foolish. The bond you feel blinds you to the truth."

"And what truth is that? That we are not join—"

Talon stopped her speech with a gentle finger against her lips. "I am a Warrior and live by a different code. On my honor, I swore to do you no harm, and I broke that vow with my negligence. I abandoned my duty and must pay for my actions."

Aria wrapped a bed cloth around her body and stood up, grasping Talon's arm with her hands. "It is wrong if duty would punish you for my mistakes. Stay here with me, and we will speak with the Elders. I am sure they will understand and help."

"How? A joining cannot be undone. Perhaps they would ask the Council to forgive my lapse in judgment?" Talon shook his head. "You were in my mind. You know I will not forsake my honor to avoid punishment."

Aria dropped her hands from his body and turned away, not wanting him to see the sorrow in her eyes. She listened as he dressed, buckling his sword and pulling on his boots. She refused to turn and watch him as he walked to the door.

His footsteps paused.

"If you truly carry a piece of my soul, you know I will broach no more dishonor for either of us."

"There is no *if*. I carry your soul, as you carry mine."

His denial was unvoiced, but she thought she heard it in her mind. He probably hoped she would forget him, forget the joining, but she knew it would never happen. She would remember her time with him whenever she looked in a mirror and saw her own dark-eyed reflection looking back at her.

"Good-bye." The door closed behind him, swinging shut with a dull thud.

She refused to cry. If he were strong enough to leave, then she would be strong enough to let him go.

She walked across the room and onto the balcony that faced towards the water. Still in disarray from last night, her hair fluttered about her shoulders. She clutched the bed cloth closer and sat on the stone railing to watch Talon as he walked towards the boat where other Warriors waited.

Perhaps he denied his heart, but she would not deny hers. If only he had considered staying, she might have told him the other reason for her physical change.

But he had not, and she could not.

She placed a hand on her flat belly and knew that soon it would grow rounded.

Trancer's eyes also darkened when new life began.

Two

He had not come back. Again.

From a window high above, Aria watched in silence as a group of Warriors departed and wondered if Talon stayed away because of her. Three seasons and three Given ceremonies had passed since she last saw him. Three seasons since she had turned from him in anger and misunderstanding. Three seasons since she had watched him leave.

Three seasons of regret.

Misery rolled over her like a water-laden blanket, and the surrounding currents of life shifted to reflect her bleak thoughts. Pain and loss dominated the flow, dragging her deeper into regret. With a mental 'oomph,' she blocked her mind. She did not need the currents to remind her how foolish she had acted.

She should have said good-bye. She owed Talon that much. They were joined. With a sigh, she turned away from the window and the sight of the festivities below and pressed her hand against her child-swollen belly.

The baby kicked. At least she carried a part of Talon within and, so, kept a piece of him close. A tiny light to fight the dark. She had not lost everything. She had their son, Tarik.

She wondered what Talon would say, what he would think, if he knew she carried his son. Would he have returned?

She knew the answer. Despite the Warrior code of never knowing their blood, he would have returned. And in doing so, given up all that he was and all that he had worked for.

He might forgive her if he did, but he would never forgive himself, and she could not permit that.

Cumbersome with her protruding belly, Aria moved over to the wooden table that occupied the middle of the room. One hand supporting the small of her back, she began sorting through the herbs, scented oils, and candles that took up one end. There were many, and all stood in wait for use in the birthing of her son.

"Everything is still there."

Startled, Aria turned, her gown swirling around her ankles. Iliana stood in the doorway, watching her.

"I know. I just wanted to make sure."

Smiling, Iliana crossed the room, picked up a bottle of pale yellow oil, opened the stopper, sniffed it, and then pulled away in disgust. "That smells like the stables after a long rain. What is it for?"

"If I lose consciousness during childbirth, this will bring me back." Aria took the bottle from her friend, put the stopper back in, and set the vial back down on the wooden surface.

"If only to get away from the stench." Iliana wrinkled her nose again.

Aria chuckled. She had not realized how much she had missed Iliana until just this moment. She embraced her. "I am glad you are here."

Iliana returned the hold. "I am sorry I have not been able to see you more." Pulling back, she held Aria out at arm's length. "Look how big the babe has grown."

Aria turned from side to side. "He is getting bigger, is he not?"

Her friend nodded and drew Aria over to a small couch covered with soft pillows. "Come, tell me how your time goes. Have you kept busy?"

Aria sat next to her friend and shrugged. "What can I do? The Healer worries about my health. I walk, I eat, and I prepare for the babe. She refuses to let me do anything else."

Iliana reached over and took Aria's hand in hers. "She has cause for concern. You are as pale as parchment and, with the exception of the babe, as thin as a reed. If he were not as large as a melon, I would not even think you carried a child within."

Aria flushed. "Do you think I neglect my child?"

Iliana's eyes opened wide, and she drew back. "No. I think you neglect yourself. I worry that you will waste away after the babe is born, if not before."

Aria took a deep breath and stopped herself before a harsh retort tripped off her tongue. Her anger was not with Iliana or the Healer. Her anger was at herself for her own physical weakness.

Her father's voice echoed through her mind, telling

her how useless she was. She still felt his hatred and anger for her being the eldest and a *girl*.

Just the opposite, Iliana's love shone like a beacon of hope, breaking through the painful memories and banishing them. How could she doubt her friend's intentions, even for a moment? Iliana offered her friendship like a child offers trust—with no strings or conditions.

It was more than her family had ever offered.

Aria smoothed her hair with a nervous gesture. "I am sorry. I find myself out of sorts and impatient now that the babe is so near to birth. Please forgive my impulsive words."

Iliana waved the apology away with a laugh. "They say women who are with child are sometimes unreasonable."

Aria's brow rose. "I am glad to see you still possess a sense of humor."

Iliana's smile faded. "Since you so rarely find lightness anymore, I try to have enough for us both."

Aria opened her mouth to reply but found no words. Instead, she stood and went back to the table, not wanting her friend to see the truth of her perceptions. "Tell me how training goes." Eyes focused downward, she lined the glass jars into a neat row. "I hear that being an Apprentice is much more demanding than being a Maiden. Is it true?"

"I take it you do not want to discuss what is bothering you?"

"I cannot," Aria replied, wishing Iliana would accept the change in subject. She moved the bowls of herbs, grouping them neatly together.

"Do you distrust me?"

Aria shook her head. "No. You are my greatest friend, but I fear that if I spoke, you would feel compelled to tell the Elders. I cannot put you in such a position. Our friendship means too much to me. *You* mean too much to me. I would not risk this."

Iliana rose from the couch, joined Aria at the table, and began to move the bottles and jars back to their original positions. Picking up a box of dried petals she sniffed, this time smiling before she put it down. "It gives me great joy to hear that our friendship means as much to you as it does to me."

Aria warmed at the words.

Iliana continued. "You can tell me anything, and I will keep silent. I was raised in the Tower, but my upbringing does not make me any less compassionate or understanding. It does not make me any less your friend. Please, believe me."

Aria nodded. "I do believe you." Her hands moved up her arms, holding herself still. "You are as close as my sister, but please, for now, let my thoughts be my own. Later, when the memories are less painful, I can answer all your questions."

"I understand." Iliana's voice softened, and she focused her gaze on the table before her. "I fear your aching soul drains your energy, but I will wait until you are ready to speak."

Looking up, she brightened. "Do you really want to hear about my Apprentice training? I can tell you what to expect when you join us."

"Please," Aria said, grateful for the change in topic. "I am hungry for news."

"You heard correctly. It is difficult. We spend much time learning to read the nuances of the currents of life." Her hands gestured in the air around her. "The Elders say that only when we can tell a sob from a wail, and a want from a need, can we move up in status."

Aria grimaced. "I shall have much to learn to catch up to you. I can only feel strong emotions and the obvious. Nuances, I fear, are hidden to me."

"You will learn. Besides, I overheard one of the Elders say that you possess a strong natural talent. It will allow you to progress to Elder status faster than most."

"Truly?"

Iliana tossed her head. "It is probably why they are so anxious to bring you into the class as soon as the babe is born. Goddess forbid that you should do something without proper training." A flip of dark hair and a matching smile belied her good-natured sarcasm.

Did the Elders know that she and Talon were joined? Aria's eyes widened at the thought. "They exaggerate my abilities." She hoped her argument did not sound as weak as her voice.

"Do not underestimate yourself. The Elders are amazed

that being raised in Laini did not extinguish your Trancing abilities. One said that only a Trancer with strong natural talent could have caught up with those of us raised here."

Every muscle in Aria's body relaxed at the explanation. The Elders were unaware of the joining. "It is nothing."

Iliana laid her hand on Aria's shoulder. "No, it is something. Have you ever wondered how you were able to come to us so late in life but function on the same Trancer level?"

"No."

Iliana shook her head in well-meant disgust. "If you would pay more attention to your training, and less time thinking you are inferior due to birth, you would know that you are special." She placed her other hand on Aria's shoulder, turning her. "Right now. Tell me what you sense."

"As you wish," Aria said and lightly touched the surrounding currents with her mind. She saw Tarik, a life spark, bright with innocence. Then, anger, misery, and pain overwhelmed her. She pulled back out and shook her head. It was as before. Her regrets buried the brighter currents that flowed throughout the Tower.

"Well, what did you sense?"

"The festival. Happiness," Aria replied, glad her friend did not look into her mind to see the lie. To carry the burden was difficult enough without foisting it off on another.

Iliana smiled. "Good. With the celebration I would be surprised if you saw anything else."

***

Thunder shook the Tower walls. Aria sat up, the wooden frame of her bed trembling with the force of the sound. Her heart beat as fast as a frightened *hari*. The room was dim, barely lit by the fire's dying embers.

Sliding her legs over the edge of the bed, she pulled a robe about her shoulders and walked to the window.

Clouds obscured the moons and starlight, blackening the night sky. She strained her eyes, waiting for the next flash of fire from the sky to signal another clap.

Nothing.

Instead, another boom sounded closer and louder, and the floor trembled beneath her feet.

Aria frowned. It was not thunder. Something was

wrong. Very wrong. She turned, and the boom sounded again, this time knocking her off her feet with its force.

She fell to her knees, the candle rolling from her grasp. Loose mortar from the stones above fell into her hair.

What was happening?

Scared for herself and the others who dwelt within the Tower walls, she reached out with her mind. The currents were the same as before—heavy with regret and anger. Now, there was another element. One that was missing earlier. There was fear.

It was not just hers. It was everyone's, and it was so thick it was almost tangible. She would have to push past both if she were to read the currents of life and find its source.

Mentally, she took a deep breath, reached out psychic hands, and parted the black. It swirled like slick webbing, flowing over her clothes and through her skin. Pain, rage, and disharmony lay beyond. She tranced deeper, sinking into the current. Letting the black bind her.

Death. The Tower. A man wanted them dead. She saw him standing, shouting out orders. A black and white mask obscured his face, its ragged stripes meant to confuse all that saw him. A black robe flowed from his shoulders to the ground. He waved a sword above his head.

His smile was death's grin.

Aria flinched, but stayed within, mesmerized by the grinning stranger and his obvious hatred of all within the Tower.

How could she have missed this? How could she have ignored the depth of the black, thinking it hers? Her darkness was but a flicker when compared to the shadows this man carried within.

She was a fool for being so careless, and now all were in danger.

Including her child.

The babe within kicked as if rebelling against what she saw. She pulled out of the darkness, her hands wrapped around her belly, protecting it. It rippled beneath her palms.

The door to her chamber flung open, slamming against the wall.

Still on her knees, Aria lifted her head to see the Healer

hurrying towards her. She wore a deep green robe with its hood pulled over her graying hair.

"Aria. Are you hurt?" The Healer bent down to help her to her feet.

"No. Merely bruised." Aria rose and then stumbled, as the child kicked harder.

One hand braced against her back, she straightened.

Pain. Shooting pain rushed from her belly to her spine and through her legs.

The Healer caught her before she fell.

"What is it? What is wrong?"

Aria groaned aloud as the sharp agony worked its way through her torso. The babe. Something was wrong. He struggled to leave her body.

She gripped the Healer's robe. "Please." Her voice was a strangled whisper as she fought to speak. "My child. He comes."

The Healers eyes widened. "Now? He cannot."

Aria's muscles contracted, and she doubled over. "No matter. He comes."

With faltering steps, she allowed the Healer to walk her to the bed. Groaning, she pressed a pillow against her rippling belly as the Healer put one under the small of her back.

The Healer's voice was urgent in her ear. "You must stop the babe. We are under siege. I came to take you to safety."

"I know, but it is too late." Aria gripped the Healer's hand in her own as another wave of pain washed over her.

"Try, Aria. Please. Reapers climb the walls. They will kill us all."

Aria's green eyes shone black in the dim light. "The Warriors. Where are they?"

"I do not know. We have lit the signal fire, but it will take time for them to arrive."

"Does not matter." Aria held a scream at bay. The bed covers crumpled under her as she twisted in agony. "The babe comes. Go. Save yourself."

The Healer shook her head. "I do not run. I heal."

In the distance, away from the agony that occupied her world, Aria watched the older woman light scented candles, placing them around the room. Once done, she sorted through the bottles and jars that rested on the table, setting them aside until she found what she wanted, making a small exclamation of success.

The Healer came back to the bedside, a bottle of oil in her hands. "I do not have time to make a tea for the pain. Can you withstand it?"

Aria nodded. "Just hurry. I can take it."

"Let us hope you are right." The Healer opened Aria's robe and pushed her short gown upwards, exposing her. "I am sorry that we do not have the time for ceremony, but we must bring the babe forth as fast as possible." She applied the oil, rubbing it over Aria's rounded belly.

Aria arched off the bed as the contractions folded over her, taking her to the peace of oblivion where no thoughts of strength or consciousness could follow.

Cold water dousing her face, and the Healer's frantic voice begging her to awaken, brought Aria back to consciousness. "I am returned," she mumbled, swiping her hair away with a weak gesture. "Continue. I will hold on this time."

"You do not have the strength to do this." Doubt tinged the Healer's voice. "I will increase the contractions to force the babe out." The Healer opened another jar, and the scent of *balt*—a powerful drug— permeated the air. "If all goes right, you will be fine."

"My child?" Aria asked.

"I do not know. The contractions will be great."

Aria grabbed her wrist. "I cannot allow this." What worth would her life be if she bought it at the cost of another? "Find another way." Her eyes focused on the sharp knife that served to cut her food. "My child must survive. Cut him out if you must."

Resignedly, the Healer nodded and set the jar down. "If there is no other way."

Aria smiled and let go of the woman. Her babe would live.

Shaking her head, the Healer applied a compress to Aria's face, dabbing the cold water onto her forehead and cheeks. "I will call one of the Elders. They might be able to help with the pain."

Aria shook her head. "You will not make it before the

Reapers find you. Their quarters are too far."

"Are you close enough to any of the Apprentices to make a mind link?"

Aria hesitated. She did not want to involve another in the danger, but she also wanted her child to have the best chance possible. Only one person would understand the risk.

"Get Iliana."

The Healer did not reply as she hurried out the door.

Aria closed her eyes, waited, and fought to breathe through each contraction that came upon her.

"Aria." Her name was whispered in the dark.

She opened her eyes to see her best friend, her hair unkempt and hanging about her shoulders, leaning over her bedside.

"The Healer told you what needs to be done?"

Iliana nodded, and Aria reached out to touch her cheek. "Thank you for being so brave. I know I ask much, but you are the only Trancer I want in my psyche. I can trust no other."

Iliana knelt down next to the bed, her sleeping shift little cover in the cool night air. "You realize that afterwards, you will be indebted to me," she said with forced mirth.

"Agreed." Aria knew her smile was just as strained. The oil that the healer used before assaulted her senses. Weaker than the *balt*, it was still potent enough to do what was necessary. The Healer bent over her again.

Sounds of the Reapers running through the courtyard, hooting and yelling, filtered up and through the window.

The Healer uncorked the bottle. "You will have to push the child forth now, or we will all die."

"I will."

The Healer looked to Iliana. "You must help her control the pain so she can keep her strength and focus on pushing. Can you do this?"

"Yes."

"Good." The Healer held the bottle over Aria. "Ready?"

Aria closed her eyes and forced her breathing to ease. Opening her mental shield, Iliana touched her thoughts and established a light mind link.

Her belly warmed as the Healer spread the oil over it.

Her muscles contracted. The tension built as her body forced itself to push out the struggling babe. The pain folded over her, multiplying and expanding. Her strength wavered. Then, the pain lessened. Dividing.

Iliana. She shouldered it.

Aria felt her friend's distress and strength as she endured the agony, giving Aria the necessary power to bring the child forth. She gritted her teeth and pushed. The Healer's voice cut through the haze. She urged Aria to be strong, to be quick, and to push harder so that the babe could emerge.

Aria cried out, her hands gripping the covers, wadding them as she bore down with all her strength. The pain ceased.

Tarik was born.

Iliana slumped over onto the bed, her face buried in the covers.

Aria fell back into the pillows. *Welcome, my son.* The Healer cut the cord that joined them, and a sense of loss washed over Aria.

Tarik screamed at the separation.

The Healer gave the babe to Aria, and she smoothed his shock of black hair, reveling in its damp, silky texture.

Iliana raised her head but did not meet Aria's eyes. "I know about Talon." The quiet statement barely reached Aria's ears.

"I know you know," Aria replied. "I also know you approve." She tickled Tarik's cheek with a fingertip, no longer caring who knew about her and Talon's joining but secretly glad that Iliana sanctioned it.

Iliana pushed her own sweat-dampened hair from her face. "The joining is a beautiful thing. More powerful than I ever imagined." She took Aria's hand in hers, their fingers interlaced. "I would be lucky to feel what you feel, if only for a day. How could I disapprove?"

"I hope that—"

Shouts of victory and screams of terror filtered up from the courtyard below, interrupting Aria. The women turned towards the window in unison then back to each other.

The Healer took Tarik from Aria and passed him to Iliana. "Get the child ready for departure."

"What about Aria?" Iliana cuddled Tarik in her arms.

"What do you need to make her ready?"

"Nothing. We stay here."

Iliana took a step back. "You cannot. Are you mad? The Reapers will kill you both."

"We have no choice. She bleeds too much. I must stabilize her before I move her. Otherwise, she dies anyway." The Healer picked up a blanket from the foot of the bed and handed it to Iliana, indicating that she should wrap Tarik in it. "You must take the babe to the boats. I will follow with Aria when it is safe for her to walk."

"No." Aria interrupted the squabble.

The Healer and Iliana both turned to look at her. "I want you," Aria nodded towards the Healer, "to go with them. Two women have a better chance of getting my child away."

The Healer shook her head. "I cannot leave you to die."

Aria smiled weakly. "I give you no choice. I refuse to let you heal me, and you cannot go against my wishes." She stopped the protests of the women with an upraised hand. The Healer was right. The birth of her son had cost more that she thought. Even now, her life force faded, and it was an effort to breathe. She would not let her weakness bring harm to another. "The Warriors will arrive soon. If I live, they can help me. But I cannot live knowing I did not give my child, and the women who helped bring him into our world, the best possible chance of survival." She held her arms out, "Now, let me kiss him good-bye."

Tears in her eyes, Iliana brought the child over. "Please, reconsider. Let the Healer stay. Let me stay," she begged.

Aria shook her head. There was no time for reconsidering. Even now, fate conspired against them.

With a sob, Iliana laid the babe in Aria's outstretched arms. Aria kissed his wrinkled cheek and stroked his hair. He was small, red, wailing, and perfect. "Tarik, my little one. Be sure to obey Iliana. Grow up strong and honorable, like your father. If I do not see you in this lifetime, I will wait for you on the other side."

She nodded to Iliana, and as much as his small weight pained her weakened body, it hurt far worse when Iliana took Tarik from her arms. She sank back into the pillows. "Now leave," she ordered the two women. "Take my child away from here. Make him safe."

Iliana held the child close with one arm and embraced Aria with the other. "Once Tarik and the Healer are safe in the boats, I will come back for you. I swear it."

A trickle of blood ran down Aria's thigh, soaking into the blanket beneath her. "I will still be here," she said, too tired to argue further.

The sounds of assault grew closer as Aria watched her friends depart. She closed her eyes and waited for fate to come to her.

***

It was still nighttime when Aria awoke. The courtyard was quiet, with only the occasional whimpering reaching her ears. She listened harder, wondering if the Reapers were gone. Footsteps sounded in the hallway outside her door. Someone ran. Someone pursued.

The Reapers had not departed. They had taken over the Tower.

She wondered how much time had passed since Iliana and the Healer had left for the boats and if Tarik was safely away.

Praying to the Goddess for their protection, she opened her mind to the currents that flowed through the Tower, looking for their sparks. Blackness and death greeted her like unwelcome visitors. She reeled back. It was too thick, and she did not have the strength to get through the dark to find her son.

I must know if Tarik is safe. Even if it means crawling to the boats to find out.

Her breathing forced, and her movements slow, she sat up. Turning over onto her hands and knees, she crawled backwards to the end of the bed and slid her legs over, her gown riding up and over her thighs.

Done, she thought with relief. She was halfway off the bed and still alert. She pushed upward with her forearms and stood. Her body swaying like grass in the wind, she grabbed the wooden bedpost to steady herself.

Something trickled down her leg. Still holding onto the bed, she bent over and watched a thin line of blood make its way over her thigh and towards her unshod foot. The sight made her stomach lurch, but she would not let it stop her.

She needed to know her child's fate.

Stumbling from bed to table to chair, she made her way towards the door, each step more jarring than the next. She did not need to look behind her to know that a trail of blood followed in the form of red, smeared footprints. After what seemed like a turn, she reached the chamber door and fell against it, the rough wood scratching her cheek. Strength fleeing, and her abdomen cramping, she slid down the frame and onto the floor where she lay in a heap.

Would physical death hurt more than the loss of her son, she wondered, as another spasm shook her. Or would it be a relief? She gazed up at the ceiling, waiting to die, and saw Talon instead. Talon? Was he dead as well?

He was as when she last saw him, his dark hair tied back with the ceremonial cloth ties from the Given ceremony. His sword was by his side.

"Aria. Our son needs you." His voice sounded distant, as if he spoke from deep within a cave.

"You know about Tarik?" Aria asked, surprised. She reached for her Giver, but he floated too far away.

Talon smiled. His teeth white against his day-darkened skin. "Of course. I know everything you do. I can feel it everyday."

Aria smiled. She had hoped as much. Their link was strong, and neither distance nor time lessened it. He knew everything, and now he would help. "Please, Talon. Our son is in danger. You must save him."

He shook his head. "I cannot."

Aria trembled with disappointment. "You are a Warrior. You have no choice. Leave me here, but take our child away from this."

Talon shook his head again. "You must do that yourself. Only you can save him," he said and then melted away.

Aria awoke to find herself still on the floor, her cheek pressed against the cold stone. Damp with sweat, her hair stuck to her in lank strands. How long had she lain unconscious? Where was Talon?

She shut her eyes and tried to remember his words. She had to save their son.

First, she had to get up.

Ignoring the white-hot pain that shot through her

body, she reached upwards and gripped the heavy metal door handle, using it to pull herself to a standing position. She needed to get to Tarik. He was in danger. Talon said so.

Her vision wavering like water running down glass, she opened the door and began to make her way through the hallway and towards the cove that sheltered the small boats. The floor kept moving from beneath her feet, confusing her senses. She gave a complaint as she slammed from one side of the hall to the other.

"Boats. Where are the boats?" she mumbled. She remembered that boats were usually in water and giggled.

Lurching down the hall on ever weakening legs, she ran face first into a wall and fell backwards, cracking her head on the stone. Reaching back, she rubbed the spot. No matter. She had a mission. Rolling over, she crawled to her knees, braced herself against the wall, and managed to stand. "Tarik." Her thin voice boomed in the desolate hallway. "Tarik, where are you?"

Turning, she continued to stumble and ended up pressed against another wall before she fell to the stone. Blood. It ran down her legs. She tasted it on her lips. Now she bled from all over. She laughed at the thought, rolled over, and saw the Healer lying next to her.

"Healer." Aria shook her shoulder. "You must rise and help Tarik. You said you would. You promised."

She plucked at the Healer's robe with feeble motions, too weak to feel pain. "Look at me. Tell me why you break your promise." She shook her again, and the Healer's head lolled over.

The woman who helped her birth her son looked at the ceiling with sightless eyes. Her throat gaped open like a macabre smile where a Reaper had slashed it with a knife

Her delirium lifted at the gruesome sight, and her stomach heaved, but there was no time for sorrow. Tarik. Where was he? She prayed she was not too late and tried to rise. Her legs trembled, and she collapsed too the floor. *Too tired,* she realized. *Too much life's blood spilled.*

Talon came back, this time not floating but standing in front of her. "Aria, my love. You must hurry."

Aria licked her lips, wishing for water. "I am trying."

"I know, but try harder."

"You are the Warrior. Why did you not save us? Save Tarik?"

He was gone again.

The cool stone, and the sound of a child's high-pitched cry, brought her from the blackness. Tarik? She started to crawl again. *Stay centered,* she told herself.

A great crash shook the very air about her. More screaming. This time, a woman. Iliana? What were they doing to her? The door at the end of the hallway stood partially open, but nothing was visible.

"Stop," she begged. Desperate, she commanded her body to push past the resistance of gravity.

The child's cry abruptly stopped. The woman's shriek was cut off.

A Reaper laughed.

It was over. They were gone. Aria collapsed back onto the ground. Beyond pain and beyond caring, she vaguely registered the motions as the Reaper emerged, his blade stained with blood. The mask of day and night covered his face, but Aria knew who he was. *It is the man from the dark,* she realized. He stepped over her, not glancing down. *He thinks me dead.*

In her heart, she was.

Three

Talon leapt from the bow of the boat the moment it plowed into the sand. The Warriors under his command followed behind him. Battle cries sounding, they raised their swords above their heads as they splashed through the salty water, prepared to meet the Reapers.

The silence of a vacant beach greeted them.

At the head of the squadron, Talon quickly surveyed the area with a practiced eye. He saw no movement. Straining to hear over the ocean breeze, his ears detected nothing to indicate the Reapers waited. Was it a trap?

Or their worst vision?

There was only one way to find out.

With a finger against his lips, he motioned his men to spread out. Quickly, silently, the Warriors broke into teams of six and made their way over the dunes and towards the Tower.

In the lead, Talon crested a dune, and his heart dropped at the sight before him. The Tower's great wooden gate hung from only its lower hinge. A black and white banner, undulating in the breeze, was thrust into the wood with a knife.

It was not just any Reaper who had taken the Tower. It was Mako. The scar that ran from Talon's eye to his chin burned at the memory of a man more ruthless than a *katah'*. A man with a heart blacker than a moonless turn.

He knew few, if any, would be left alive inside the Tower.

He whispered a silent prayer to the Goddess to let Aria be among the living.

"Do we go in?" Lore asked, waiting for Talon's decision.

With a nod of approval towards his second in command, Talon pushed open the broken door in response and stepped into the still smoldering courtyard. Even though he knew what to expect, he gaped in horror at the destruction that lay before him.

Women, ranging from early in years to ancient, lay strewn about. Like unwanted dolls left in the mud, their bodies were ravaged and torn.

Talon wanted to howl at the loss. His jaw clenched, and the muscles in his neck corded and strained, as he held his emotions in check. He would mourn later. Right now, he had to find the living and secure the area.

The sound of gagging reached his ears, and he turned to see one of the younger Warriors on his knees, retching. The boy would be embarrassed by his actions. It was not the lad's fault. It was his first trek as a Warrior, and to see such barbaric destruction was horrifying.

"You." Talon pointed with the tip of his sword at the kneeling boy. "Comb the beaches for survivors. If none are found, stay with the boat and guard it."

Wiping his mouth with the back of his hand, the boy nodded and stumbled to his feet. Talon pointed at two of the other recruits, young and in obvious distress by the green tinge to their cheeks. "You two, go with him." The three trotted off, not sparing a backward glance.

The remaining men waited as Talon scanned the area, deciding what to do first. Quickly, he assigned teams to areas, and the squads began searching for any signs of life.

Leaving his sword unsheathed, he motioned for the rest of the men to follow him.

Silently, they wove through the courtyard, turning body after body over, hoping for a breath of life. Disappointment greeted them at every turn. In pairs, and always ready for a Reaper ambush, the men separated, entering the different buildings in their search.

"Do you think she lives?"

Talon turned at Lore's hushed question. His closest friend, only Lore knew of the still tender feelings he carried for his Given, Aria. "I do not know, but I hope," Talon answered as the pair walked toward the smaller Tower where the Apprentices lived.

"Can you feel her in your mind?"

Talon gave a sideways glance at his friend. Was Lore perceptive enough to know that he sometimes thought he felt Aria? Heard her thoughts and dreams? "I used to think so. Sometimes I would swear she thought of me. Directed thoughts to me."

"But now?"

"I am not so sure." They turned a corner in unison,

swords at the ready. The door to the Apprentices' Tower was swung open. "I think I would know if she was dead, but I am not a Trancer and cannot trust those feelings. I deal with the tangible." He reined in the anger that threatened to flow outwards at the thought of his beautiful Aria killed like an animal. "But know this. If she is dead, the Reapers will suffer. I will make sure of it." His eyes narrowed as he envisioned choking the life out of Mako.

Lore raised a brow. "Are you sure you do not feel more for her than you would like to admit?"

Talon shot his friend a wary glance. "I neither admit nor deny my feelings, since I cannot explain them myself, but because of me she loved carelessly. I am bound to protect her."

"Ah, an answer that is not an answer," Lore commented, his wry smile a sharp contrast to the carnage surrounding them. "I thought only Trancers could be so obscure. Are you sure you have no Trancer blood?"

"Yes," Talon replied. The pair entered the Apprentices' Tower. Talon motioned Lore to follow him towards the room where he had last seen Aria. They turned a corner, and his heart stopped. A girl lay on the ground at his feet, her red hair stiff with blood. His lips moving in a silent prayer to the Goddess, he turned the still figure over.

It was not Aria. Unaware he held his breath, it came out in a gasp. Guilty with relief, he closed the girl's eyes before he continued.

Perhaps Aria was safe, hiding in her room. There were fewer bodies in this area. Some might have lived. His lips continued to move as he prayed, but he knew that if Aria already lie slain then she was beyond even the help of the Goddess.

Still, he took comfort in the thought that if she lay hurt the Goddess would assist her until he arrived.

Why did I wait so long to come back? he asked himself as he made his way down the hall. He should have returned earlier—if only to beg forgiveness for opening his mind to her. Now, he might not have that chance.

So many chances lost, and so many things left unsaid. It was a bitter thought.

He turned another corner and stopped. A Healer lay on the stone, her throat slashed.

Aria lay beside her, one arm flung over her chest and the other lying palm up on the floor beside her. Blood covered her robe and thighs.

Talon dropped to his knees and gathered Aria's still form in his arms.

"Aria, wake up. Open your eyes," Talon implored, looking at her pale face for any signs of life. She did not stir, but lay in his arms, her limp form unmoving. He bowed his head and begged the Goddess to spare her life, promising anything if she would save his Given.

"Let her go, Talon. She is beyond us now."

Stricken with grief, Talon focused his eyes on Lore, who stood on the other side of Aria. "No. I will not let her go."

He kissed her pale cheek. Lore was wrong. The Goddess would not let this happen. "Open your eyes for me. Breathe for me," he begged, letting his head rest against Aria's lank hair. Goddess, how could she be gone? Hot tears filled his eyes, stinging. He had not cried since he was a boy. It was not fair. Not now and not like this. Talon gave another cry, the sound of a wounded animal, as he rubbed his rough cheek against her smooth one.

"Please." His whisper was a prayer as he held her closer, willing his breath into her lungs and his life force into her heart. "Please, do not leave me."

A weak thud sounded in his ears. Talon's head shot up. Just as quickly, he bent down to listen.

Another dull thud sounded. She lived. Barely, but it was enough. *Thank you, Goddess.* "Lore, get the Healer from the boat. Now."

In one swift movement, Lore nodded, sheathed his sword, and turned on his heel, running down the hall.

"Hold on, little one. Just hold on. If you can do that, I swear I will make sure no one ever hurts you again." Talon stroked her bruised forehead with his hand before he placed a kiss upon it. His movements slow and gentle, he pulled her matted hair away from her cheek. The last time he had seen her, the strands shone like a fiery beacon in the night. Now dulled with blood, the red was a garish caricature of her real color.

He touched a bruise that stained her cheek. She moaned, and her body twitched as if struck.

Carefully, he pulled her against him, hoping his presence would signal safety and allow her to awaken. "It is Talon. I have returned."

Her chest rose with a deep sigh. Her eyes opened, and he saw the same deep green that haunted his dreams.

"Talon?" Her voice was barely a whisper.

"I am here." He gripped her hand in his and brought it to his lips, grazing the scraped knuckles with a kiss.

Her eyes went from the hand that Talon held, to his face, and back again. "Are you real this time?"

"Yes." He kissed her hand again, not caring that her life's blood stained his lips.

She sighed again and her eyelids closed.

"Do not fall asleep," Talon begged. She did not answer, and Talon watched in horror as her face went from pale white to bright pink. He placed his palm against her cheek. She burned. She was back from beyond, but fever racked her small frame.

"You are not real." Aria's voice was distant, and her eyes were still closed. With more strength than he thought possible, she began to shake. Hoarse screams issued from her throat, and she twisted, fighting whatever haunted her fevered mind. Her small fists beat weakly upon Talon's chest. "Where have you taken Tarik? Give him back to me." Her sobs tore at him. "I will do whatever you want, just please give him back."

Tarik? Who was Tarik? Talon held her tighter, rocking her in his arms. She screamed for Tarik again, howling as if demons chased her. *Tarik.* Perhaps she had taken a lover after he left. The hair on the back of his neck stood on end at the thought, but there would be time to deal with that later.

He grabbed her hands, not wanting her to hurt herself further. "Aria, you must listen to me," he said, trying to break through the dreams. "You are imagining things. It is I, Talon. There is no Tarik."

Her face went lax at his words. "No Tarik?"

"No. You imagine things."

"No," Aria cried, twisting in his grasp. "You lie." She took a weak swipe at his face, and he caught her hand in his.

Her strength ran out, and her breathing slowed. Still,

her skin burned so hot he felt it through his leathers. "Where is that Healer," he muttered. Aria was getting worse, and he was helpless. He was a Warrior and knew only how to kill. He wished he at least had some cool water for her forehead. Anything to soothe her. *Goddess, get the Healer here soon!*

***

"Master Talon. Move aside. Let me see the girl."

He looked up. He had been so lost in prayer that he had no idea how much time had passed, but Lore stood next to him with the Healer by his side. She carried a medicine bag in a pouch at her waist.

Talon laid Aria back down onto the stone floor, putting his cloak under her head. Hovering, he watched as the Healer examined Aria. Her slim hands were sure and deft as she searched for broken bones and opened wounds. Finally, she stood.

"Will she live?" Talon asked, afraid of the answer but even more terrified to not know.

The Healer shook her head. "I cannot be sure. She has lost much blood. She also has a fever. It must come down. Her body cannot take the stress of both."

Talon nodded, grateful for a plan of action. "Tell me what I must do to help."

"Do you know which room is hers?"

"Yes."

"Good. The soul finds it easier to heal in familiar surroundings."

Keeping his cloak under her head, Talon picked Aria up. He marveled that she seemed so light—like a wraith with no more substance than the morning mist over the trees.

Almost running, and with the Healer and Lore in tow, he headed down the remembered hallway. The smell of blood, metallic and thick, saturated the air.

Arriving at Aria's room, he walked inside. His heart almost stopped when he saw her bed—the same bed where they had made love, laughed, and joined—was soiled with blood. The covers were disarrayed and shoved to one side. Her pillows were flung carelessly to the floor. Something had happened here, of that there was no doubt.

He looked at the blood that covered her robe, her hair,

and her thighs. His eyes narrowed. He would kill all the Reapers for abusing not just her flesh but also her gentle nature. Holding Aria with one arm, he used the free one to pull the soiled sheets off the bed. Carefully, he laid her upon the bare mattress.

"Stand away." It was the Healer. Talon walked to the end of the bed where he could guard but be out of the woman's way. The Healer stripped the ruined garment from Aria's body. Talon held his breath, fearful of the damage done to his Given.

"I am sure she will be all right." Lore stood next to him.

Talon acknowledged the comment with a grunt before he spoke to the Healer. "Is there anything I can do?"

The Healer tucked a blanket around Aria's nude form. "Boil some water and bring it to me. You." She pointed at Lore. "Gather some clean cloths, rip up clothes if need be, and bring them to me."

Both moved, commanded by the slight woman. Looking in the kettle that hung over the hearth, Talon was relieved to see it still contained water. He poked at the dead ashes in the fireplace until he found some embers. Placing dry grass from the firebox over them, he blew until a small flame leapt up, and then placed small twigs upon it until he could add larger pieces. The fire roared to life. He stood close until the water churned.

Using a thick piece of cloth, he carried the kettle back to the Healer.

She gestured with her head. "In the bowl."

Talon saw a blend of leaves and flowers scattered in the bottom of a wooden vessel.

"Mix it until it is well blended then add cooler water until it is still hot but not scalding."

Talon nodded and prepared the mixture.

"It will bring down her fever," the Healer explained. "You must hold her up while I make her drink."

"As you wish," Talon replied. He dipped a finger in the water, testing the temperature. "It is ready." He handed the bowl to the Healer.

"What is her name?"

"Aria."

"You were her Giver?"

Talon's face grew hot. Was their relationship that transparent? "Yes."

The Healer nodded. "Good. She will recognize your voice. I want you to call to her. Tell her to drink."

Keeping Aria covered, Talon sat on the bed and pulled her upright against his chest. She lay lifeless in his arms. "Aria, wake up. I have medicine to make you well. You must drink."

She did not respond.

"Again," the Healer demanded. "But she is far under. You must open your heart and call to her if she is to awaken."

Talon took a deep breath. Open his heart? How could he do that when even he did not know what he felt? Still, he had to try. "Aria," he whispered in her ear. "I have returned to you. Awaken."

A hair's breadth of body movement told him that she was emerging from the depths that claimed her.

Then, she settled again, going limp.

The Healer glared at Talon, her disgust obvious. "Do you want her dead?"

He could not let her die, not after the Goddess had granted him the chance to save her. Talon took a deep breath. "I cannot live without you. Please do not leave me. I need you."

He was rewarded with a fluttering of eyelids, and her eyes looked into his once more. "Talon, are you real?"

"As real as life." He whispered a thank you to the Goddess.

"I thought I dreamt you. I was in the hall. You were there, but you left. There was screaming and an evil man."

"Shh," Talon murmured. "We will talk later. Now, you must drink. We have something to make you better."

Aria opened her mouth and drank.

Talon clapped her lightly on the back when she choked on the last few drops, and then he laid her back down, satisfied that she would live. Holding her hand, he sat on the edge of the bed until her eyes closed. His own eyes were hot, sticky with sudden weariness, as his defenses relaxed. The Tower was lost, but Aria lived.

Placing her hand at her side, he moved to stand and was stopped when, with surprising strength and speed,

Aria reached out and grabbed the hem of his tunic. "Do not leave me again."

Talon's lips tugged downward at the fear that lit Aria's eyes, and he caught the rung of a chair with his foot, pulled it over, and sat down. "I will not. Now rest, and let the Healer work."

"I do not want to rest," Aria protested, even as her eyes closed.

"Shh." Talon stroked her hair. "Sleep will heal you."

"I have bad dreams."

Talon kissed her forehead. "I will protect you," he assured her as her breath slowed, and she sank into a more natural slumber.

"We must clean her wounds."

Talon looked up, startled at the Healer's voice. He had forgotten she was present.

"More water?"

"Yes, but you will need to move while I bind her."

"I promised I would stay by her side."

"You will, but not just yet," the Healer said. "Now move so I may perform my duties, or would you rather she remain unclean and uncared for?"

Standing, Talon walked over to the hearth to let the Healer have the room she requested. He watched as she poured the rest of the water into another bowl. Lore handed her the clean material he had found then joined Talon while the Healer worked, affording the women privacy. "Be patient, my brother," Lore said, one hand on the hilt of his sword and the other on Talon's shoulder. "The Healer is well trained, and Aria is stronger than you think."

Talon tried to take comfort from the words, but failed. "I should have been here."

"Then what? Could you take on an entire Reaper army?"

"No, of course not." Talon's rising voice was subdued with a scathing look from the Healer. "But I could have saved her from this tragedy. I could have kept her safe," he finished with a whisper. Troubled, he ran a callused hand through his hair before it came to rest on his sword. What did Lore know? Had he ever cared for a Given beyond the ceremony? Talon looked into the blue, concerned eyes of his friend and knew he judged unfairly. Lore used wit as a weapon and shield, but it did not lesson his depth of feeling. Talon rubbed his still stinging eyes, knowing he would do better to keep his anger directed where it belonged—at the Reapers. "How goes the rest of the Tower? Any survivors?"

Lore shook his head. "Not that I have heard of, but I directed the others to keep looking until we are sure."

Talon fingered the pommel of his sword. Aria's escape from Mako, and death, was more than a fluke. It was fate. The Goddess spared her for a reason, but for what?

"This is odd." Both men turned at the Healer's comment. Still partially covered, Aria lay in exhausted sleep as the Healer tended her.

Talon strode over to the bed, fear racing through him. "What is it? What is wrong?"

The Healer continued to clean the blood from Aria's body. "Other than some scrapes, she does not have any serious wounds. I did not find any earlier but thought it due to the speed of my exam."

"Where did all the blood come from? Is it not hers?" Glancing at the soiled sheets on the floor, he feared the answer.

The Healer did not reply but continued washing, silently assessing her patient. Dipping the rag into the now red water, she pulled the blanket aside and began washing the blood from Aria's thighs. Talon did not turn away, dreading what the Healer might say but needing to know.

Finally, she stopped, placed the rag back in the bowl, and left it. Standing, she covered Aria with Talon's cloak.

"Well?" Talon asked.

"It is hers."

His instincts for revenge and protection rising to the surface, Talon bristled. A question weighed heavy on his lips but had to be asked. "Was she violated?"

"No." The Healer's smile was a mixture of both sorrow and relief. "She bore a child."

Four

Aria's scream pierced the morning air, jerking Talon awake from his uneasy sleep. He pulled his sword even as he leapt from his makeshift bed. In two short steps, he was at Aria's bedside, awake and ready to protect her from harm.

He glanced around in the room. No foes attacked. No Reapers lurked in the shadows. There was only Aria, fighting her nightmares.

She screamed again, a cry of anguish and loss. He sheathed his sword and leaned over her, holding her bruised and scraped hands between his palms.

She continued to shriek as she fought to break free from the sleep that claimed her. With surprising strength, she pulled her hands from his, holding them in front of her like a shield.

Anger at the Reapers sprang anew in Talon's blood. His sword arm tightened in reflex. *Later,* he promised himself and held his anger in check. Now, Aria called for rescue from the demons that tormented her. "Shh, you are safe," he whispered. "Nobody will hurt you while I am here."

Calming, her eyes fluttered and opened, their dark green shade accenting the shadows beneath them. She looked up at him in confusion. "Are you real?"

Thank the Goddess. He was beginning to wonder if she would ever waken. Smiling in relief, Talon stroked a damp curl away from her forehead. Leaning down, he kissed her hair. "Yes."

Her mouth curved in a weak smile as his hand came to rest against her cheek. "I thought you were a dream. Another vision to taunt me."

"I am real enough." He kissed her fingertips. "Can you not feel me?"

She nodded, and for a few heartbeats, both took solace in the silence.

Finally, Aria spoke. "What happened? Was the Tower taken?"

He shook his head. "Later, when you are strong, we will talk."

"No." Her hand tightened around his. "Tell me now."

Sighing, Talon sat on the edge of the bed. As much as he wanted to protect her, to keep her safe from death's destruction, she had the right to answers. Sadly, there were no easy ones.

Aria pressed him. "My sisters? Are they safe?"

The words stuck in his throat. How could he speak of total devastation? He could not. Not while she was weak. Not now. The agony of loss would find her soon enough. He stood. "I will find the Healer and tell her you have woken."

Aria grabbed his tunic with her hand. "Tell me now."

He untangled her fingers from the cloth and laid her hand on her chest. "Later. I promise I will tell you all later. Let me find the Healer first."

"No. Now. What do you hide? Were many killed?"

He ran his hand through his hair. Panic stroked her face, and he knew the lack of knowledge made it worse, but how could he tell her that the truth was so much more horrifying than anything her mind could imagine? *Oh Goddess. Help me find the right words.*

There were none. "You are the sole survivor."

"Dead? They are all dead?"

Her shock, her look of disbelief, pierced Talon like a spear. "I am sorry," was all he could say, and even in his own ears, it sounded inadequate and pitiful when compared to the anguish that he knew welled in her heart.

Sudden tears deepened her eyes and traced a path to the pillow beneath her head. "All dead? It cannot be." Beneath the thin gown, her shoulders shook. She turned her stricken gaze to him. "Why do I live? Why me?"

There was but one explanation. "I think they thought you already dead. We arrived a few suns ago, and I found you in the hallway. You were covered in blood and unconscious." He hesitated. "You almost did die in giving birth to our son."

Aria closed her eyes, her lashes dark upon her pale cheeks. "You know."

"Yes." He wanted to comfort her, but did not know what to do. How could his sense of loss compare to hers?

"I wanted to tell you."

"I know." Both knew it would have been impossible.

The Elders would have stopped her. It was not for Warriors to know their sons. Only the Trancer mothers gained that privilege.

"It was a difficult birth." Aria's eyes glazed over as if she looked into the distance—or the past. "He was a large baby and stubborn." Her voice cracked.

Talon's heart ached. He wanted to know about his son, but he also knew the knowledge would bring a greater pain. Still, he did not stop her. She needed to speak, to say the words so she could begin to grieve for her loss.

His grief could wait.

"I needed Iliana. You remember her, do you not? She was the one who chose you as my Giver."

"Yes, I remember," Talon whispered. An ebony-haired maiden, she had called his name across the sands for Aria to hear.

"I was not strong enough to push our child forth. So much pain." Aria grimaced, her delicate face twisting at the memory. "Pain that the Reapers brought when they invaded our Tower. I could not get past it. Iliana helped me. She gave me strength."

Talon flinched as her shoulders heaved and tears choked her voice.

"I named him Tarik. What a temper he had. He was so mad at being taken from his warm home and brought out into the world." She laid a hand on her stomach.

Talon wiped her tears away with his thumb, knowing she remembered their child and how the babe had felt when within.

Aria shuddered, but continued. "I gave him to Iliana and the Healer to take to the boats. I tried to save him, Talon." Her eyes opened, dark green and desperate. Her voice rose in panic as she relived the deadly night. "I tried to save him, and I failed. I found the Healer in the hallway. Her throat cut. She was left like an animal. Like she did not matter."

Barely breathing, Talon's very being cried for Aria to stop. It was inhuman torture to hear of his son's birth and death in the same breath.

Still, he said nothing.

"The last thing I remember is hearing Iliana shout and our baby cry. They were cut off in mid-scream, and a

Reaper walked out, grinning. His sword was stained with their blood." She threw her hands over her face. "I failed him, Talon. I should have saved him, and I failed. I killed our son."

Pushing his pain aside, Talon pulled her to him, resting her against his chest, unable to bear her anguish. "You did nothing of the sort. There was nothing you could have done save die alongside him."

Aria struggled. Talon released her, and she fell back onto the bed. Turning away from him, she buried her face in the pillows. "I should have died. What right do I have to life? What did I earn other than shame?"

Talon shook his head. "Do not blame yourself. Do not take all the pain and rage and heap it upon your shoulders."

"Where would you have me put it?"

"On the Reapers." He hesitated, not wanting to speak his heart, but she deserved to hear the truth. "And on me."

"You were not here, and I was. I am the one who failed."

"Do you not understand?" Talon said, his voice harsh. "I should have been here, keeping you safe. If I were, our son would be alive. It was my duty to protect you and our son, and I failed. Not you." He pounded the bed with a fist.

Aria laid her hand on Talon's, opening his taut fingers with a delicate touch. "You are a Warrior, not a Trancer. How could you have known to return?"

"I should have known. I should have come back."

Aria took a deep breath. "I cannot have you blame yourself."

"And I cannot have you shoulder the burden."

She held his hand to her cheek.

With his other hand, Talon unbuckled his sword and set it on the floor. Pulling the covers aside, he settled in next to Aria, keeping her safe, keeping her close. Silent, the only sound was his heart beating in time with her breathing.

She turned in his arms and pushed a strand of hair away from his face. "Talon?"

He jumped, caught in dreams about what would not

be. "Yes?"

"Over by the fountain is a shade garden. I think Tarik would like to meet the Goddess in such a place. I would place him in Iliana's arms. She was my friend in life and committed to his safety." Her voice quivered but did not break. "I know she will do the same until we meet in death."

Talon pulled her closer. Hearing of the destruction was horrific enough. He had hoped to avoid this part of the conversation for a while longer, but now that she asked, waiting was not an option. "I wish I could say yes to your desire, but his body is not here."

Aria's head jerked up. "What do you mean?"

"Reapers often take those they kill and either fling them into the ocean or leave them in the woods for the wild animals to dispose of. It is a final act of cruelty, leaving the survivors to wonder and worry."

"Oh my Goddess," she whispered. "Who else? Who else did they take? Who else will I have to leave unspoken and unburied?"

"No one other than Iliana and Tarik." It was as if Mako had known how to hurt Aria, the single survivor, in the worst possible way. "We will have a service and commit him and Iliana to the Goddess. I swear it. I will make the Reapers pay for what they took."

"Only Tarik and Iliana?" Shakily, she pulled away from Talon and managed to push herself into a sitting position. "Do the Reapers take prisoners?"

He rose beside her, shaking his head. "No. Never, but that is what they would have you think."

"Perhaps it was not Tarik and Iliana I heard."

He frowned. She did not hear him, but instead, wanted to believe the unbelievable. When he found Mako, he would pay for this added pain. Pay for making Talon be the one to crush her dream.

"Perhaps they live," she murmured. Ignoring Talon, Aria leaned back against the headboard, crossed her legs, and shut her eyes. She drew a deep breath, and her hands relaxed and fell to her knees where they rested palm-up.

Trancer position. He had heard of it, but not seen it since he had never dealt with Trancers other than the Given ceremony. Was she strong enough to do this? He reached out a hand to shake her and stopped himself.

Would he hurt her if he broke her trance?

Moments ticked by as he watched. Her expression, far from passive, changed as she wove her way through what he understood to be the currents of life. He waited, watching her frown change to anger, and her anger to confusion, then the confusion to beatific. She smiled. What had she found?

Swaying, she fell sideways. Talon caught her in his arms. Grabbing his tunic, she managed to remain steady. She opened her eyes. She still looked tired, but the tears were gone. In their place was a profound expression of comfort and hope.

"I do not feel him, Talon."

Or was it desperation? What had she seen, or thought she saw, when she looked for their son? "Tarik? His body is gone."

She shook her head, her impatience obvious "No. That is not what I mean. I feel his energy, but not his death. He is alive."

"You found him?" Goddess help him, Talon wanted to believe her. Wanted to believe their son lived. Wanted to believe his failure was not complete.

Aria shook her head. "No, I am too weak, and the Tower," she hesitated. "The currents are corrupt with death. It will be seasons before they will help a Trancer and not hinder."

Talon's brief flicker of hope died with her excuse. No matter what he wanted, and no matter what Aria thought she felt, their son was dead. Of that, there was no doubt. Why would the Reapers, a group that depended on their ability to move quickly and silently, take a newborn babe?

"No. You are wrong." He whispered the denial.

"He lives. I know it," Aria insisted.

Talon rested his head in his hands. "I know you wish it true, but wishing does not change what happened. Why would they take him?"

She shrugged. "I cannot answer what I do not know. I only know that I do not feel his death. Just his life."

Talon fell back onto the bed with a groan. What should he do? He did not want to encourage her belief, but she had been through so much already. Perhaps it would not hurt to let Aria believe Tarik lived. Then again, was it right to let her dream and hope for the impossible only to have it taken away again? He did not know.

Uncrossing her legs, Aria lay back and snuggled into Talon's arms. "I know you do not believe me, but you will."

**

Standing at a window overlooking the courtyard, Aria watched as the Warriors below performed the ceremony for the dead. Pushing the windows open, she leaned out to hear the liturgy. Masculine and low, their voices rolled over the phrases and songs. She closed her eyes and listened as the final good-byes were said.

The chanting stopped, but Aria did not need to open her eyes to know Talon now stood in front of his Warriors, saying the farewell to Tarik. Alone. It was supposed to be her, but the Healer refused to let her leave the Tower.

Besides, her son lived, and the chant was unnecessary.

Turning away from the scene below, she wandered the communal room, her robes dragging on the floor behind her. *I should be down there, sending my friends to meet the Goddess*, she thought. Her son lived, but many others had died in the Reaper raid. So many sisters and Elders.

She breathed deep as memories overwhelmed her, threatening to send her to the floor in their intensity. Stumbling, she recovered. She could not mourn. Not yet. If she mourned now, if she remembered what happened, the tears would never cease. Later, after she recovered Tarik, she would sing for her friends. Until then, she would have to bear the silence of the almost empty Tower.

It would help if she could walk outside. Perhaps assist in the restoration of all that the Reapers destroyed. Her lips turned downward as she remembered the Healer telling her that under no circumstances was she to exert herself. The sounds of song stopped. The ceremony was over. Aria sighed and walked back towards the window, letting her fingers trail along the tops of the cushioned chairs as she walked past. Her patience wore thin with the confinement.

The squad of Warriors walked away from the graves, returning to duties. They had spent much time on making the Tower habitable once again. Soon, word would be sent to the other Towers, and a few women from each would arrive, ready to finish the work the Warriors had started. Their presence would bring the Tower back to life, and they would bond as a group.

Aria wondered if it would ever be the same, but she already knew the answer. No. Not for her. This new group of Maidens, Apprentices and Elders would see the Tower as their new home. They would know its past, but it would not touch them like it touched her. She would never see the Tower in the same way. Once, the sturdy walls kept her safe, and her friends made her happy.

Now, her friends were gone—and she knew that no walls were impervious.

"I brought these for you."

Talon stood in the doorway. He carried a bundle of fresh *shanta* flowers.

He walked over and placed them in her hands.

She inhaled their spicy scent. Since her recovery, his attention to her was both consistent and charming. "Thank you." She stood on her toes to kiss his rough cheek. He colored at the gesture, his discomfort endearing him to her.

Talon touched the spot where she had kissed him. "You are welcome. I hope these make your confinement more pleasant. I know it is difficult."

"Boring would be more accurate." She placed the flowers in a vase. "I know the Healer means well, but I would like to go outside and sit under the trees. I feel strong enough to make my way down to the yard and back again." The Healer did not understand that she had grown up in a place where grass grew up to the door, and in some cases, even served as a roof. To be stuck within stone walls was intolerable.

"Only a few more days. I promise."

Talon did not understand either. Resignedly, she nodded and went back to him, placing her cheek against his chest. He hesitated then put his arms around her.

"I suppose I can wait a while longer," she replied with a sigh. Happy to be in the safety of his embrace, she wrapped her arms around his waist.

Talon stroked her back with a firm hand, kneading her still-sore muscles. "I offered sweet oil for our son." He whispered the information like a deep dark secret.

"Why?" Aria asked.

"It is said that the Goddess is most appreciative of such a gift. I wanted to make sure she would care for him as we would have."

He deliberately misinterpreted her question, but in doing so, he acknowledged their bond. Anger and elation warred within her. Patience called a truce. She held him tighter and chose her words. "My Warrior, I thank you for the gift to the Goddess, it was most thoughtful, but our son lives."

"I know you believe he does," was his cautious reply.

"Then why do you persist on ignoring my words? I know you do not misunderstand."

Talon disengaged himself from their embrace and unbuckled his scabbard. He hung it on a nail that had been pounded into the back of the door, went to the table, and poured deep-red wine into two goblets. Without a word, he offered one to Aria.

Both drank deep, and the silence took on a life of its own, filling them room. Talon sat in a chair by the fire. "You are right. I know what you meant."

"Then why act unaware?"

"I think our son has gone to meet the Goddess. You feel differently." He swallowed another mouthful of the tart red liquid. "Who is to say which of us is right?"

Aria's ire flared at the patronizing tone and all thoughts of patience fled. "I am right."

"I know you think you are." He looked at her like a misled child. "I hoped we would save this conversation."

"Why wait?"

"You are still frail."

Frail? Childhood wounds opened at the accusation. "I am stronger than you think. Speak your thoughts."

"As you wish," Talon said. "But I have only a question. Why would the Reapers take a newborn with them?"

Aria clenched the goblet, her knuckles white, desperate to make Talon understand that grief did not blind her. "Perhaps Iliana talked them into it."

"And why would they take her and no one else?"

Aria's grip tightened further. "I do not know their motivations, but I know they took our son."

"If you knew their ways you would not be so sure in

your conviction."

"Do you know them so well that you are positive of yours?"

His face darkened at the question. "I know them well enough to know that they would not take a newborn. It would be inconvenient at best, deadly at worst."

Aria let his words wash over her, reminding herself that he was a Warrior. He relied on what he saw, not the intangible emotions that all possessed. For Warriors, feelings were suspect. "You are right in that I do not know their ways," she conceded. "However, my ignorance does not mean I am wrong."

Talon set his goblet down upon the stone hearth. "I do not think you ignorant, merely optimistic."

Optimistic? Perhaps, but she was also a woman changed by pain and loss. She wondered what it would take to make him see the changes she had undergone in losing both her child and friends. "How do you propose we resolve this matter?"

"You are the one who believes he lives. Tell me your thoughts."

"I would like to find him. I can be ready in a few suns."

"You will do nothing of the sort."

Taking a deep breath, Aria focused on remaining calm, knowing anger met with anger only grew. She reminded herself that his denials were born from concern over her well-being. However, he overlooked the fact that keeping her in her room would not keep her safe. Or happy.

"Would you have me do nothing?" She asked. "Would you ask any mother to ignore the fact that her child was in peril?"

Talon crossed his arms and turned away. "*I* will hunt down the Reapers. If our son lives, *I* will bring him back."

With a Trancer's sight, she saw an echo of black and a swirl of dark fury surround Talon, engulfing him. He lied. Aria sat down, stunned. He did not go to find Tarik. He went to find the Reapers and destroy them all. Perhaps he denied it to others, but he could not deny it to her.

She rolled the goblet stem between her palms, the metal cool against her skin. She could not lose him again. Not like this. Not to pain and destructive passion. She would have to save him from himself. She gulped some wine to fortify her resolve for the battle to come. "Then I will travel with you."

Talon whipped back around, his face blank. The mask of a man who has all the answers. "No. I forbid it."

Aria's jaw dropped at the audacity of his words. "You *forbid* it?"

"Yes. You are too weak to travel and would slow me down."

She wanted to fling her goblet at his head, but resisted the urge. "I will not. Besides, you need me. I can follow their trail. Once I feel Tarik, there will be no way they can hide my child from me."

Talon strode over and gripped Aria by the arms, pulling her too her feet. "I lost my son to those butchers. I will not lose you."

Aria did not try to move away but looked her Giver in the eye, fighting the hysterical laughter that trembled on her lips. They both wanted the same thing—to save the other. He wanted to save her body, and she wanted to save his soul.

She laid a gentle hand upon his forearm. "You will not lose me. With my Trancer abilities and your Warrior skills, we will prevail over all that try to bar our path. Together, we can find Tarik."

He shrugged her away. Aria's heart cried out at the dismissal.

"My decision remains unchanged. You will wait here. Do I have your word?"

She shook her head. "No. You do not. I will not give my word, and you should not ask for it."

Talon took a step forward, his eyes softening. "I beseech you, Aria. Do as I ask. Please."

Aria walked towards the window, avoiding the pleading look he gave her and the truth that surrounded his emotions. Perhaps he was a Warrior, more comfortable with a sword than a battle of words, but if she were not careful, his honest distress would win this fight.

She could not let him win. If she did, she would be safe, but Talon would lose his soul to the destructive forces within.

If that happened, he would not be able to live with himself, and then her loss would be complete. Perhaps it was selfish, but that possible future frightened her more than the edge of a Reaper's blade.

She braced herself for Talon's wrath. He would not like her decision, but it was for the best. "I know you wish to keep me safe, but I cannot agree to what you ask."

Talon walked up to the window to join her, caressing her shoulders with his palms. She shuddered. He would be easier to deny if his concern were not so genuine.

"What if I give you no choice?" he asked.

"You would not do such a thing." Aria turned around, appalled at the implication.

"Yes, I would, but please believe me in that I do not wish to do so. I am not your master and have no desire to play the role. I am your Warrior and wish to keep you from harm's way."

She shook his hands off. "Pretty words from one who would control me."

She heard him chuckle, and her skin burned. "You mock me? That is beneath you."

"I do not mock. I admire. When we met, you were but a naive maiden, fearful of touching my bare skin. Now you stand defiant." His chuckle quieted. "I would give my sword to bring back that innocence."

Her heart swelled at the tenderness in his voice, but she refused to let it sway her. "Much has happened."

"Too much. Your innocence may have vanished, but you are still more unfamiliar with the ways of the world than you might imagine."

"I know enough, and I am a Trancer. Do not forget that."

"I do not forget."

"Then you will let me travel with you?"

"No."

Aria broke away, her pace loud on the stone as she measured her anger in footsteps, "Do what you must, but do not ask me to do any less." Deliberately, she turned away, ignoring him. He approached her from behind. His warm breath disturbed her hair as he leaned in.

He kissed the top of her head. "It will be as you say," he whispered.

Turning on his heel, he sheathed his sword and left the room. The door slammed closed like a coffin's lid.

***

"I cannot believe how uncooperative and stubborn Aria has become." Talon paced the room while Lore watched, grinning.

"What did you expect?"

Talon wanted to throw his hands in the air, but he refrained from such a useless gesture. Aria made him want to tear his hair out, but he would overcome his own impatience if it killed him. "I expected her to be reasonable."

"Reasonable or malleable?"

Talon stopped in front of Lore. "What do you mean, malleable?"

"When you met Aria she was ignorant enough to do anything you said. Took your every word as truth. She believed in you completely. She was a maiden, a girl. Now, she is a woman made strong by suffering."

Talon glared at his friend. "Do you suggest that I want to keep her ignorant?"

Lore held up his hands. "I am saying that maybe she was easier to deal with before the Reaper's raid, and now, you are at a loss as to how to behave."

Talon frowned. "Nonsense. I want to keep her safe. She is a woman, yes, but she is still inexperienced."

"And you would keep her in such a condition."

"No. I would show her the world," Talon replied. He would place the moons at her feet and the sun in her hands if he could. He continued, "But I would not have her gain more world-experience at the hands of the Reapers."

Lore shrugged in acquiescence. "Agreed. I cannot argue your logic in that wish. No woman should be subjected to that kind of knowledge."

Talon whipped around. "So, will you help me?"

"What would you ask of me?"

"Keep Aria here while I ride to find the Reapers."

Lore raised a brow. "I can, if that is what you want of me, but I thought to travel with you. Two Warriors stand a better chance against a Reaper army."

Talon clapped his friend on the back, wanting to accept the offer, but knowing it was impossible. "Thank you, but I must decline. I think Aria is strong-willed enough to try to follow me, and I need someone I can trust to prevent such an occurrence."

"Surely another Warrior could fulfill such a simple request."

Talon held back a sigh of exasperation, but decided to speak his thoughts, hoping to make Lore understand his reasoning. "The Council will be angry at my leaving, but my motivation is strong. There is a chance they will be lenient in punishment when I return." *If I return.* "As for you, they would banish you from the Keep. Friendship is not a reason to slaughter."

Lore's expression grew stony. "So you do not plan a single confrontation? You desire total revenge? Obliteration of the Reapers?"

Talon made a careless gesture, but his heart was not so flippant. He was a city dweller long before he became a Warrior, and some of the codes ran deep. The Reapers would not go unpunished. Any of them. "I will do what is necessary to make the Tower—all Towers—safe from their evil doings."

Five

Hands bound in front of her, Iliana lurched forward, physical weariness overcome by Reaper strength. Though the destroyed Tower was four suns behind them, the band of Reapers showed no signs of slowing and stopped only to sleep at night.

Another tug from her captor and Iliana stepped on her already battered sleeping robe, stumbling to the ground. She landed with a cry. A rock gouged her hip and dirt imbedded itself into her bruised skin. She saw the leather boots of other Reapers as they passed, ignoring the scene.

"Get up, *Trancer*," her captor commanded. "Or lie there forever."

Instead, Iliana ignored both him and her throbbing hip and closed her eyes, grateful for the lack of movement. *A moment of rest. Just a moment, and I will get up.*

"I said move." He emphasized the command with a kick to her ribs, and Iliana cried out as pain shot through her side. Out of the corner of her eye, she saw his foot go back for another swing, and she rolled away, rising to her feet.

"Son of a *raja*," Iliana muttered through gritted teeth. "I am up."

"What did you call me?"

"Nothing." Iliana turned away to continue her march.

"That's not what it sounded like." Grabbing her by her braid, he swung her around until she faced him. "You look at me when I speak, *Trancer*, and you better watch your mouth, or I'll cut out your tongue."

These Reapers were barbarians. Animals. No, below animals. Animals would never show such contempt for life. She pulled away, her captive braid tugging at her scalp. The Reaper laughed. "Stay with me, and maybe I'll forget what you called me."

Was he going to hit her again?

He pulled her closer. The hardness of his erection pressed against her as he ground his hips into hers. No, he had plans far worse than a simple beating. Anger welled up from deep inside, replacing the need for survival and the fear of the situation. How dare he? She was a Trancer. A daughter of the Tower.

Leering, his free hand moved to her waist and made its way up her chest. Hot anger burst from deep within. She was not a common village whore he could paw and fondle. Rearing back, she spit at her captor. The sticky glob struck his cheek.

He wiped it away with the back of his hand, and in the same motion, cuffed Iliana across the cheek, sending her reeling into the dirt.

"What did I tell you about our guest?"

Iliana looked up from the ground to see Mako, the leader of the Reapers, staring down at her from the back of a black *rohha*. She swore again, but this time only in her mind. She did not want to attract his attention any more than she already had.

He would kill her if he felt the need. She had seen the depths of his ruthlessness when she was marched past the bodies of her sisters. Hidden behind his handsome, almost regal face, was the heart of a madman.

If he had a heart at all.

"You said to make sure she did not run."

Mako tilted his head in acknowledgment. "I also said to treat her well, Bruin. Do you see how hitting her will not help me towards that goal?"

Bruin nodded. "My apologies, but she is insolent."

Mako raised a dark brow, and Iliana flinched, regretting her hasty actions.

"Bring her to me."

Bruin punched her in the small of her back, shoving her forward.

"Trancer, do you know why you live?"

"Yes." Bile rose in her throat at the memory she already worked to forget.

She lived because of a bargain. Let her, the Healer, and Tarik live, and she would help him. She would use her Trancer abilities to give him an advantage over the other Reapers.

Mako, eyes black behind his mask, had agreed, but given her a choice—only herself and one other. Tarik or the Healer. Not both.

If she refused to choose, all three would die by his

blade.

So she chose, and the Healer died, her ancient eyes forgiving Iliana even as they cut her throat.

Iliana swallowed hard, knowing any reaction other than cool disdain would be perceived as a sign of weakness.

And weakness was not tolerated by the Reaper leader— it was *dealt* with.

"You remember what I hold as collateral, do you not?" Mako's *rohha* danced beneath him.

"I remember." How could she forget? Iliana peered around the side of the beast, looking for the small bundle that was the baby. The poor child was too quiet.

A horrible thought crossed her mind.

What if she had sacrificed the Healer for nothing?

"Let me see him," she demanded. "Let me know he still lives, and I will trouble you no further."

Mako gave a sharp whistle. One of the other Reapers rode forward, stopping when he came to Iliana and the leader.

"Show her," Mako commanded. His cool eyes never left hers.

Reaching behind him, the Reaper pulled a bundle off his back and presented it to Iliana. Tarik lay inside the wrapping. Fast asleep, his cheeks were pink with life, and his tiny chest rose and fell with each breath.

Iliana breathed a sigh of relief that went all the way to her toes.

"We will have no more of this nonsense, will we Trancer?"

Iliana nodded her acquiescence. "As long as Tarik is safe, I will do as you ask."

"Good." Mako turned his *rohha* around to leave, stopped, hesitated, and turned back. "Punishment. I forgot."

The Reaper leader nodded to Bruin. "Turn her."

Hands like clubs grabbed her, forcing her around, and she was once again inhaling Bruin's foul breath.

"I am going to like this," Bruin whispered in her ear.

She felt her head tugged back by her braid. What was Mako going to do? She squeezed her eyes shut, prepared for a blow. It did not come. Instead, he caressed her hair, his hand curved around her ear and ran lightly across the back of her neck like a lover's caress.

Before she could cry out, he pulled her hair straight up and away from her scalp. Iliana opened her eyes in time to see the flash of a sword, razor sharp and deadly, as it came towards her. Her head snapped forward. The pulling was gone.

So was her hair.

With a cry, she looked to see Mako holding the long, thick plait in one hand and his weapon in the other. "Do as you promised, or next time it will be your head." He smiled, letting her hair fall beneath the hooves of his *rohha.*

Muffling a sob, Iliana nodded, knowing he told the truth.

Mako reined his *rohha* in towards Bruin. "Now it is your turn. Step forward."

The Reaper looked up, startled.

"You disobeyed my orders. What shall your punishment be?"

Bruin shuffled forward and knelt before Mako. "It will not happen again."

The air around Iliana grew silent as others stopped to watch with expectation.

Mako grinned the same death's smile Iliana remembered from the Tower. "That is right. It will not." Raising his sword, he ran Bruin through.

Without a sound or a sigh, the Reaper fell to the ground. Dead.

Wiping his sword on his cape, Mako sheathed it and bowed his head to Iliana. "My lady, you ride with me."

There was no choice. Iliana let herself be pulled onto his saddle.

Six

"Was that a lunge, or did you stumble?" Talon taunted his opponent. He shifted his body, ready to move in an instant. Sword in one hand and short dagger in the other, he waited for the other man to attack.

He was rewarded moments later as Lore rushed forward with a battle cry. A surge of energy raced through Talon's blood. He stepped aside and whacked his friend with the flat of his sword as he went past.

Lore fell forward, rolled, and jumped to his feet with a grin.

"A worthy try," Talon goaded.

Lore, his body dusty and his smile wide, charged again, not allowing Talon a chance to step away and prepare. Within seconds, the clash of swords rang throughout the courtyard.

Talon reveled in the clean energy of battle as Lore rained blow after blow at his head and torso. He moved backwards into a defensive position. Sweat ran down his face and into his eyes, obscuring his vision. He blinked once, twice, three times before it cleared. He shook his head. Sweat spun outwards.

"You should have worn a head cloth," Lore commented with a grunt as Talon blocked a thrust. "Such a simple mistake could get you killed if we truly fought."

"Perhaps," Talon replied, his voice even and steady despite the exertion of sparring. Lore lunged. Talon stepped back and sideways. Lore misstepped. It was all Talon needed. Within seconds, his mind unerringly calculated his next move. The surge of power that came with winning roared through him. "But not today." With a tuck and turn, he rolled past Lore, rising to his feet.

The fight ended with his sword pointed at Lore's back.

Lore raised his hands and dropped his sword in defeat. "Once again, you are the victor." His tone held no hint of malice, only good-natured acceptance. Turning, he bowed in acquiescence.

Talon sheathed his sword. "I am glad to see my maneuver was successful."

"I did not think a man of your size could move so

quickly. It was a bit of a surprise."

Talon's brows went up. "My size?"

Lore grinned. "You know, as big as a *rohha* and about as graceful."

"You fight much better with wit than with sword," Talon said, unable to resist. "Perhaps if you practiced more, you might best me in both."

Lore took a step back, clutching his chest. "You wound me with your words."

Clapping his friend on the back, Talon laughed.

"Master Talon!" Talon saw a young Warrior walking in his direction. Still chuckling, he wiped his sweaty brow with the back of his hand and waited while the young man made his way across the courtyard.

"What is it, lad?"

The young Warrior bowed before speaking. "The Council has arrived, and they wish to speak with you."

Talon sheathed his sword. He had been expecting the summons. His impending quest for vengeance was common talk around the Tower. It had been only a matter of time before the Council heard the rumors.

"Would you like me to stand at your side?" Lore asked.

Talon shook his head. "Thank you, but this is my battle."

"Perhaps, but as Warriors we either stand together or fall alone."

"I am grateful for the offer." Warriors lived, fought, and died with their brothers. They relied on each other for protection in battle, but this battle was private. "This is something I must do alone."

Lore nodded. "As you wish. I will be in the dining hall if you care to speak later."

Turning on his heel, Talon accompanied his escort to the main Tower chamber—the one where the slain Elders had once governed. Other Warriors occupied the courtyard, some helping the new arrivals from the other Towers settle in, and some still repairing Reaper damage. Silence followed in Talon's wake as his comrades watched him walk past, fully aware of the summons and its meaning. He ignored the sideways looks, preferring to ready his wits for the verbal battle to come.

Seven Warriors made up the Council. The members

were older and past their prime for physical battle, but they were unequaled in verbal skills and tactical strategy. Still fearless, they commanded the Keep that the Warriors usually occupied.

Talon's muscles tightened into battle readiness as they strode closer. The Council of Seven would try to talk him out of his chosen path. It would take all his determination to deny their request and all his skill to gain their approval. They only sanctioned fighting the Reapers when the outlaws invaded the land, and were not willing to give the Reapers the advantage by fighting them in their own territory.

The thought that the Council had grown soft flickered through Talon's mind. He reminded himself it was not his place to issue judgment on them. After all, they were not the enemy, not in the way the Reapers were. The Council sought to preserve, not destroy.

His escort stopped in front of the large double door to the chamber where the Council waited. Without hesitation, Talon thrust the heavy wooden portals open and entered. His nose wrinkled. The room smelled stale and dank from disuse. A deep blue rug marked a path to a chair placed in front of a table. Made of a deep, brown wood, the table was barely long enough to accommodate all the members who sat on the far side.

Talon walked to the chair, but remained standing, alert and ready for the verbal battle he knew would be waged. He placed his hand upon the cold metal handle of the weapon that rested against his hip.

Knowing there would be no pleasantries, he waited for the Council to make the first move.

"Master Talon, do you know why we have summoned you?"

Talon turned to face Councilman Reef. His brown hair flecked with gray, he was the youngest member of the Council.

"Yes."

The Councilman looked grim as he surveyed Talon from sweaty hair to leather-clad foot. "Let me first say we understand your anger and desire for revenge."

Talon frowned at the comment and quelled the urge to scoff. They understood? They did not feel Aria's shame in survival when her world was destroyed. They had not seen the grief and sorrow in her eyes when she was told of the death of her son. They had not held her as she cried over her loss. They did not share in her anguish.

Or his.

"I see you doubt my words," Reef commented.

Talon nodded. "Do you have a son?"

Reef shrugged. "I do not know, but that does not negate my empathy and understanding for your situation."

"I do not doubt your intentions are worthy, but you err when you speak of understanding my situation. You have never lost a child to violence."

Reef gave a curt nod. "True. However, you would be as unaware as I if not for this unfortunate turn of events. Aria erred in telling you of the boy. Regardless of the situation, her son's death was private and should have remained so."

The hair on the back of Talon's neck rose. "Her loss is mine. You would do well to remember that. I will not have you speak ill of Aria or discount the death of our child."

The Council buzzed at the statement. Reef silenced them with a gesture. "It is true? You care for the Trancer?"

Talon hesitated, knowing he must speak the truth, but also knowing the consequences of such an act. He could not define his feelings for Aria, but he knew that because of the joining, they went beyond the boundaries of custom. "She is the mother of my son and my Given." He hoped it was enough to satisfy the Council as far as Aria was concerned.

"*Was* your Given," Reef corrected. "When the ceremony ended so did your obligations." The rest of the Council nodded in agreement.

Talon did not deny the truth of the statement. When he departed after the Given ceremony, he should have left Aria and all she meant to him.

He had tried, but his determination to dismiss her only seemed to entrench her in his mind and bring her deeper into his thoughts. He had found himself alone in the dark of night, remembering her cries of delight and the excitement of discovering her own body's responses. When he rode through the forest, every leaf was the color of her eyes. When he saw a flame, he saw her hair.

Joined or not, she was unforgettable. An innocent enigma that haunted him.

"It was my hope this issue would not rise." Reef interrupted Talon's thoughts. "But I see now it is the crux of the problem."

"What issue do you speak of?" Talon asked.

The Councilman rose and walked around the table while the other members whispered among themselves, evaluating the conversation. "In addition to the talk of your desire for revenge, we are aware of your lack of participation in the Given ceremony since you were with the Trancer."

All conversation stopped as seven pairs of eyes watched Talon for a response.

Talon challenged each Councilman, one by one, as his gaze met theirs, staring until they backed down. What he did or did not do was none of their business.

Reef paced in obvious agitation, waiting for Talon to speak, but finally breaking the silence. "Master Talon, I am sure you are aware of the covenant between the Trancers and the Warriors in regards to the Given ceremony."

"Of course."

"Explain it to us."

"Why? You know the pact as well as I."

Reef sat in his chair, folding his arms across his chest. "Indulge me."

Talon shrugged. If the Council wished to humiliate him, let them try. He knew the law as well as one born to the Warrior code. "As Warriors, we use our physical strength to protect the Trancers and all who lie within their Tower."

"And in the Given ceremony?"

"Only a Warrior may assist the Given in becoming a woman, for only a Warrior has the mental shield to withstand the Trancer onslaught that occurs in her first encounter."

Reef did not rise, but motioned Talon to sit. He glared at the Councilman, defying the request.

Reef rose from his chair and walked around the table, stopping in front of Talon. "I have never had reason to ask this, Master Talon, and never thought I would have reason

to. Especially of you, one of our most noble Warriors."
The Councilman stepped closer until he was nose to nose
with Talon. "Did you join with her? Did you break the
pact? Is this the reason you declined the other
ceremonies?"

Talon closed his eyes. After the joining, he had planned
to confess but could not. Instead, he had kept silent,
hoping to spare Aria any repercussions.

Now his silence served to convict him.

The air pulled outward as Reef stepped away. "Why
did you not speak? There are ways to repair the damage.
Why did you not come to us?"

Talon opened his eyes to see the rest of the Council
staring at him, their shocked expression more cutting than
words. "I would not trouble my brothers with personal
problems."

"Your silence had nothing to do with the Trancer?"

Talon's head dropped, knowing his answer was not
the one Reef wanted to hear. "I did not want her disciplined
then, and I will not allow her to be disciplined now. It was
not her fault."

Reef's face colored. "It is not up to us to discipline to
the Trancer. Her mistakes are between herself and her
people if she would choose to tell them. However, you must
be aware we cannot allow you to continue on this path.
You are a Warrior and must act as such. If you persist in
an inappropriate relationship with this Trancer, you will
be forced to leave the Warrior brotherhood."

"I understand."

"No, I do not think you do," the Councilman continued.
"The same consequences apply if you persist in seeking
revenge for a son you should never have known about.
This path you walk ends here and now!" The table shook
as the Council slammed his fist onto it.

Talon took an involuntary step towards Reef at the
decree. "You cannot do this. I must find his killers. Honor
demands it."

"Not Warrior honor, which you seem to overlook at
convenience. So, do not speak to me of honor. I will strip
you of rank and title if you force me to. We can forgive a
mistake if it is small, but you broke one of our most solemn
vows and now propose to break another."

"What do the other members say?" Talon searched the faces of those who judged him, but their eyes were blank, their lips pressed firm, as they watched him and the proceedings. "Will you deny me satisfaction?"

Cloak swirling with a flourish, Reef swept away and made to speak with the Council of Seven. He went from one member to the next, holding whispered conversations. When he reached the end of the table, he walked back to Talon. "We are in agreement. Return to the Keep. Forget the Trancer."

"And my son?"

"Him as well. A Warrior fights when necessary and does not take life without just cause. Revenge is in opposition to everything we stand for."

"If I refuse?" Talon asked, although he knew the only answer possible.

"You will be disavowed." Reef's expression was earnest but firm. "Now leave, and consider what we have said. You have until the next rising of the sun to decide if your life as a Warrior is worth the price of revenge."

"My decision is already made." Unsheathing his Warrior's sword, Talon held it at arm's length. The polished metal glowed pure silver in the room's dim lighting. He opened his hand. It fell to the floor. The clang of metal on stone ripped through his soul. He was a Warrior no longer, not in title and not by right.

He walked away.

***

Aria stood in the doorway to Talon's room and watched as he thrust clothes into a pack. Rumors of the Council's decision, and his reply, had spread though the Tower, and she had feared they were true. "By the way you are stomping about, I would say my fears were justified," she murmured.

Talon turned at the whispered comment. "You should not be here. I am an outcast. You only hurt your reputation." He closed the pack and flung it onto the bed where another waited.

Aria shrugged. "Perhaps you are unaware, but others' opinions mean little to me now." She crossed the cold stone floor and stopped a hairsbreadth away from Talon, her eyes searching his.

Talon pushed a strand of hair from her eyes. "You should care."

Burning from the fire that raged within, the heat of his skin singed her Trancer soul. "Why? These people are strangers to me."

"They are your people." Talon's hand dropped away. Taking bread and fruit from the table, he filled another pack.

Aria walked to the window and pulled the curtain back. Down below, both men and women worked in the garden. She watched one of the newly arrived Elders, her hair white with age, as she bent over to water a young plant. "What do you see when you look out this window?"

Leaving the pack on the table, he walked over and stood beside her. "I see what you see. People working. Warriors and Trancer bringing your Tower back to life."

"True, although that is but a cursory observation." She leaned on the ledge and took a moment to take in the view as the massive gates opened and a band of Trancers walked through—more recruits for the Tower. "Do you know what I see?"

"Tell me."

Aria heard the indulgence in his voice. She ignored it. "I see the same thing."

With a *harrumph,* Talon turned away. Aria stopped him with a gentle hand upon his forearm. Now was not the time to allow him to humor her, not when so much was at stake. "Wait. I have yet to tell you the difference between your vision and mine."

He stopped, obliging her request.

She tried to smile. "The difference is not in what is seen but in what is *not* seen. I do not see my friends or my son. I do not see the women who taught me to be strong. I do not see my home." Her voice cracked before she caught herself with a reminder that she could not allow herself to be crippled by grief. Not yet. She forced herself to finish, to speak her thoughts before she lost the chance to make Talon understand. "This is still a Tower, but it is not *my* Tower."

"I know how you must feel."

"No, you do not." Aria gripped his arm harder as memories of that night resounded in her ears. The screams, maniacal laughter, and pleadings grew louder with each breath. She shut her eyes, but it only served to intensify the experience. "You cannot possibly imagine what it is like to lose everything. To have everything, *everyone,* taken away. To never get the chance to say good-bye."

Talon placed a hand over hers and squeezed. "Yes, I can."

His voice and comforting strength brought her back to the present. She glimpsed the empty scabbard on the bed. Her face colored in shame. He knew loss all too well. "I am sorry. I did not think."

He shrugged. "At least I was given the choice and the chance to say good-bye."

"When did you plan to say the words to me?" Aria asked, "Or were you going to just walk away?"

He reached into his shirt and pulled out a crumpled piece of parchment. "Everything I needed to say, I said in this."

Aria took the paper from his fingers, wadded it into a ball, and threw it to the ground. "Perhaps you are of the Warrior guild no longer, but your heart is not so easily changed. A letter of explanation is beneath you." She touched his cheek. "Do I mean so little to you?"

"No. Never. I only thought to save us both the pain, but you are right. It is a coward's way." He caught her chin with a forefinger and tilted her face upwards. "I could not bear to do it. I could not bear the look on your face as I left."

"Then do not. Take me with you."

Talon brought her hand to his lips and kissed a fingertip. "I wish I could."

"Then do," Aria urged. "I promise you will not regret it."

Talon shook his head. "It will be a rough journey. I do not know where the Reapers reside. He hesitated. "And barely a moon has passed since Tarik's birth. You are still too weak to travel."

"I am not as delicate as you would believe. Do not make the mistake of assuming that muscle and willpower corresponds to height and strength." She drew herself up to her full height, but she barely reached Talon's chin. "Do not leave me because I am a woman. Take me because

I am a Trancer. With my abilities to read the currents, you will locate the Reapers faster with me than without me." She could also take the time to talk some sense into him and save him from dishonoring not just his code but also his soul.

"Speed is not the issue. I will find them no matter how many seasons pass."

Aria gritted her teeth. "Leave me and I will follow."

Talon ran a hand through his hair. "You are more stubborn than I thought." He paced away, and she heard him murmur as if talking to himself or, perhaps, the Goddess. "Perhaps she can do what she claims. Who am I to decide her fate? Is it up to me to tell her what she can and cannot do?"

He continued to pace. Aria watched, waiting to see the outcome of the conflict that raged within her Giver—to keep her safe or to let her decide her own fate. What would he do?

His voice rose, catching her off guard. "Have you been able to read the currents since your recovery?"

Aria worried her lip. "No, but no one can. Not until the Elders perform a cleansing ceremony to banish the negative currents the Reapers brought upon the Tower."

He frowned, and she hurried to explain. "Once I am away from the Tower, I will be able do so again."

The silence as he mulled over her words almost broke her. His pacing ended when he stopped in front of her. "Are you sure?"

Aria nodded. "I am positive."

She was rewarded with a resigned sigh. "If you cannot keep up, I will have to send you back."

Her heart leapt that reasoning had managed to penetrate her lover's rigid ideals. "You will take me?"

"Against my better judgment, yes." He shook a finger at her. "But I mean it when I say I will send you back if you cannot keep up. Do you agree?"

"Agreed," Aria replied. Standing on her toes, she reached upwards. "A kiss to seal the bargain. I know we will succeed and find our son." She placed her lips on his mouth, and he crushed her to his chest and tasted her with his tongue. She rose into the heat that rushed from their bodies, her hands tangling in his hair, and for a moment, all the pain went away.

He pulled away, and she crashed back to reality. But the residue of his feelings for her caressed her skin, giving her strength. Her head reeled.

"Go pack." He kissed her on the forehead. "We leave in the morning."

Aria let a grin curve her lips in the first truly happy moment she had experienced since the Reapers took her world away.

Playfully, Talon swatted her on the bottom as she rushed out the door.

"I will be waiting," she called over her shoulder, her mind already preparing and planning all that needed to be done before she departed.

***

The pounding on the door grew louder, invading Aria's dream. She rolled over. It was time to begin the quest.

Her feet were running before they hit the floor.

The smooth leather of the leggings she had stolen from a young Warrior hugged her legs as she ran for the door. Perhaps the reason for the journey was serious, but excitement coursed through her at the thought of adventure. Finally, after years of being the obedient daughter, and then the dutiful Trancer, she was going to be able to prove she was strong. She would be able to quell the voice in her head that told her she was weak and insignificant.

She would show her father that a first-born daughter was worth as much as a first-born son.

Her eyes caught the letter she had placed on the table. Sealed with candle drippings, it described her reasons for departure. She hoped it would help ease the worrying of the newly arrived Elders. Even if it did not, she knew what she and Talon did was right.

She flung open the door.

It was Lore. He stood alone.

Her eyes widened, then narrowed, as she understood the situation.

"Aria—"

She held up a hand, stopping him. She recognized the expression of guilt that clouded his perfect features—she saw it every time she saw her own reflection. Granted, hers was more pronounced, but his downcast eyes told her more than mere words ever would.

She turned away, unwilling to let Lore see the pain of betrayal in her eyes. "When did he leave?"

"Last night. He asked me to watch out for you."

She chewed her lip. Perhaps Talon was worldlier, but it did not give him the right to his overwhelming arrogance. It did not give him the right to lie.

"I do not need a keeper. I am not a child." Running a hand over her hair, she smoothed the waist length braid.

"I know. I told him as much."

"Really? I thought all your kind tended to agree when it came to matters of women."

"We disagree and agree as much as anyone else."

She dismissed Lore with a flick of her hand. Walking over to the table, she picked up her letter and tore it into pieces. The sound of paper ripping did little to satisfy her anger at the betrayal. "Your words are nothing to me. Just more talk, more lies, from a Warrior who would control me." She threw the paper pieces into the fireplace.

"I know what he did seems wrong but it is for the best. You have been through much, and he would not see you go through more." Lore placed his hands on her shoulders. "He will be back soon, and in the meantime, you will have me to keep you company."

"Small consolation." She jerked away, turning to watch the rest of the letter burn.

Lore chuckled.

Her frown deepened.

"You are stubborn. I can see why Talon worries." Lore's breath sounded in her ear. "It will not be as bad as you think, pretty Aria. I am pleasant enough."

He pinched her bottom, and Aria jumped, turning in midair. "How dare you," she shouted. "Get out."

Lore backed up.

Picking up a goblet, she threw it at her keeper's head. He dodged and went for the door, shutting it behind him. "At least you are not angry with Talon anymore," she heard him call as he turned the key, locking her in.

"Lore, you are an insufferable *raga,*" Aria screamed, throwing another goblet. "Let me out of here." Laughter was the only response, and it faded as Lore walked away.

Aria screamed again, a wordless cry, and beat on the heavy wooden portal until her fists were red and sore. Talon had left her behind. Left her to wait for him to either die or return a killer. Hope dissolved at the thought, and she leaned her head against the wood, as her pounding grew weaker.

Tears of anger flooded her eyes. The betrayal went deep.

Seven

Lore stood at Aria's doorway with a tray of food in his hand. "Is it safe to come in?"

"Yes," came the muffled reply.

He hesitated, remembering his earlier encounters with the Trancer. "Are you armed?" he called out, partly concerned, but mostly amused. For two suns, he had asked the same question. For two suns, when he entered the room, Aria waited with a weapon in hand, and he had ended up pushing her tray through the partially open door.

"No." Her voice sounded closer as if she waited just on the other side of the door.

"How can I be sure?"

"I promise. I will not try to hit you," was the muffled answer.

Perhaps the beautiful Aria was over her snit. Lore chuckled. It was more likely she was waiting to brain him into unconsciousness. Still, she had to eat, and so did he. Balancing the tray with one hand, he placed the key in the lock. The sound of tumblers turning signaled the end to Aria's confinement.

Pocketing the key, Lore backed into the room, kicked the door shut, and feinted to the right. Nothing whizzed past his head. Empty-handed, Aria gazed at him with contempt. She was still dressed in the stolen clothes.

He feinted again. She did not smile at the joke. If she wanted to sulk, that was fine. He shrugged and walked over to the table to lay her morning meal out. "I am sorry I locked you in, Mistress Aria, but under the circumstances it seemed best." He continued to place food on the table, but stopped with a pitcher of morning wine. "Goblets?" he asked, unsuccessfully hiding a smile.

Aria did not return the grin but bent to retrieve the cups from the floor. "For whom is my confinement better?" Walking over, she thrust them into Lore's hands with a ferocity that surprised him. "You and Talon? Or for me?"

"For all concerned." Lore filled the dented cups. He noticed Aria's eyes were rimmed in red. Her cheeks were raw and damp. "You have been crying."

Aria rubbed her face with the palms of her hands.

"What did you expect?"

A pang of shame pierced Lore, but he ignored it. What he did was for the best. No matter what Aria believed, she was not equipped to handle the unforgiving path Talon walked. Besides, he had promised his friend he would keep her safe.

"Do my tears bother you?" Aria asked.

Lore walked around the table and escorted Aria to a chair. Tossing a small square cloth into her lap, he placed a plate of food in front of her before going to his own seat. "I do not like to see women cry. Especially when I am the cause."

Aria took up an eating tong and picked at her food. "You can stop this by taking me to Talon."

"Perhaps, but I will not." He bit into the still warm bread.

Aria jumped to her feet, the cloth fluttering to the floor. "Why not? It is as much my right to find the Reapers as it is his."

Lore took a sip of wine. She was a fiery one. No wonder Talon's feeling ran so deep and strong. However, the same spirit that had pulled her through tragedy could also get her into trouble. Trouble prevented only by constant vigilance. "You are not a Warrior, Mistress Aria. You are a Trancer. Can you wield a sword? Can you ride a *rohha?*"

Aria sat back down with a thump, arms crossed. "No, but I can learn. Besides, with you and Talon by my side, I would not need to know how to fight."

"That is precisely why he did not want you to go. Warriors must be sensitive to their surrounding. We must remain vigilant or die. To guard another splits our attention. If you were with him, you would be a distraction. One that could kill him." Lore raised his cup and sipped his wine, waiting for Aria to reply. He wondered if his speech made a dent in her resolve.

The weight of her door's key reminded him that if she refused to be sensible, he could keep her locked in her room. It was not the best alternative, but it would keep her safe while Talon pursued his quest.

If only he could have done the same to Talon.

"With my Trancer skills, I can tell you and Talon of danger before it arrives. I can read the currents and give the safest route."

Lore set his goblet down and leaned over the table. The ineffectiveness of his explanation was not a surprise. "Then we would lose our edge and later, when we traveled alone, we would be more vulnerable. Is that your wish? Would you sacrifice Talon's future for the ease of today's journey?"

Aria shook her head, and two tears ran down her cheeks, dripping off her chin into her food. Lore's heart twisted in sympathy. *She is really a child. No matter what has happened, for all the horror, she is innocent.*

"Do not cry, Mistress Aria. Talon will return soon, and everything will be better." He reached over the table and patted her hand, relieved when she did not pull away.

"What if I try to leave on my own? Will you stop me?"

Her eyes pleaded with him. Lore took a deep breath before he replied. "Yes, I will stop you. You are unused to the wilds. I doubt you have ever tracked a man. If I let you go, you will be lost by the next sunrise." Her shoulders slumped, and he knew he called it right. "Aria, do not make me lock you in here to keep you safe. I have no wish to be so cruel."

"I will climb down from the balcony. Even you cannot stop that."

Lore pushed away from the table and walked over to the doors that opened onto the stone palisade. Pushing them wide, he walked over to the edge. Could she climb down? He skimmed the stone with a callused hand and smiled. The walls around were smooth with age. It was a straight drop to a stone court. Climbing down was not an option, and if she jumped, she would break her legs and possibly her neck. She was not that foolish. He walked back in, leaving the doors ajar so the sunlight shone in, brightening the room.

Aria stood next to her chair, shifting from one foot to another, waiting for his response.

"You will hurt yourself if you attempt such a foolish idea," he said.

Her nervous shifting stopped. Bending, she picked up the fallen cloth and dabbed at her eyes. "I am not as backwards as you may think."

"That is not what I think." Sitting, he sipped his wine

and raised the goblet to Aria in salute. "I think you are a smart, sensible, beautiful woman who is persistent as a Warrior when she wants something. I admire your tenacity, but wish you would put it to better use."

"Your opinion means little to me, Warrior." Her hands clench into rigid fists at her sides. "I ask you one more time to take me where I want to go. Do not do keep me here against my will."

"I will do what I must." He drained his wine.

Aria sat back down and picked at her food some more. Silence prevailed, but not a comfortable one. Pouring another glass of wine, Lore took a deep draught, and then stretched his arms above his head, yawning.

"Do I bore you?" Aria flashed him a sly smile, a knowing grin that spoke more than words. Lore's eyes widened. He had seen a similar smile before—on Talon's face when he bested an opponent.

Lore shook his head. The room spun. He must be more tired than he thought. His arms fell to his side, heavy and useless. What was Aria up to? He tried to ask her what was happening, but all that emerged from his lips was an unintelligible groan. Unable to remain upright, he fell forward. His head hit the table with a dull thud.

The conniving wench.

It was his last thought before the world went black.

Aria's mouth fell open. She had not thought the drugs would act so quickly. Left over from Tarik's birth, the powder did anything from relax the user to bring unconsciousness. She had poured it into Lore's wine so quickly that she was not sure of the dosage. She ran to the other side of the table and shook the Warrior's massive shoulders. "Lore. Lore, are you all right?"

The only reply was incoherent mumbling.

Aria held her ear to his back, hoping she had not killed him. He seemed to be breathing steadily. His heartbeat sounded strong. He would feel like a fool when he wakened, but he would live.

Satisfied, she gathered the remnants of the meal and stuffed them in a sack. Digging through his pockets, she retrieved the key to her room, shut the door behind her, and locked it. Nobody would search for her until Lore wakened. He would eventually get out, but his forced confinement might buy her a little more time. *It will also teach him a valuable lesson about locking people up,* she thought, pleased with the small retaliation. She hefted the small sack to her shoulder. Now, all she had to do was steal a *rohha,* track a trained Warrior through the forest, and save her son.

***

Aria stopped at the edge of the forest and dismounted with a groan. She had never ridden so far or so long. Still, it was only a day's ride between herself and the Tower. Not nearly enough to feel safe. So, weak knees were the least of her worries. Ignoring her aching muscles, she tied her stolen *rohha* to a tree, running her untrained hand over its dull-colored hide. Its owner would be outraged at its loss.

She was outraged that it was so uncooperative and ill-tempered. As if reading her thoughts, the beast whipped about and snapped at her. Aria snatched her fingers back before the creature managed to connect. She raised a brow, reassessing the owner's reaction to the stolen animal. Outraged? Perhaps not. The owner would more likely be grateful she had stolen the cranky pack animal. A chuckle began deep in her gut, rose through her throat, and emerged as a howl of laughter. The beast lunged again, and she dodged away, but not before it tore her sleeve.

"I think I shall name you Cossa." She fingered the rent garment. "It is an herb that they give to children as a tonic. It is quite bitter and unpleasant." The *rohha* laid his ears back. "I see it is a name you are familiar with," Aria teased as the animal took another, final, desperate, but unsuccessful lunge.

Still chuckling, Aria retrieved a threadbare cloak from her pack, being careful to stay clear of Cossa's teeth, and carried it into the tall grass. Spreading the garment onto the cool ground, she lowered herself into sitting position and took a deep breath. An evening breeze pulled at her hair, rustling the loose strands. The breeze tasted like rain.

No matter. She had a job to do. Blocking the surrounding noises, she let her head drop forward and relaxed her neck. Resting her hands palms up on her knees, she took a deep breath. Focused, nothing entered her consciousness but the sound of her breath as it traveled in and out of her lungs.

She disconnected from her body.

Thick with the life that comes from wild things, the currents swelled around her. Her first thought was that they were too crushing. Around her ankles and over her skin, they swirled like silk. Iridescent beams of light pulsed and throbbed with the rhythm of her heartbeat. From the newest blade of grass to the bird soaring overhead, all living energy vibrated, scattering power from one to another, connecting them.

Aria breathed deep, inhaling the color, letting the vibrations fill her from head to heel, cleansing her. As the purity of nature replaced a corner of the horror that still haunted her nights, she breathed a psychic sigh of release. Here, creatures killed for need, not joy. Life was an honor, not a lesson. The beauty both shattered and rebuilt her.

It was too much. Too overwhelming.

She pulled out of the trance. Air whooshed from her lungs. Sweat dripped from her brow, and her chest heaved with exertion. She would have to be more careful. The forces were strong. Stronger than either at the Tower or her hometown. Was it because of the extent of life that surrounded her, or was it something inside her? Had the events changed her? Made her more sensitive? Aria tucked a stray hair behind her ears and back into her braid, letting the mass fall down her back. Whatever the reason, she would have to be more careful.

Shutting her eyes, she delved back into the currents, mentally turning away before the forces overwhelmed her once again. Stretching her vision, she rose above the forest to look for the spark that was uniquely Talon's. It would be like him. A dark light, hard to see and even more difficult to understand. It would be even darker now that he was on a quest for revenge.

Nevertheless, there was still goodness within him. His sense of responsibility and duty glowed with the deep, bright light of a Warrior's soul. She remembered it from when they joined.

The joining. Its memory and its effects were a part of her now. She remembered how his spark had touched her. Like thick stone and hot steel. Like a soft blanket and a warm kiss.

Enough reminiscing. She had to find him.

Once again, she entered Trancer consciousness. Time was both everything and nothing as she flew over the landscape, weaving a path through the life forces. Watching the rivers of color, she searched for Talon's spark, questing, and feeling for his presence.

She sensed an intensity below. A distinct throbbing that touched her. A churning that drew her. Talon. She dove, swimming through color to see him as he bedded down for the night. She watched, mesmerized by the colors that emanated from him. Jewel-tones and black, the shifting and contrasting shades hypnotized her. A white light pulsed from deep within, shining through the dark for but a moment. She knew what it was—*his love for Tarik*, and it was so deep, so swallowed by pain of loss, that it broke her heart.

She had to help him, could not let him be consumed by the anguish that ravaged her own soul. She had to find Tarik and show Talon that his son lived.

Could she? Now that she was away from the wounded Tower, could the currents carry her to her son? Much time and distance stood between them, but the thought of a quick resolution and Talon's pain drove her. She had to try. Up she flew until she was above the plains. *Focus.* The mountains called her. Through the currents she swam, soaring like light, faster and farther than she had ever gone. Tarik's spark was not visible to her, but she knew he was close. A mother's bond to her babe was invincible. A Trancer's bond to her babe was unimaginable.

Or so she thought. In a breath, a psychic wall loomed in front of her, stopping her. Darker than fear, it stood like a fortress in the currents, keeping her from Tarik. Angry and desperate, Aria reached out with psychic hands—-

And awoke screaming.

By the Goddess, what was that wall? That barrier? She shuddered. Whatever it was, it was blacker than Talon's thoughts and wider than the world. It was not natural.

And her son was behind it.

Still shaking, Aria uncrossed her legs and stood.

Perhaps later she would be able to breach its depth, but not now. If she tried now, before she was ready, she knew the wall's power could do more than keep her at bay. When they were closer and she was rested, she would try again. Meanwhile, she would follow her original plan and travel with Talon, keeping him from harm until she proved herself right.

She stretched, groaning aloud at the stiffness that saturated her muscles. Cossa snorted behind her. The animal sounded both impatient with being made to wait and amused at her discomfort.

Working in the moonlight, she managed to untie Cossa, pleased when the beast did not snap at her, and struggled up onto the leather pad that served as her seat. The *rohha* pricked its ears back and danced beneath her, making Aria wonder if it was anxious to be gone or annoyed with her lack of experience. No matter, it would adapt, and so would she.

Grasping the reins in her hands, she turned Cossa in Talon's direction. He was at least two suns ride away. It would be awhile before she caught up with him, but in the meantime, she could figure out she would do when she did. As much as she wanted to be by his side, until they were far enough away that it would be a greater hindrance for him to take her back than to keep her with him, she would have to follow him at a distance.

With his stubborn nature, that meant trailing his path in silence for at least a few extra suns. It would be a test, of sorts, to see if a Trancer could fool a trained Warrior. The thought of succeeding made her feel both wicked and proud.

***

Talon pulled at Cam's reins as a new sound broke the silence of the woodland trail. Both *rohha* and rider stopped. Another thunderclap rippled through the air, and a splash of water struck Talon's arm. Rain. It slipped through the spaces between the trees like a thief, small drops striking all things beneath the canopy of leaves.

Reaching into a pocket sewn into the inside of his cloak, Talon pulled a piece of dried meat out and wrestled a bit off with his teeth. He pulled his cloak over his head and patted Cam's neck, wondering if nature mocked him by reflecting his dismal mood. "Let's go, my friend. I want to make Zaraza by nightfall."

The *rohha* tossed his head and broke into a trot.

Zaraza. Home. That is, if anything could be called home. There were aspects of his life he would rather forget—things he had done before he joined the Warrior clan, things he was not proud of—and almost all centered on Zaraza. And Mako. No, he could not forget the dark city because it was the connection. His tie to the past.

Zaraza and Mako. The memory of either left a bitter taste in his mouth. He would see one or both by nightfall.

Would Mako be there, waiting for him? If so, then the confrontation would be over soon, and he could return to the Tower and Aria.

But Talon knew Mako would not be so foolish. After such carnage, he would travel back to his fortress to let the wrath of the Warriors fade. A few raids for food and slaves, that would be all anyone would see of the Reaper leader for a few seasons.

Then, confident in his superiority, he would emerge with his Reaper clan and commit more atrocities.

And nobody wanted to stop him. Nobody wanted to prevent the death of one more child.

Except me, Talon thought. *And Aria, if I allowed it.*

Amusement lit his face, wondering how Lore was bearing up under the brunt of his Given's anger. He would not be expecting such a fiery reaction from so petite a Trancer. Talon chuckled aloud as he envisioned the names Aria would heap upon Lore. She was much tougher than she looked, but still, the need to protect her drove him.

He needed to keep her safe.

Talon's stomach turned, remembering the moment in the hallway when he had turned her over and found her covered with blood. His life had come to a halt in that dreadful instant in time. His grief had been so overwhelming that his heart had stopped beating in his chest, and he had wanted to join her. Perhaps it was a poor excuse, but he could not go through that again. That was why he left her behind. He admitted the truth to himself if to no one else.

Cam tossed his head, and Talon peered through the confines of his hood to see a clearing beyond the edge of the trees. He pulled on the reins and gave a soft command. The *rohha* stilled, and both waited as Talon listened. Water. Not just the pouring of the rain, but the sound of rushing water greeted his ears.

"That explains your reaction." The *rohha* loved water and would swim given the chance. "Sorry, Cam, but now is not the time." Talon stroked the damp, black mane that flowed from between Cam's ears and down the ridge of his back. "We have a mission to complete, and from the sound, I doubt it would be either a pleasant or relaxing swim."

The *rohha* gave a snort, as if it cared more for the water than any mission Talon might have or any danger that the water presented.

Talon patted Cam's sleek neck. "Later. I promise." He kicked Cam's sides with the heels of his leather boots and guided his mount across the clearing. He stopped at the beginning of the bridge that crossed the watery torrent below. Flashes of river were visible between the wide cracks that separated the boards. Held together by taut rope, the rickety structure might hold the weight of a few *rohha*, but no more.

Talon guided his mount over the bridge. Cam, a well-trained battle *rohha*, picked a safe path across the boards, instinctively testing each before he set his full weight upon it. Both man and animal tried to ignore the water as it flowed below them, churning and white, making its way through the rocky ravine and down to the sea. Talon silently pitied those with a less trained creature. Between the swaying of the bridge and the sound of the water, most *rohha's* would balk from the passage.

Talon breathed an audible sigh of relief when Cam's back hooves passed over the last board and both were safe on solid ground. "See, I told you the water was not calm enough for swimming." Cam rolled a brown eye and picked up to a trot at Talon's command.

Ten spans from the bridge, the hair on the back of Talon's neck rose.

He was being watched. The person who trailed him was not visible, but he was there. Talon trusted his senses. Reapers? He unsheathed his sword. Scarred from battle, it was from a past he had tried to forget. A past filled with dishonor and rage.

Still, the weight of the unadorned dull-gray weapon was familiar. Comfortable. It was perfect for what he had to do—especially if it involved a Reaper.

Talon rode until the bridge was out of sight behind him. He stopped Cam with a nudge. Reaching around, he held a large hand over the *rohha's* muzzle, a signal for silence. Cam tossed his head in understanding and did not make a noise.

Dismounting, Talon tread silently back towards the bridge. Using the trees that surrounded him for cover, he watched through the downpour, waiting. From there, he would see if his follower traveled alone. If he did, then he would best him in battle and perhaps gain some knowledge. If not, he would slash the bridge bindings and buy time to escape.

The thought of running from a fight twisted his gut. He ignored it. He could not risk dying in an uneven battle. Not now. Not when he had a mission to complete. Not while Mako breathed.

His pursuer came into view. A lone rider, and only one, unless his friends were in hiding. Talon peered harder. From his size, the rider looked to be a young boy, but Talon could not be sure. The lad wore a mismatch of clothes. A Warrior's leggings and villager's boots. A cloak and blanket covered his clothes and head, but both were so worn that Talon had doubts that either sufficed to keep the lad dry.

He watched in silence as the boy dismounted, and his *rohha* tried to dance away, pawing and pulling. Over the rain, Talon heard the lad shout at the creature, trying to force it to cross the bridge. Talon shook his head. The mount was too ill trained to make the crossing, and the rider was obviously too young to know better than to try. He was also alone. If comrades waited in the trees, they would be out to help by now, and not allow the escape of a good pack animal.

The *rohha* pulled on the reins, but the lad held on.

Goddess. He would have to help before either the beast or the boy was hurt. Sheathing his sword, Talon stepped onto the bridge and called out.

It all happened at once. At Talon's call, the *rohha* shied

away and bolted back the way they had come. Caught off guard, the boy stumbled and fell towards the bridge's railing. The cloak fell away from the lad's head revealing long red hair. The sound of splitting wood and a woman's scream rent the air, as Aria tumbled into the icy waters below.

Eight

"Cam! To me!" Talon's shout was automatic, a trained response, as Aria fell into the pounding water. In the same instant, he ran towards her. The current carried her away before he reached the edge of the bridge. Judgment honed by Warrior instinct, he knew it would be a mistake to jump into the river after her. Her only chance was for him to ride ahead and pluck her from the rapids as she passed. It was not much of a chance, but it was all she had.

In what seemed like a turn, but was probably just a breath, Cam galloped towards him. Showing no signs of slowing, he swept towards his owner. Talon grabbed the *rohha's* mane and swung onto the animal's back as it passed. Signaling Cam with his knees, they raced along the edge of the ravine.

Leaning forward, Talon put his boots to Cam, urging the *rohha* to greater speed. At the same time, he grabbed a rope and tied it to one of the straps on his leather seat.

"Faster, Cam," Talon urged his mount. "We must get ahead of her." The *rohha* stretched its neck and gave its master what he asked.

Talon searched for Aria as they sped along the edge of the steep bank, focusing on the water that roiled below. Every nerve in his body sang with adrenaline. Where was she? The raging water obscured all. Was she under its surface and far ahead, or had he not reached her yet? He prayed to the Goddess for the latter.

A flash of brown cloth and red hair caught his eye. "Aria!" Talon shouted her name, praying she heard it over the rush of water and would keep faith that he was coming to save her.

Powerless, he watched as she bounced off a rock and disappeared under the surface of the water.

His heart sprung to his throat. "No! Aria!"

She bobbed back to the surface again, as if answering his plea.

Sharp relief flowed through him, and he urged Cam on until they passed her. Cam flew along the ground. Talon visually scouted ahead, searching for the best place to stop and make a rescue attempt.

His eyes widencd. There was no place. The land sloped downward and ended, changing from river to air as the water flowed over a cliff.

All options were at an end.

Talon pulled back on the reins, and Cam came to an abrupt halt. Swiftly, Talon wound the rope around his hand, slid off Cam, and leapt off the edge of the embankment.

The bitter-cold water enveloped him. Jerked and pulled by the raging torrent, Talon winced as the cord bit into his flesh. He bore the pain with a grimace, knowing the thin line, and Cam, were the only things keeping him from washing over the edge of the cliff and into space.

He kicked as the current pulled at him. Muscles straining with the effort to stay afloat and sight blinded by water, he begged the Goddess for help. If he could not see Aria, he could not save her. If he could not overcome the strength of the current, she would plunge to her death.

He pleaded for a miracle.

Aria slammed into him, knocking them both under the surface. Arching and turning, Talon reached out and grabbed blindly, searching for her before she slipped away. His numb hands closed around a bit of cloth. He kicked to the surface, dragging Aria by her threadbare cloak.

Both sputtered as they broke free, gulping fresh air into their burning lungs. Praying her thin cloak held, Talon pulled Aria closer until she was in his arms.

"Hold on to me," he shouted to make himself heard over the raging torrent.

Aria responded by wrapping her arms around his neck.

Holding onto the rope with one hand and Aria's waist with the other, Talon jerked on the rope. "Cam! Pull!" he shouted. A rough tug on his arm and both moved upward, inching past the rock sides of the ravine as Cam dragged them towards the top of the wall. Aria's grip around Talon's neck tightened.

"Do not worry. I will not drop you," he assured her.

With her head buried in his neck, she nodded, but her grip remained strong and unyielding.

They reached the top. Solid ground. Talon's sigh of relief echoed Aria's.

"Cam. Hold."

The *rohha* ceased pulling. Talon unwound the rope and rolled onto his back, taking Aria with him.

He lay with her pressed against him. One thought ran through his mind. He had almost lost her. Again.

Cupping her face with his hands, he stroked her lower lip with the pad of his thumb.

"Talon." She whispered his name, her breath hot against him, and he was lost.

"Aria." Her name was a prayer of thanks as he slanted his mouth across hers, and she returned the kiss. All gestures of tenderness gone, he took her mouth with a savage intensity, and her lips parted beneath his. She groaned, and he swallowed the small sound, taking it into his mouth and intensifying it with his own sounds of satisfaction. He pulled her closer, one hand tangled in her damp hair, and the other cupping her bottom.

Aria shrieked and pulled away.

His hand flew to the hilt of his sword before he opened his eyes.

It was Cam. He was above them and had a lock of Aria's hair in his mouth. Aria shrieked again as Cam yanked harder.

It would be a horrible irony if Aria survived the water only to be slain by a jealous *rohha.* Talon held back a chuckle. "Hold, Cam," he commanded.

Obediently, the *rohha* ceased his tugging and waited, keeping Aria suspended by the red strands. She struggled, balancing on Talon with one hand and using the other to make a futile swipe at the *rohha.*

"Hold still," Talon told her. Reaching around her, he tapped the beast on the nose to show his displeasure.

Cam's mouth opened, and Aria fell against Talon's chest, all pain gone from her expression, as well as all signs of passion. She rubbed her head. "I thought he was going to take my scalp off." Aria shot Cam a look of loathing. The *rohha* simply tossed his head and trotted off.

"No damage done?" Talon asked.

She shook her head, and Talon lay back. A pang of disappointment at the interruption tugged at his psyche, but Cam's interruption was probably for the best. Lust brought on by a near death experience was intense and satisfying, but it would complicate things. Besides, Aria was wet from head to toe, and so was he. They both needed the comfort of a fire and dry clothes. The comfort of sinking into each other was not an option, although his body thought otherwise.

Later, he would thank Cam for his unintentional intervention and give him some extra grain.

Aria settled against him with a contented sigh. Her life pulse beat against his flesh as he watched a bird soaring above them, casting shadows over their soaked forms.

She finally broke the silence. "I almost died."

"Yes," Talon replied. He closed his eyes and breathed deep, welcoming the small weight of her body, vital and alive, against him.

"But I did not."

"No, we are both very much alive." Aria shivered in his arms, her damp clothes clasping her body like a second skin. He tightened his hold, willing his body heat to warm her.

She snuggled closer, her breath warm against his ear. His chest constricted as his body responded again.

He gave a muffled groan.

Aria rose up to look at him, balancing on her elbows. Her hips fitted neatly with his. "Are you hurt?" she asked.

"No, I am undamaged," Talon replied, his voice hoarse with need.

"Then what is wrong?"

Talon reached up and stroked Aria's damp hair, willing his hunger to vanish. The fire within subsided at his will, but still waited, smoldering, ready to roar back to life. "Nothing is wrong. I am merely grateful we are both alive."

"You are not angry?"

He shrugged. "I should be, and most likely I will be later on, but for now, I am relieved. However, I would like to know why you are here and not at the Tower."

Aria's lips were pale with cold, but her eyes flashed fire. "You should not have left me behind."

"I did so for a reason. I had hoped you respected that enough to wait for my return."

"Do not talk to me of respect. You lied to me."

Talon winced at the truth. "You would not have let me leave otherwise."

"True," Aria agreed. Wriggling out of Talon's hold, she rolled away and into a sitting position with her legs tucked under her. "But we could have avoided this."

All vestiges of passion disappeared as Talon's temper rose. "I can say the same thing. We would both be dry and warm if you were where you were supposed to be."

Aria's eyes narrowed, and the corner of her lips curved downward. "I am exactly where I am supposed to be."

"You are a Trancer. Your place is with the Tower."

"My place is where I choose to make it. I may not be a Warrior, Talon, but this quest is as much mine as it is yours." She crossed her arms, muscles tight, as if preparing for battle.

Talon started to retort, but stopped himself before the first syllable passed his lips. He did not want to fight with Aria, and if he spoke his mind then they would be arguing until the rising of the moons. She was tired and needed a fire. He needed food and rest as well. With a deep sigh, he placed his hands under his head, crossed his legs at the ankle, and closed his eyes.

He had fought in battle, killed men, and ended many a day covered in blood and dirt. But nothing had ever sapped the strength from his body like seeing Aria fall in the river.

"Do not ignore me, Talon."

He opened his eyes to see her standing over him, her body shaking with cold despite her heated temper.

"I am not ignoring you."

Hands on her hips, she stared down at him in obvious disbelief. "Then why are you lying there with your eyes closed?"

His shirt stuck to him, clammy and wet. "I am not in any mood to bicker and fight. I would prefer the comfort of a fire and a soft bed to lying here in the cold and being scolded by the woman I rescued." He shut his eyes again, annoyed. "When you are ready to leave, let me know."

The grass rustled as Aria knelt beside him. "Talon?"

Her voice sounded as weary as he felt. His irritation dissipated as he reminded himself of her inexperience. "Yes."

"Perhaps you are right in that this conversation can wait." Trailing her fingers up his arm, she stopped to tickle his ear before she reached his hand. Pulling it out from under his head, she kissed his knuckles, soft lips against rough flesh. "Thank you for saving my life."

He turned his hand over to grasp hers, and brought it to his mouth, returning the sentiment. "You are welcome." He opened his eyes to see her smiling in spite of the damp, and his spirits lifted despite the situation. "Are you too tired to ride?"

She shook her head. "No, but would it not be better to stay here? We can shelter in the woods."

With a Warrior's ease and grace, Talon rose to his feet and pulled Aria with him. "We could, but there is a town up ahead. I planned to shelter there for the night. Can you ride that far, or are you too weary?"

"I can make it," Aria assured him.

"Good." Talon turned to see Cam cropping the grass at the edge of the trees, patiently waiting for his master to make a decision. "Cam, come," he called.

The *rohha's* ears flicked up, and he walked over to the pair, pushing Talon with his soft nose.

"He is a wonderful *rohha*," Aria said and reached out to stroke Cam's skin

Cam rolled his lips back, baring his teeth, and Aria jerked her hand away.

"He does not like to be called a *rohha*." Talon ran a hand down Cam's glossy black hide. "A *rohha* is like that mount you rode. Worn, ill-tempered and undisciplined. Cam is a *Sorriia*. Loyalty to me is part of his breeding and training. I trust him more than my brothers, save Lore."

Talon stopped stroking Cam. "Speaking of Lore, how did you manage to elude him? Did his charm and good looks not win you over?"

"I shall tell you about it as we travel," Aria said, her expression gleeful. "But be assured that if he follows he is far behind."

Talon's brow went up. Perhaps Aria was more resourceful than he thought, but she was still out of her element and would have to go back.

Even if he had to take her himself.

***

Pungent, unwashed, and thick, the smell of the city roused Aria. Still half asleep, she almost fell off Cam before Talon caught her and settled her securely in front of him.

"Where are we?" She held her cloak in front of her face, using the cloth to filter the smells. It did not work. She coughed, choking and gagging, as they passed a stall of fish.

"Zaraza," Talon answered, guiding Cam through the throngs of people.

"Zaraza?" Aria tried to turn around, but only succeeded in sliding sideways.

"Sit still," Talon commanded, righting her once again.

"We should have retrieved Cossa, then this—" She shifted in the seat. "—would not be a problem."

"Cossa is trained to pull a cart. I would not put my life in peril, much less yours, by using a beast that was not trained for endurance and bravery."

She remembered the look of sheer terror in the *rohha's* eyes when faced with the bridge and the raging water. Talon had a point.

"Then perhaps we can purchase one. A trained one."

"Perhaps, but even that would not be needed if you had stayed at the Tower."

After her rescue, Talon had mentioned that he would probably be angry later. It appeared that later had come.

But his anger changed nothing. She was here with him, and she would not be dissuaded—especially by something as insignificant as the lack of a mount.

Letting the cloth fall away from her face, she gripped Cam's black mane in her hands, winding the long strands through her fingers. Remaining silent, she breathed through her mouth as they made their way through the crowded streets.

"Stop gawking," Talon whispered in her ear after a few minutes. "You mark yourself as an *ouseta* when you stare."

"What is an *ouseta*?" Aria whispered back.

"An outsider. Someone who would be easy to steal from."

"What kind of place is this?" Aria spoke over her shoulder, making sure her voice stayed low. "Why did you bring me here? I thought we were going to a safe place to sleep. Not a town of people who rob those they do not know."

"No," Talon corrected her. "I said was that it was a town, and I wanted a fire and soft bed. I never said it was safe."

"We should have stayed in the woods," Aria muttered. "At least we would not have to worry about getting killed."

"Is this more than you bargained for?" Talon asked. "Perhaps the Tower looks more inviting now that you see the places I must travel."

Aria bit back a sharp retort and gripped Cam's fur tighter, making the *rohha* toss his head and roll his eyes. Contrite, she murmured a word of apology and relaxed her clenched fingers, focusing her annoyance towards the true perpetrator—Talon.

Holding onto Talon with one hand and the leather pad with the other, Aria turned sideways until she saw Talon's face. Then, she hooked her outer knee over the horn on the leather pad, using it to help stabilize her precarious balance. "I am not so easily sent away, Talon. Do I seem like the kind of person who would run away from a threat?"

"You would be wise to do so." Talon's voice was low in her ear. "Lore was one person, and he was only trying to stop you, not kill you. Do not think that because you bested him that you are ready for the road and all the dangers it presents. Zaraza is not a nice town, like your home of Lanai, or full of good people, like the Tower or the Keep."

She winced as his lips curled over the words, mocking her. "I know that I am inexperienced, but that does not lessen my desire."

His eyes narrowed as he continued, ignoring her words. "People here will kill you for your cloak. If you were not under my protection I can guarantee that you would be dragged into an alley."

"Which is why I travel with you." She poked him in the chest with her finger, emphasizing her words.

He grabbed her hand. "Stop it."

She pulled her hand from his and placed it on his chest for balance. It was bad enough that Talon's temper raged, but it would do neither any good if she lost hers also. "Do you hope to scare me into returning to the Tower?"

"No, I speak the raw truth hoping to knock some sense into your pretty head. I grew up in this city. I know what these people are capable of."

A memory from her joining with Talon flashed through her mind—an image of a short, wicked blade cutting towards her face. Aria shuddered and squeezed her eyes shut, banishing the vision.

"Are you going to be sick?" Talon asked.

The hopeful tone of his question rankled Aria. "No. My eyes sting from this rancid air," she lied, keeping them closed.

"That is my point. You must understand that where I go is neither clean nor safe. Anything can happen."

She felt, rather than saw, his hand wave through the air as he gestured. "These people are more of a threat than a river will ever be. Even one that ends in a waterfall."

Aria swallowed as bile rose in her throat, and another memory flashed through her mind. *Talon and another boy, running through garbage-strewn streets. Running to escape. Shouts accompanied their passage. Cries of "Thief" and "Stop" overshadowed their frantic breathing as the pair scaled fences and ducked through doorways.*

She shuddered and opened her eyes, wondering how long she had been remembering.

"Aria, do you understand?"

It must have been more than a moment. "What was the question?"

His eyes flared. "Zaraza is no place for inattention. You would do well to remember that."

"Yes, you are right," Aria agreed quickly, hoping he would not ask why her thoughts had drifted. Her knowledge of him had made him cautious of her before, and she would not give him another reason to take her back to the Tower by reminding him of that fact.

"I said that I plan to take you to an inn I know of. You will stay there while I try to find information on Mako."

"Mako?"

Talon placed a hand on the pommel of his sword. "He is the leader of the Reapers who destroyed the Tower."

"What makes you think that?" Aria asked.

"His banner was found impaled on the door of the Tower."

He knew who had taken Tarik, and he had not told her? She knew her mouth hung open, but it seemed of little consequence. Finally, she managed to speak. "Why did you say nothing to me about this?"

"The knowledge would not have eased your grief or brought Tarik back. I thought knowing the killer's name would disturb you more than was necessary."

The anger she had worked so hard to control erupted. "It was not your right to decide. Not your right at all. How *dare* you keep such information from me? I birthed Tarik and should have been told everything. Do you understand? *Everything.*"

"It was in your best interest."

"I will decide my best interest. Not you." Her voice shook with rage. "I am a Trancer as well as a woman, and you will treat me with the respect my station demands. Do you understand?"

For a moment, Talon looked taken aback, but his look of apology disappeared behind the emotionless mask that Aria had come to know as meaning he no longer listened. "I apologize for upsetting you, but I still think you make too much out of such a small issue."

"If you had told me it would not be an issue at all." Aria crossed her arms, holding in the anger and disappointment. He was so focused on protecting her that he crossed the line from helpful to controlling. "Your lack of faith in me is quite distressing. I survived the death of my Tower. Do not assume that I cannot manage a bit of knowledge. What I cannot—*and will not*—bear is you treating me as one would treat a child."

Talon shrugged. "I will consider what you have said, and again, I apologize for causing you distress."

Was he telling her what he thought she wanted to hear, or was he honestly contrite? His lack of expression told her nothing. "Accepted," she said cautiously. "But under the circumstances, you cannot expect me to wait in a room while you ask questions. You need me beside you. I deserve to be a part of this."

Aria knew her plea was ignored even before he spoke.

"I am sorry I neglected to tell you about Mako, but

that does not change the current circumstances."

"I thought you said you would consider my words."

Talon scowled. "Your words change nothing about what I must do here. If I am to discover where Mako hides his men, I need to keep my guard up and my thoughts focused. People here will not want to talk to me about such things. You are inexperienced and will complicate matters."

"I can help you. I am a Trancer."

Talon scowled. "In Zaraza, you are a woman. A potential bed partner, nothing more."

Talon was from Zaraza. Is that all she was to him as well? The sliver of doubt pricked her thoughts, but she pushed it aside before the question reached her lips.

Besides, it looked like the discussion was over as Talon pulled the hood of his cloak over his head, shadowing his eyes and signaling an end to the conversation.

***

A painted sign, too worn to read, hung over the door of the shabbiest structure Aria had ever seen. This was where Talon proposed to leave her? With its sides bleached gray by the sun and the porch missing its railing, the building appeared abandoned. Still, Aria slid off Cam and stood at the base of the three stairs that led to the door. Behind her, Talon gave instructions to a stable lad about the *rohha's* care.

"Is it what you expected?" Talon asked as he walked to her side.

"I did not know what to expect," Aria replied. She hoped her doubts did not show in her expression. "Is it safe?"

"Yes. I know the people here. It may not look like much from the outside, but they run a clean, safe inn."

Following Talon, Aria walked up the stairs and through the large wooden doorway.

It was amazing. People of all kinds sat at tables eating and drinking. Women carried pitchers of drink and huge platters of food, distributing both as they navigated their way through the crowd.

Aria's gaze swept across the scene, taking in the group of men playing a game with rocks and sticks at the corner table. Another group cheered and shouted as two men wrestled hand-to-hand, their elbows on the table as each tried to push the other's arm down.

She had never seen anything like it.

"Come on." Taking Aria by the arm, Talon wove through the crowd and towards the back of the room. People parted before them, but most ignored the couple. Aria's eyes narrowed as one of the serving girls stared at Talon with obvious desire.

Aria gripped his arm tighter. The quick journey ended at the back of the large room where a beefy man in a stained shirt poured mugs of ale and glasses of wine.

Talon pounded on the worn wooden bar top. "Hey, barkeep. How about some service."

"Keep your leathers on. I'll be th—"

The barkeep's shout ended in mid-sentence when he saw them. Putting down his half filled mugs, he walked over. Grinning, the man clapped Talon on the shoulder, and the pair shook hands—wrist to forearm. "Talon. Glad to see you."

"You too, Barias. It has been too long."

"Where have you been? I heard some nonsense a few years ago that you had joined a Warrior's clan."

Aria took a step back as Talon's eyes darkened. "I did. For a time. But that time is over."

The barkeep shrugged. "Whatever. All that matters now is that you are here." Barias shouted over his shoulder, "Hey, get some food over here for my friend."

Aria called up her nerve and stepped forward.

"Hello." She thrust her hand out. "My name is Aria."

The barkeep's eyes darted from Aria to Talon and back again. "So, you finally did it." He addressed Talon, but his smile and gray eyes never left Aria's face. "You finally took the leap and found a mate."

Leaning over the bar, he kissed Aria on the cheek. "Congratulations," he said. "You've got a good man. A little domineering but priceless in a fight." His eyes sparkled. "I've also heard he knows how to keep a woman happy— if you know what I mean."

Aria face grew hot, and she knew she was as red as the wine.

"Barias, quit teasing Aria and give us a room."

The barkeep smiled. "I have the perfect one with a bed large enough for whatever you might desire." He chuckled, as Aria's blush deepened. "I'll even throw in dinner."

Talon nodded. "Thank you, but dinner only for Aria. I have questions to ask around town and will not return until late."

"No."

Both men looked at Aria.

"No," she said again. "I already told you that I will not stay and wait while you search for news of Mako."

"Mako?" Barias frowned.

Talon nodded.

Aria watched as the two men reached an unspoken agreement. Barias nodded and pulled a key from under the counter.

Talon took her arm. His grip was gentle, but firm. She knew her fight was lost, at least for the moment.

Nine

Iliana sat alone in her darkened room, the silence of the Reaper's Keep punctuated by the jingling of swords and steel as the night watch made its rounds.

With a sigh, she ran her hands through her shortened hair, smoothing it away from her face, both wishing for and dreading sleep.

Because with sleep came dreams, and her dreams were worse than reality. In dreams, she relived the horrors of Mako's raid on her Tower. In dreams, she watched as the Healer was cut down before her.

In dreams, she left Aria. Betraying all that she knew to be good and right by abandoning her best friend.

And each night, when she woke, sweaty and with the stench of fear on her skin, she wondered if she should have—*could have*—done more to save her people.

She knew the answer. She had failed, and that was why she dreamed.

Did Aria live? She hoped. She prayed. If Aria lived, maybe there was redemption for even her—a deserter of family and killer of Healers.

She hugged herself, refusing to give in to the roar of pain.

She wanted Aria to live so badly that she hurt with the want. Still, wanting did not make it true, and now, she had no way to find out. She was blind to the currents—deaf to their call—ever since Mako kidnapped her. Ever since she saved herself and let the others die.

With a sob, Iliana stretched out and pulled the covers over her, hugging her pillow, pressing it against her chest to hold in the anger and fear that threatened to spill out.

She listened, praying for rescue. Nothing. No shouts of battle answered her plea.

The only noise was Tarik murmuring in his sleep, dreaming the dreams of the innocent.

Innocence. When did that end? When had hers departed? Was it with the destruction of her Tower? Choosing her life over the Healer's? The death of her friends? The loss of her talent? Was it like a parchment where she could point at it and say, "There, that line, that word. That is where my innocence died."

She buried her face in the pillow. Or worse, was it being slowly sucked away with each breath she took while in bondage, or each morning when she woke up still under Mako's rule?

She did not know. There was too much anger, too much fear, clouding her mind.

The door swung open.

She sat up, clutching the covers around her.

"Having trouble sleeping, Iliana?"

Goddess, help me. "No, Lord Mako." What did he want? Was he here to claim her, as she always knew he would?

"Why so restless?"

She hugged the pillow tighter, trying to think of an answer, an excuse, anything to make him leave her alone. "I am nothing of the sort, but am merely contemplating the dark."

A deep chuckle floated over to her. "The dark? That is my domain."

The sound of footsteps approached, echoing like the pace of death.

He sat next to her, the bed shifting with his weight, and she knew she would have done better not to have replied at all.

"Tell me, what is it you want to know about the dark?"

She scooted over to the far side of the bed, wishing he would leave but unable to speak the words—not with her life, and Tarik's, in the balance. "Nothing in particular."

He followed her, sliding across the bed until he sat next to her with only the thin coverlet separating them. He placed a kiss on her bare shoulder.

Could he taste her bitter fear? She prayed he did not feel her shaking at his nearness.

His hand brushed against her cheek. "Nothing in particular? Let me enlighten you. Teach you the ways."

She quelled the urge to pull away.

Leaving her cheek, his hand traced a path to her hip. "What shall be your first lesson? Shall I describe to you how the dark can hold you like a lover?"

She shut her eyes, trying to concentrate on her breathing, the rapid beating of her heart.

His voice grew closer. "Or maybe I should tell you of

its strength. How it can help you, give you power, if you but open yourself to it."

She knew he spoke not of the night, but of the dark within, and for a brief moment, she understood. Understood how anger could consume. How wrath could obliterate all the goodness within. No. The dark was not what she wanted. She pushed the dreadful, horrible thoughts away.

He pulled her against him, almost into his lap.

Would he take her against her will? She knew the answer. She did not have to read the currents to know what lay in store for her if she let him continue.

The dark within Iliana flared into being. Her heart beat loud in her ears. How dare he try to take her? Seduce her with words of evil like they were a lover's sweet poetry. The rage built, flowing through her like fire. She gritted her teeth, her jaw tight, as she fought her inner demons and pushed back the urge to either claw him with her hand or pound him into dust beneath her feet.

She could do neither, not if she wanted Tarik to live to be a man. Instead, she pulled away, almost falling off the edge of the bed.

He chuckled, his mirth as black as the shadows he described with such passion. "What is wrong, my sweet Trancer?"

She managed to force an answer through her clenched jaw.

"Nothing is wrong. Leave me."

"Is my company not pleasant?"

By the Goddess, he baited her with every word. Why? What game did he play? She pulled the cover tighter around her. "I wish to sleep."

He pulled her closer, using the covers like a net. "I am not stopping you."

Anger won over judgment, and her hand shot out.

He caught her fist before she made contact with him.

She screamed a wordless, soundless cry and tried to hit him again.

He caught her other wrist.

"Let me go!"

He laughed. A true laugh, not the evil murmuring he normally dealt her. "Or what? You will run away?" He pulled her closer, so close his every muscle matched with hers. "I could take you, Iliana. You know it. I know it."

"What is stopping you?" she asked through gritted teeth. If he was going to bed her, she wished he would do so and end the waiting.

He traced a path along her jaw with his mouth. "I need you. Need your talent, and I know from experience that a Trancer taken against her will is useless."

From experience? Bile rose in her throat.

He continued. "I am not a man governed by lust, and I am willing to give you awhile longer to prove yourself." He stopped at her ear. "But I will not give you forever."

He rolled away.

Relief rolled over her, binding her in its warmth, forcing back the rage.

The bed shifted again as he stood and walked away. The door opened, and for a moment, the torch in the hall silhouetted him. "Make no mistake. You will be mine."

He shut the door behind him. She heard bolts click as he locked her in.

Or did he lock others out?

Either way, she was safe for a night. Safe from Mako. Safe from the other Reapers.

If only she were as safe from herself.

Ten

Aria sat in the hip-deep bathtub, her temper hotter than the water. Exhausted from the day's events, both she and Talon had laid down when they arrived in their room. She had meant to rest her eyes for but a moment. When she opened them, the sky was dark, and she was alone in the bed.

His departure was not a surprise, which infuriated her even more. Her hands clenched, she struck the water, sending drops flying.

"Mistress Aria," the voice behind her chided. "If you keep that up I shall be as wet as you."

Aria crossed her arms over her chest. "I apologize, Marri."

The woman chuckled. "I suppose I would be angry if my man left me to go off on his own, but do not worry. Talon is a good man. He will return soon."

Would he? Aria wondered. Or would he use the opportunity to leave her again?

The woman picked up the wet length of Aria's hair and began lathering it. Aria closed her eyes with a sigh and leaned back, allowing herself to enjoy the attention despite her ill temper. The sweet scent of flowers filled the small room.

"Have you and Master Talon had a pleasant journey?" Marri's firm hands massaged Aria's scalp.

"Hardly," Aria answered. She grimaced, as she thought about all that had happened in a single day. "I lost my *rohha* and almost drowned. Cam tried to pull my hair out. Talon does not want me with him, and now he is treating me like a girl fresh out of the village."

"Well." Marri acknowledged the list of complaints with the single word.

"I suppose," Aria answered, feeling awkward at her outburst and the woman's quiet, efficient conversation. Goddess, Marri probably thought her a whimpering weakling.

Marri removed her hands, and Aria recognized the sound of water pouring into a metal pitcher.

"Lean back."

Aria tilted her head, making sure no more complaints passed her lips. Clean water cascaded over her.

"I'll bring your dinner up after your bath so you can go straight to bed."

Aria sat up again and frowned. Dinner and bed? She pulled her hair forward and twisted it gently, squeezing the water from it. She had risen but a while ago, and she had no desire to return to sleep. How like Talon to make sure he was in control of the situation by planning her evening for her. Irritation tugged at her again, and she gave her hair an especially hard twist.

"Will that be all right?" Marri's voice interrupted her thoughts.

"What?"

"Bringing dinner up here?"

"You mean I have a choice?" Aria asked, her voice tinged with sarcasm despite her vow to behave.

"Of course. You are a guest."

"Talon did not tell you to keep me in my room?"

Marri's eyes widened. "No, of course not."

"How about Barias? He is Talon's friend and will do what Talon asks."

Marri tossed her head, her blonde curls bouncing despite the pins that held it. "I am Barias' bonded mate, and he knows that I would never agree to such a thing. This is an inn, not a prison."

Aria smiled, her anger dissipating as her planned defiance grew. If she were a guest, then she would act like one, despite Talon's plans. "Please hand me a drying cloth. I will eat in the main room with everyone else. Who knows, perhaps I will make some new friends."

Marri handed her the thick towel, her smile sly. "I could use a bit of ale myself."

***

Talon let the door to the last tavern slam shut behind him. Aria was right. The people's fears ran deep, and none were willing to talk about Mako for fear of retribution. Talon's sword hung heavy on his hip. If he drew it and reentered the establishment, he could learn what he needed to know. He fingered the hilt but a moment and let the thought pass. He could not harm people for protecting themselves.

Sounds from another tavern filtered through the night air. Briefly, Talon considered visiting it, but dismissed the idea. He could stop at every bar and brothel in Zaraza and would walk away with as much information as he currently possessed—which was none.

He ran his leather-gloved hand through his hair. It was time to visit Ciella. A companion from childhood, now a prostitute by trade, she was a good friend and sometimes more. He had hoped to avoid her. He did not have the desire or the time for the games they usually played.

Five streets later, he stood outside the door of a well-kept house. He pulled a rope, and a bell rung inside. Within a few moments, a panel in the door opened, he heard a cry of delight, and the panel slammed shut.

The door opened to reveal a small woman gowned in a frothy robe. Her black hair was loose and pulled to one side so it cascaded over her shoulder. Holding a candle and a smile, she ushered him in.

She set the candle down on a table, flung her arms around Talon, and planted a kiss on his mouth, her red lips forcing his apart.

Talon waited, stonily enduring the display of affection, until Ciella pulled away with a confused expression. "Is that any way to act?" she asked. "What is wrong?"

Reaching up, Talon unlocked her arms from around her neck. "I do not have time for play tonight. I need information, and I need it fast."

She thrust her bottom lip out in an exaggerated pout. "Is your Warrior clan so demanding that you cannot spend a little quality time with an old friend?" She reached out to trail a long, red fingernail down the front of this shirt.

Talon grabbed her wrist, stopping her before she reached the buckle to his scabbard. "I said I was in a hurry. I have a mission to complete."

"Really?" Her eyes widened in mock belief. "A mission. How fascinating." She reached out and began undoing the buckle to Talon's scabbard with her other hand.

He pulled away. "Not this time."

"Why not? Is your mission a secret? One I will have to *persuade* you to share?" She ran her hands down her stomach and over her hips.

Talon shook his head. "My mission is personal. I need

your help."

Ciella's lips went from an exaggerated pout to an equally exaggerated smile. "Personal?" She walked away, her hips swaying provocatively from side to side. "Come on, lover. I'll help you."

"Ciella," Talon called as she went down the hallway towards her bedroom. "I do not jest."

Her husky laugh echoed back.

"Goddess," Talon muttered in frustration

The light from her candle disappeared as she rounded the corner and entered her bedroom. Annoyed, he followed to find her already sitting on the bed, her robe open and showing her shapely legs. She leaned back, resting on her elbows with the sash to her gown in one hand where she toyed with its tasseled border.

She crooked a finger at him. "Come sit beside me."

Instead, Talon walked over to the fireplace and sat in one of the overstuffed chairs that rested before it. Its wooden frame groaned under his weight. How could he make her understand, short of telling her about Aria and Tarik? The loss of his son was still a raw wound, and he wanted to say as little about Aria as possible. Their bond was private, and it felt like a betrayal to discuss it with an old lover.

Ciella laughed, low and husky, interrupting his thoughts. "Lover, why do you ignore me? Is that any way to treat the woman who has what you need?"

Talon frowned. Since she became a prostitute, Ciella related to most men almost entirely on a sexual level. His relationship with her was different—more friendship than lovers. Still, the sex was there, or had been there, until Aria. Now, the desire for casual intimacy was as lost as his Warrior's sword. "You are a beautiful, desirable woman—"

"That is what I wanted to hear." Rising from the bed, Ciella walked over to Talon.

Talon continued. "And you are a good friend, but that is all you are. A friend. No more and certainly no less."

She shrugged. "That is all we ever were, but that does not mean we cannot enjoy ourselves. Why only have information when you can have this?" In a single motion, she pulled the tie to her robe and shrugged the garment off her shoulders to reveal her naked body. "You can't tell me you are not tempted." She straddled him, settling down in his lap.

She ran the tip of her tongue over her full lower lip, her hands planted on his shoulders as she waited for Talon to make a move.

"Ciella, get off me," Talon said, his voice quiet.

"Make me." She wiggled her bottom, laughing.

He silently cursed her trade. It shadowed reality with games, making both hard to define. He needed her to listen. "You are acting the whore with someone who has no need of such a performance."

The laughter in her eyes died as shock took its place. Without saying a word, she stood up and gathered her robe from the floor, pulling it around her slender form.

He rose, feeling like he had kicked a child. He should have found a better way, better words, but need and time drove him. "I am sorry, but I must make you understand that things are different now."

"How?" Her voice was choked, and he knew she held back the tears she let nobody see. "I never felt like a whore with you. Never. Until now. Did the Warriors add celibacy to their many rules of conduct, or is it only to stay away from prostitutes?"

"It is neither you or the Warriors who prevent pleasure. It is only myself." He laid his hands on her shoulders and turned her to face him. "You are my friend. If circumstances were changed, I would spend the night in your bed. I am different now. My life is different now. Forgive me, but I had to make you see this."

Talon waited as she mulled over his apology, debating on whether to accept or deny him. She pulled her robe closer and tied it. The small smile on her lips spoke forgiveness, and Talon breathed a sigh of relief.

"You are lucky we are friends. If any other man spoke to me in such a manner Kar would toss him into the streets."

Talon raised a brow. Kar was Ciella's bodyguard, and although not Warrior trained, he was a master at street fighting. He was also as big as a *rohha*, and even Talon would think twice before a confrontation. "I thank you for your understanding."

Ciella acknowledged the comment with a nod. "I assume a woman brought this great change."

Was he that transparent? "Yes."

"Does she wait for you?"

"At Barias'."

"Do you love her?"

Talon hesitated, shaken at the abrupt question. Love? He wanted to protect Aria, care for her and even make love to her, but was that love? He was not sure he could feel that warm emotion anymore. Pain and loss surrounded him like a shield keeping all else out. "She is the mother of my child."

"Not exactly the answer to my question, but you always were close-mouthed, Talon S'Diro." Ciella frowned. "What is her name?"

Talon hesitated, but she deserved to know some of the truth. "Aria."

"Aria." Ciella rolled the name on her red lips. "A beautiful name. What is she? A village girl?"

"A Trancer."

Ciella's jaw dropped. "You travel with a Trancer? Have the rules changed so much that Trancers and Warriors now follow the same path? What of her Tower?"

"They are all dead," Talon replied, grateful for a chance to turn the conversation away from his Given. "Which brings me back to my reason for my visit. I need information."

Ciella held up a hand. "Hold. I would like a glass of wine before I hear your story, and I think you could use one as well." Walking over to a table, she filled two goblets, returned, and placed one of the cups in Talon's hand.

"Thank you." He raised the ornate metal rim to his lips. The wine was pale and sweet on his tongue.

Ciella went to the bed and patted it with the flat of her hand. "Now, come over here, and tell me what happened."

Talon raised a brow at where she sat.

"I will not try to seduce you again. I promise. Before, I thought you were playing. A new love game for me to solve." Ciella smiled. It was a smile Talon had not seen on her lips in a while. It was one of friendship, and nothing more.

With relief, he walked to her bed and sat next to her.

Ciella took the glass from his hand and set it on the bedside table. "Now, tell me of your Warrior's mission."

Talon leaned forward, elbows on his knees and hands clasped. "My mission has nothing to do with the Warriors."

"Really? I was not aware they offered that much freedom."

"They do not."

Ciella did not speak but picked up Talon's glass and handed it back to him. He took a long swallow, knowing she waited for an explanation. "I am no longer a Warrior. I left the clan." He winced at the disappointment in her expression. Of all the people from his past, she was one of the few he had told of his profession.

She took a deep swallow from her own glass. "What can I do to help you make it right?"

Talon shook his head. "Nothing. I yielded my sword of my own free will." He remembered when he first presented his Warriors sword to her. Proud of him, she had marveled over its brightness and 'aahhed' over the ornate hilt. *A beautiful sword for a beautiful man,* she had said.

What would she say now? Slowly, he pulled the Reaper sword from his scabbard and held it out in front of him. Ugly and dull, its only ornament was a single bloodstone. He turned the blade, looking down its perfect length.

Ciella stared at the weapon in his hand. Her eyes narrowed. "Is that from before?"

He sheathed it. "Yes, but that does not matter." He was no longer the angry youth who challenged all, and he did not want to hear the lecture he knew was coming. What mattered now was information. Information that only Ciella could provide.

Ciella's full lips thinned at the indifferent comment, and she moved to speak, but Talon interrupted. "What matters now is that I need to find Mako." He waited for her reaction.

"Mako?" Ciella echoed, her voice querulous.

"Yes."

"Why?"

Talon rested his head in his hands, his fingers laced through his hair. Ciella knew Mako as well as she knew him and, in fact, had once pledged a vow of love to the Reaper. To hear of Mako's atrocities was going to hurt her, but there was little other choice. "Mako attacked a Tower just over a moon ago. He killed all save a single Apprentice."

"Mako might be a Reaper, but he is not a butcher. He would never do such a thing."

Talon saw the denial in her eyes, plainer than any words she might speak, and he could not blame her for the disbelief. Mako used to be a decent man, if not a good one, but the illusions were over. He was no longer the boy they knew.

Talon pulled the slender banner from one of the pockets on his vest. "I found this stuck in the door." He offered it to her.

Silently, she took it from him and opened it out on her lap.

"He killed my son," Talon continued.

"Your son?" Slowly, she smoothed the cloth with her hand, flattening it.

"Yes."

"I thought Warriors never knew their children."

"I did, or at least I would have, if he had lived."

"Oh." Now wadding the cloth in her fist, Ciella twisted the black and white banner in her hand, winding it around her palms and unwinding it again as his words sank in.

Talon reached over, his large hand covering her small one, stopping her. "Where is Mako?"

Ciella stared at the banner twisted around her hand. "He killed them all?"

"Save Aria. She was the Apprentice he left alive."

Ciella met his gaze, her eyes bright. "Why did he spare her? Perhaps he knew and held his sword at the last minute. Perhaps it was not even Mako who killed your son, but one of his men."

"It does not matter. They were under his command, and he bears the blame." Perhaps Mako had known what, and who, he hurt. Talon would not put it past him. As to how he knew, Talon would ask—right before he killed the Reaper leader.

"I ask again, why spare the girl?"

Talon heard the hope in the question. Hope that Mako had a heart or at least some sense of goodness left. Goddess forgive him, but he had to crush that hope. He pulled away. "She had just given birth to my son. She almost died. I do not know why she was spared, but I can only assume they thought her already slain. She was covered in blood and only a whisper away from the Goddess when I found her."

"But she lived?"

"Yes, but only by the grace of the Goddess, not Mako." Talon hesitated and then made the final blow, cutting away Ciella's hope. "He killed them all. Old women and young girls. Children. Would you sacrifice another babe to his sword? Would you let friendship blind you to what he has become? He is a beast that must be stopped before he causes more tragedy."

A sob broke from Ciella's throat. The sound of someone whose heart was breaking. She unwound the banner, freeing her hands. Slowly, she stood, and with the cloth fluttering by her side, she walked over to the fireplace.

She stared at the flames. "What do you want to know?"

"Where Mako resides. How many men he has. Everything."

She threw the cloth in the blaze. It flared to life, consumed by the flame, then was gone. Ciella walked back to Talon. "I do not know much, but what I have is yours."

***

Talon opened the door to Barias' tavern and hesitated as his eyes adjusted from the darkened streets to the brightness of the room. Stepping over the threshold, the combined smells of cooked meat, ale, and burning oil assaulted his nose. His stomach growled in response. With any luck, Aria had left some dinner. If not, then he would have one of the girls bring something up. When his eyes had adjusted, he entered the great room and made his way through the crowd and towards the stairs leading to the second floor and the array of sleeping quarters.

A roar of laughter sounded, catching his attention, and he glanced to see a group of young men gathered on the far side of the room. Years ago, he would have joined them in their gambling, wrestling and bragging. He would have drunk until dawn and still found the energy to please a woman.

Now, he felt old in both soul and body. His feet dragging

with weariness, he made his way up the stairs. Another round of laughter sounded from the young men, he smiled, taking one last glance at the group. They were engrossed in something. Or someone. He caught a glimpse of red hair glinting in the light from the overhead candles at the same time the figure laughed.

He squinted.

It could not be. He leaned over the railing. A small figure stood in the center of the group, all but obscured by the height of the men.

The group parted, and Aria came into view. In one hand, she held a goblet. The other rested on a young man's leather-clad chest.

With a growl, Talon spun on his heel and stormed down the stairs, two at a time. What in the name of the Goddess was she doing down here? He had told her to wait in the room. He walked past the bar, and Marri waved at him in greeting. She pointed towards Aria with a tilt of her head. "Your woman's over there," she shouted over the din.

Talon did not answer as he made his way through the throng and past the crowded tables. He should have told Marri that Aria was a Trancer, and perhaps she would have kept a closer watch on her.

Aria's laugh cut through the noise, and he shoved his way through the crowd of men.

"Talon," Aria cried, raising her goblet to him. "You're back."

All heads turned to look at him. Talon ignored them and took the goblet from her. Overflowing with wine, much of it spilled on his shirt. Ignoring the mess, he let it drop to the floor and pulled her close. "Why are you not in our room where you belong?"

"Because," Aria said and fell against him, laughing.

Talon gave a great sigh of exasperation. She was as drunk as a Warrior on the first day of the Blessing Season. He mustered his patience. Men who could not hold their wine were annoying, but in his opinion, women were even worse.

Taking her hand in his, he started to pull her though the crowd. "We are going to the room."

"What about all my friends?" Aria slipped from his

grasp. "I don't want to leave them. We're having fun."

"Yes, who are you to take her?"

In front of Talon stood a young man, his face full of youthful arrogance.

"Her companion," Talon replied.

"So?" the youth barked. "That does not make her yours to command, and she does not want to leave."

"Right," Aria said, and with another giggle fell back against Talon. "Let's stay here. You can have a glass, too."

Talon growled again, and in one fluid movement, he picked Aria up and slung her over his shoulder. Her giggles jostled him. He ignored her. He had a more pressing issue in front of him—Aria's self-proclaimed defender. "Tell me, *boy*, what is your name?"

"What is it to you?"

"I always like to know the name of the men I kill. It saves time in delivering the body to their families." He did not have the time nor the desire for a fight. With his free hand, Talon moved aside his cloak, showing the blade by his side.

The surrounding crowd grew silent, waiting like carrion eaters to see who would attack first.

The lad did not flinch but straightened. "My name is Adrik, and do not worry about my family name, since I will win."

The boy had spirit. If he were not careful, that spirit would get him killed. "Tell me, Adrik, have you ever fought a man?"

"Plenty," the youth answered. He took a step forward.

Carrying Aria, Talon matched the step with one of his own and closed the gap even further. The crowd mumbled in unison, and the wagering began.

Talon ignored them and focused on Adrik. "Have you ever killed a man? Felt his life force slip through your fingers as your blade slipped through his ribs?" He gave the boy his most menacing stare, hoping to scare him into backing down.

The boy stood firm, but hesitated before nodding an affirmative answer.

Talon smiled. The boy lied.

Aria whacked Talon's back with the flat of her hand. "I can't breathe," she said, her voice muffled in his cloak.

Talon ignored her and took another step forward.

Adrik came to the bridge of his nose, but no further. His shoulders were broad but still had the thinness of youth. He was so close that the smell of his fear tickled Talon's nose, and the tremble of the boy's lower lip was obvious.

The lad was scared, but he stood his ground and met Talon's penetrating gaze. Talon's smile broadened.

"What are you smiling about, *old man?*"

Talon's left brow went up. *Old man?* The boy was as cocky as Lore.

"Talon, he was just being nice." Aria's muffled voice called out. "Don't make me hurt you," she said and hit him again.

Talon sighed. "Answer me this. Is she worth it?"

The boy gave him a quizzical look.

"She is drunk," Talon said.

"Perhaps, but she does not want to go with you, and I cannot allow you to take advantage of her."

"I'm not drunk," Aria protested. "Put me down, and I'll show you how not drunk I am."

Talon ignored the request. "She is under my protection."

"Then why does she deny you?"

"Because she is stubborn."

"I am *not* stubborn," Aria protested. "I just know what I want, and I want to stay here with my friends."

The crowd laughed in encouragement.

Talon ignored her outburst. "Tomorrow, she will be appalled by her behavior, and I would save her from embarrassment. I swear by the Goddess that my intentions are honorable, and other than putting her to bed, she will remain untouched."

Adrik hesitated. "Why should I believe you? You carry her like a sack of flour, not a person. You degrade her even now."

The youth made a point. Talon set Aria on her feet.

"Thanks, friend," Aria said, waving at Adrik. "I was getting dizzy back there."

The crowd roared again, enjoying the drama.

Talon pulled Aria close, but ignored the comments. "I pledge that I speak the truth. She will sleep at my side, nothing more. Now, let us pass or blood will spill."

"You claim honor, but are you sure it is not fear that drives you?"

Adrik was cocky, untrained and probably deserved a beating.

But Talon drew his cloak, covering his weapon, as he realized what this boy was—what he could be. Perhaps it was foolish, but the chance to give someone from Zaraza an opportunity to be more than a thief or a drunk overshadowed the desire for anonymity.

Besides, he and Aria would be gone before any of them thought to use any information against them.

"Positive. I have no fear of an untried youth and will be more than willing to kill you, if you so desire. However, I think your life would be better served as a Warrior."

The crowd grew silent. Adrik took a step back in surprise. "Me? A Warrior?"

He had the boy's attention.

"Good idea, Talon," Aria interjected. Swaying unsteadily, she slapped Adrik's chest with her palm. "You'd make a great Warrior."

Talon shook his head, wishing Aria would shut up. "Go to the Tower that lies on the water four suns ride from here. Ask for Lore, and tell him that Talon sent you to be trained."

Adrik's eyes narrowed. "Why should I believe you?"

Talon shrugged. "You probably should not, which is good instinct." He nodded towards Aria. "But why would a drunk lie?"

Talon waited as Adrik sized him up and then took in Aria's drunken form. "What makes you think I could be a Warrior?"

"You are the only one who tried to stop me from taking Aria upstairs."

"That is it?"

Talon saw the suspicion rise again in the boy's expression. It pleased him. "Not because you stopped me, but why. You wanted to protect her, and that is admirable. If I thought you tried to stop me because you wanted to bed her, I would not suggest Warrior training, and you would be on the floor nursing your wounds."

The boy hesitated, then nodded acceptance. "His name

is Lore?"

"Yes." Talon swept Aria into his arms.

With a small bow, Adrik moved aside. "Perhaps we shall meet again."

"Perhaps," Talon answered as he walked past Adrik and up the stairs.

The laughter of the crowd followed him until he shut the door behind him. In less than five footsteps, he reached the bed and dropped Aria onto the mattress.

More giggles ensued as Aria bounced on the springy surface.

Talon pulled the blanket out from beneath her and tucked it around her shoulders. "Sleep," he commanded. The night's conversation with Ciella had wearied his soul, and he did not have the desire to deal with Aria anymore. He simply wanted rest.

"No." Aria pushed the blanket off. "I'm not tired."

"We have a long journey ahead of us, and you need to rest." He put the blanket back.

She wrapped her arms around Talon's neck as he leaned over her. "Where are we going?"

Talon removed her arms and took a closer look at his drunken companion. Her pupils were dilated and all but covered the green of her eyes. She was more intoxicated than he had thought. Between the battering her body took in the river and her wine addled mind, she would be miserable tomorrow.

Perhaps the physical discomfort would drive her back to the Tower. He grinned at the thought. "We travel to the Broken Mountains." Sitting on the edge of the bed, he removed his boots.

Aria crawled close and snuggled up next to him. "There's only one bed."

"I am aware of that," Talon replied.

Her small hands reached to undo the fastening on his cloak.

"Stop it." Gently, he pushed her away.

"Why? Don't you want me?"

Talon saw her eyes, dark and half-lidded, and her lips lush with desire. Her tunic had slipped off her shoulder revealing a patch of smooth skin that begged to be nibbled. His body responded despite his weariness. He groaned.

Even drunk, she aroused him.

Nevertheless, he could not take her. Not under these circumstances.

The mattress shifted again as she righted herself. "I know you want me." Her voice came from behind him, and she kissed the back of his neck.

"I said, stop it," he commanded again.

No more drunken giggles ensued, only a husky laugh as Aria scooted around to sit beside him. Ignoring her, he pulled his other boot off and threw it to the floor.

"How about I help take off the rest," Aria suggested. Laying her hand on his thigh, she slid it upwards until it rested on his hardened member.

Talon groaned again. "You are drunk, and I am not interested."

"Are you sure?" She rubbed his length through his leather leggings.

Talon's breath hissed through his teeth, and he jumped to his feet, knocking her backwards. "This has gone far enough. If you were sober, I would take you here and now, but I will not take advantage of you while you are incoherent."

"But I want you to take me."

"Would you say the same if you were not full of wine?"

She nodded her head with enthusiasm, then abruptly stopped. Her eyes widened, and she gulped. "I don't feel so good."

"Are you going to be ill?" Talon asked, remembering the first, and only, time he had drunk himself into blackness. Lore had held his head all night as he retched and then laughed the next day when Talon complained that birds sang too loudly and that the sun was too bright.

"No, I don't think so," Aria said and gave a little moan.

Talon unbuckled his scabbard and set both sword and sheath on the table. He would have to find something to set next to the bed in case she did become ill. He sighed.

A thunk sounded behind him, and he turned back around. A smile curled his lips. Aria would not be ill. She had passed out.

Eleven

Aria opened her eyes to bright sunlight, groaned, and flung her arm over her face.

"Ah, you are awake."

Talon's words echoed like bells in her ears. She nodded and groaned again as the movement made her senses spin and ache. Had Cam danced upon her head last night? It felt as if he had. Moving as slowly as possible, she pulled the covers over her, blocking out the world.

The thin blanket was jerked back off. "It is time to rise."

Still curled up, wanting desperately to go back to sleep, she managed to open her eyes. Talon stood at the side of her bed, already dressed.

"It is time to leave."

She noticed one of his packs was flung over his shoulder. "Where are we going?" Her voice sounded rough. She ran her tongue over her teeth and shuddered. It seemed as if Cam had not only danced on her head but had also bathed in her mouth.

"There is a Tower a short distance from here. I am taking you there until this matter with the Reapers is resolved." He stared down at her. His left foot tapped impatiently.

Aria bolted upright. A yelp of suffering escaped her lips before she could suppress it. "No. I travel with you. Once, you gave me your word. Now I hold you to it"

Talon shook his head. "That was on the condition you would not be a hindrance."

"I will not be." She held her head in her hands.

The tapping stopped. "You already are. I am ready to leave and have no time to deal with a wine-sickened woman." He turned away. "On second thought, stay here. I will have Barias take you to the Tower when you are able to travel."

"Wait."

He turned back.

She had not broken their bargain. Not yet. All she had to do was get up, get dressed, and spend the day on a *rohha* that loathed her. Another shudder shook her. It did not matter. "Give me my clothes, and I will be ready to travel in a few moments."

Talon gave a snort of amusement. "You are wearing them."

Aria saw she was dressed in her stolen leggings and tunic. She ran a hand through her hair and found it a tangled mess. What had happened last night? Why was she still dressed? Searching her memory, she found nothing but a blur of events. "What happened?"

"You drank too much wine." He shot her a smug, knowing, grin. "I found you surrounded by young men and quite happy with the attention."

She had never been addled before, but she had seen others in such a state. The hot blush of embarrassment heated her cheeks, and she wanted to crawl back into the comfort of the bed and hide. She did not. Instead, her mother's words echoed in her head, *No one ever died from embarrassment.*

Unfortunately, her mother was right. One only *wanted* to die. Ignoring the emotional discomfort, she replied, "My head is clear now, and while I may be uncomfortable, I am ready to leave."

Talon's dark brows rose in disbelief. "Yesterday, you were dumped in a river, rode all day, and drank too much. You cannot walk this morning, much less ride. Perhaps you think you can, but I know from experience that you will slow me down."

He wanted her gone. Well, he would be greatly disappointed. "I will manage," she replied through gritted teeth.

Talon sighed and ran both hands over his hair, smoothing it back even though it was already bound behind him. "You do not know what you say. It will be a harsh ride. We will not stop until the evening."

She met his gaze. "I said I can do it."

He dropped to a chair and leaned forward, elbows on knees, his expression earnest. "Do not pursue this. You are in pain, and I cannot bear to see you hurt. Let me take you to a Tower. When this business is over, I will come back for you. I swear it."

Aria shook her head. No matter how her head ached,

she would not let Talon do this alone. She had made a promise to herself and their son. For that, a day of discomfort was but a small price.

He continued, "You have already been through much. I know you must have the favor of the Goddess, or you would not be alive. What will you do when her favor ends?"

Leaning forward, she placed her hand on his forearm. "Whatever I must."

Talon stared at her hand as if it held the secret to life itself. "I ask you again, will you let me take you someplace safe?"

"No." Perhaps she did have the favor of the Goddess. Perhaps not. It did not matter. She had vowed to help Talon and find Tarik, and she would do so. The Goddess' will be done. She would follow her path to its end.

His sprang to his feet, tipping his chair backwards. "You cannot move without wincing. How do you expect to sit on Cam all day? I do not have time to humor you."

"I will manage." Some of what he said was true. With her state of body, the ride would be torture. But if she proved herself, maybe he would cease his relentless campaign to leave her behind. "Talon, if I ride all day with not a single complaint passing my lips, will you take me with you without a word of complaint passing yours?"

She saw her challenge sparked him. He took in her disheveled clothes, and what she was sure was a pallid complexion and dull hair. She did not have to be a Trancer to know his thoughts. He thought the wager already won.

He would learn just how wrong he was.

"As you wish," Talon replied, accepting her challenge.

Underneath his words was the self-satisfied sound of victory.

***

Cam stumbled, came down hard on his front foreleg, and recovered with a jolt. Aria stiffened, a muffled cry emerging from her lips. Talon stiffened as well, fighting his natural instinct to halt Cam and ease her suffering.

She had been sitting in front of him since daybreak, and then again after the midday meal. He knew the position was awkward and uncomfortable under the best of circumstances. She shifted in an attempt to make herself comfortable, and once again, the urge to take her into his arms assailed him.

He ignored it.

She settled at last, leaning back against him. With an internal sigh of relief, he glanced at her. Trying to rest, her eyes were closed, but her expression was far from relaxed. Her jaw was set. Lines of strain marred her smooth forehead, and her expression grew tighter with each step. However, other than her earlier startled cry, she made no noise. Not a whimper. Not a sob.

Why did she not stop this? Why go through this torture if it were preventable? He knew she thought him wrong about Mako, wrong about Tarik, but why pursue it in this manner? If she would just listen to reason and let him do what he must, then she would have her answers. She would know the truth.

Why did she have to be so stubborn?

Her hands caught his attention. Clenched into tight fists and resting on the tops of her thighs, a trail of blood trickled from between her fingers where her nails dug into her delicate skin.

The reality of the situation struck him, imbedding itself all the way down to his bones. *She was not going to give in.* She wanted to help him, and she would, regardless of anything he said or did, regardless of the danger. He cursed himself for thinking victory would be either easy or fast, and for ignoring his instincts. He held a piece of Aria inside his heart, and because of that, he knew she was more stubborn and stronger than anyone imagined.

He had known it and ignored it.

Now, what to do?

There were few options. Keep her close or take her to a Tower and leave her?

The latter was the most pleasing choice. She would be safe, and he could focus on the job at hand.

However, it would not work. If he left her behind, she would simply follow him again.

He would have to take her with him. She would slow him down, as well as split his caution, but the situation seemed unavoidable.

Besides, he had accepted her wager—something he would not do so readily again.

Cam stumbled again. A drop of blood formed on Aria's

bottom lip where she bit it to keep from crying out. Talon grimaced. It was time to end this charade. If she were going to journey with him, it would be in both their best interests to make sure she remained healthy.

He signaled Cam to go into the trees.

Aria straightened and looked over her shoulder at him, her green eyes wide. "Where are we going?" Her voice rose in panic. "You gave your word that if I rode without complaint you would not take me to the Tower."

Talon put an arm around her. The flat of his hand rested on her stomach as he held her against him. "We do not go to the Tower. We go to make camp."

"Camp? The day is not over."

"I know," he replied. "I also know that you would continue without a word of protest, win the bet, and then collapse tomorrow."

She stared at him in disbelief. "So, I win?"

"Yes." Talon chuckled. "I concede the victory. You win."

She nodded, but the strain around her eyes remained. Without a word, she leaned into him once more.

Talon knew he was right in his assessment. She was beyond fatigue and hanging on by sheer determination of will.

Would Tarik have had her strength of will? Talon's fingers tightened around Cam's reins, and he forced the uninvited musings from his mind. At present, it was essential that he concentrate on Aria.

Revenge would come soon enough.

They moved deeper into the woods, and within moments, the trees surrounded them. Light, filtered green by the thick covering of leaves overhead, barely lit the forest floor. Talon squinted at the shadows, ever vigilant to an ambush. However, as Cam picked his way through the trees, no one crossed their path.

Soon, the sound of running water broke the air. The *rohha* moved towards it before Talon gave the command. "I see your penchant for water overrides even my will." Dropping the reins, he let Cam guide himself.

The forest opened ahead of them. Using the flat of his sword, Talon lifted the mossy vines from their path, and they rode out into a small, open glade.

"Goddess," Aria uttered in awe.

Talon echoed her sentiment.

They had found the source of the water. It was a small stream and across from it was a statue of the Goddess herself. Carved in pale stone and three times as high as Cam, she sat under a canopy of trees. With her eyes closed and her hands carved palms up and resting on her knees, she assumed the pose of a Trancer.

Behind her lay a building carved from the same pale stone and covered in vines, a massive structure that stood forgotten and neglected.

"It is most remarkable. What do you think it is? A temple?" Despite the brightness of her voice, Aria's eyes remained dulled by the fatigue she fought so hard to hide.

Her bravery broke him. A temple. A palace. It did not matter, not when Aria suffered. Signaling Cam, Talon sent the *rohha* splashing through the stream, not reining in the great beast until they stood at the base of the stairs. Talon slid off Cam's back then tugged at Aria's leg. She fell into his arms with a small "oof." He set her on her feet.

Both stood silent, overwhelmed by the temple's power. It was obvious that this place was holy. It was not just that the stone Goddess protected the area, but it was the building itself. It remained intact and sealed from the world, wooden doors and shutters closed, despite the forest that surrounded it.

It also emanated a strength and quality that even Talon sensed.

In unison, they stepped forward.

Graceful columns arched towards the sky, their bases carved with stories and scenes. The walls were just as ornate and inlaid with colored stone. He recognized a scene to the left of the entrance. The Silver Maiden, her hair imbedded with iridescent shell, and the Warrior lay under the moons, legs intertwined. Her back was arched, and his sword was in his hands, completing the Given ceremony.

"I am not sure we should enter." Aria broke the silence. "This place is of the Goddess."

Talon hesitated. As holy as the temple was, Aria needed rest. The Goddess would understand. "She brought us here," was his reply as he led Aria to the stairs.

She stumbled, falling to her knees.

She is too brave for her own good, Talon thought. Without a word, he swept her into his arms, grateful that she was too tired to protest or struggle as he carried her to the landing.

He stopped at the wooden entrance. Would it open, and was the temple safe? He took a moment to listen to his instincts. No one was coming back. This place, for all its power, also had the air of a building long empty. Nothing would bother them here. Still holding Aria, he pushed the latch with his thumb. The wooden door swung open.

Talon walked through and stopped at the surprising brightness that greeted them. A large glass dome, three times the width of a man, was centered on the roof, allowing light to filter in.

The room itself was empty. No chairs. No tables. Nothing other than a large pool, still full of water, that cut a round patch from the middle of the floor.

Still, the empty space, with its pale walls and equally pale-colored floor, emitted a sense of simplicity rather than bleakness. The only hint of color was the mural painted on the far wall.

His footsteps echoing off the walls, Talon walked across the floor to see it. A continuation of the carving by the door—the mural continued the tale of the Silver Maiden and the Grey Warrior. From left to right, it flowed from their secret meetings, to his battle for her hand, and their bonding ceremony.

It was a story all knew well, and it made him think of when he had first met Aria. He gazed at her.

Smudged and sleepy, his own Maiden, not of silver but of flame, rested in his arms, more beautiful than a carving and warmer than stone. The light from above illuminated her hair like fire in the dim.

She sneezed.

She was also going to become ill if she did not rest and eat. He set her on her feet. "Wait here."

She nodded, not arguing. He hurried outside and relieved Cam of his load, telling the *rohha* to rest and stand guard.

When he came back through the door, he found Aria sitting on the edge of the pool, her feet in the water, and a real smile on her lips.

Talon set the supplies near a wall and walked over. Pale blue and white tiles covered the bottom of the pool and continued up the walls in a simple spiral design. The water was as clear as if it were just poured from a pitcher. Kneeling, he ran a hand through it. It was warm. The builders of this temple must have been skilled. Or blessed. Or both.

"Do you think it would be safe to take a bath?" Aria asked.

He doubted she would ever be safer than in this holy place. "Take your bath, and I will prepare a place for you to rest." He stood, walking to unpack his gear and prepare a place for Aria.

The sound of her tunic falling to the floor caught him off guard, but he did not turn around. Instead, he opened a blanket and spread it on the ground, ignoring her sounds of satisfaction as she slipped into the warm water with a splash.

Another sigh echoed off the stone walls. He glanced over his shoulder. Floating on her back, she pushed herself away from the wall—her scarlet locks a sharp contrast to the blue of the water and the ivory shade of her skin.

She looked like bliss, like redemption. He would sell his soul to make love to her.

It was not to be. Now was not the time.

He returned to his work.

Why not?

This was not the place.

Of course it is.

The voice echoed in his head, unfamiliar, unwanted, and not his own. Yet, far from disturbing, it soothed him in a familiar way—like a mother's voice telling her small child that it is was all right to take the leap. That if he jumped off the cliff, she would catch him.

He wanted to. He wanted to leap into the unknown waters of his own soul. He wanted to love Aria again, to show her the part of him he kept hidden.

But she was as tired as a Warrior after battle, and he had other duties. No matter what the voice said, love would have to wait.

No excuses, Warrior. Not here. Not in MY temple.

A rush of heat surged through him, laying bare his

soul.

Go to her.

Talon shut his eyes. When he opened them, he was in the pool.

***

Aria floated in the water, finding peace for the first time in days. She pulled her hands over the surface. The movement sent her towards the pool's far wall. Bumping against it with her feet, she pushed off with a gentle shove and floated back to the center of the pool.

The water was amazing—invigorating and relaxing at the same time. Life giving, it filled her with an energy. It was also as warm and comforting as the womb.

Soothed, she let her mind relax. Not Trancing, not thinking, but just being one with the blue liquid that surrounded her with its tranquility.

She wished she could share it with Talon.

You can.

Truly? She was not so sure anymore. It was almost four seasons since they joined, and Talon had yet to express any deep emotion for her. Perhaps the joining was gone, never to be experienced again.

Her heart wanted to break at the thought. With or without the joining, to never experience the depth of Talon again was unbearable.

How could she have been so wrong?

Do not doubt, Trancer. Your talent is true.

Sisterly and reassuring, the voice soothed her, but was it right?

The water rippled, and a small wave lapped over her face. She stood up sputtering.

Still in his clothes, Talon stood in the hip deep water, waiting, as if wearing his clothes to swim were a natural occurrence. What did he wait for?

He waits for you just as you wait for him.

Talon's eyes, free from pain, reflected his hunger for her. His lips curved up in an unguarded, almost vulnerable, smile. In a gesture so tender it made her cry, his hand reached out and smoothed her wet hair away from her cheek.

"No tears, Aria," he whispered. "Not here. Not now."

She nodded. He was right.

The voice was right.

Tonight was about emotion. About tenderness. About love. About that which both Talon and she craved, but of which they dare not speak. She took a step towards him and placed her hand upon his chest. Although still covered in cloth, every muscle, every ripple of flesh burned itself into her palm. His need was as tangible as the water—as eternal as the Goddess.

Shivering, she responded in kind. She wanted to bite and taste the sweetness of his need like ripe fruit on her tongue.

His eyes never leaving hers, Talon took her hand in his and placed a kiss inside her palm.

Aria's world shifted. Her senses sang and danced.

He turned her hand over in his and grazed her knuckles with his mouth. He wanted her. He wanted to share that which few ever experienced. He wanted to join with her. She knew it in her heart and her body. She knew it by the currents that surrounded them, and by the way the Goddess spoke to her of bonding and comfort. Protection and passion.

Aria shut her eyes. So much had happened since the Reaper's massacre that neither she nor Talon had considered making love, but now images bombarded her. Like the mural at the door, she imagined herself intertwined with her Giver, her legs wrapped around his hips.

And like the lovers of legend, she wanted more. She wanted to go beyond the boundaries of society and beyond the boundaries of her heart.

Could Talon read her thoughts? Could he taste her desire as she tasted his? Did he hear the Goddess as she did—her holy voice urging them towards destiny?

Working his way down her hand, Talon bit the inside of her wrist.

Aria opened her eyes and found her answer in his erotic expression. He wanted her more with every passing breath. *As much as she wanted him.*

In unspoken agreement, she met his mouth halfway, her arms twining around his neck as they tasted each other, reveling in each other's touch for the first time since the Given ceremony. For the first time since the loss of their child over a moon ago.

He traced her lower lip with the tip of his tongue then drew a path along her lower jaw, savoring her like a sweet, until he reached her ear. "Aria."

Her name was more than a name. She heard the question in it. All the questions. Did she love him? Was she angry that he failed to save her Tower, her friends, and her family? Would she let him love her?

She ached with the sincerity of his emotions, with the honesty of his desire. She nuzzled his jaw and whispered, "Talon." It was the answer he needed.

He wrapped his arms around her waist, pulling her closer. With a gentle, yet possessive touch, he bit her neck, claiming her.

Desire pulsed through her, and she pulled at him, wanting to touch him.

"More."

Was that her voice or his? It did not matter, and he bit her again—a *katah'* claiming his mate. With a moan, she stepped back. She needed his skin. She needed his flesh pressed against her. No, pressed *into* her. With trembling fingers, she tugged at his shirt, trying to pull the wet garment free from his body. He reached up and stilled her frantic hands, kissing them again. "Let me," he whispered.

She did not answer, but nodded.

He pulled the wet shirt over his head and flung it. It landed on the floor next to the pool. He did the same with his boots. Next, he unbuckled his wet leathers and forced them down. Pushing them off with his feet he stepped out of them.

Glory to the Goddess, but he wanted Aria.

Taking a deep breath, Talon sank to his knees in front of Aria, resting his head against her stomach while she tangled her hands in his hair. He stroked one of the thin white lines that proclaimed her motherhood then planted a tender kiss on it. She had bore his son in silence, never telling him. That would not happen again if she became heavy with child. This time, he would stay with her and celebrate each moment, each sign of the child within.

Each blessed change in his Given.

"Your will be done, my Goddess," he whispered, not knowing or caring if he spoke to the Goddess herself or to

Aria. He kissed Aria's skin, savoring the stray drops that dotted her flesh like tiny crystals. His hands stroked her, kneading and massaging, working their way from her shoulders to her knees and back again.

She responded with a deep sigh, and he sensed her desire for more, felt it in his blood. With her hands still tangled in his hair, he tilted his head up, his tongue leaving liquid crystal for the hard pink peaks that topped her breasts.

Pulling a nipple into his mouth, he caressed, savoring the sensation as it hardened between his teeth, relishing the sweet turmoil he knew he caused in Aria's body. Unhurried, he traced a path with the tip of his tongue to lavish the other breast with the same attention.

Aria's hands moved from his hair to his shoulders, holding and pushing at the same time, as if the torture was too unbearable to continue, but even more unbearable to stop. Grinning, he rubbed a hard peak between thumb and forefinger. She flung her head back as a cry ripped from her throat.

He smiled, loving the sounds of her passion. He wanted to make her moan and want and scream until she was breathless. He wanted her wild. Wanted to join with her both body and mind.

He wanted what they had had before. The joining.

With only Aria's breathing and the calm lap of the water for sound, he left her breasts, anxious to savor more of her. With exquisite slowness, he kissed her bare skin again, first her stomach, then her sides as he remained low in the water and circled her, holding her with firm hands that stroked her skin as they followed the path of his mouth.

He stopped at her back, and smiled again as, like lost birds, her hands fluttered between water and air, searching for purchase. Her back was perfect, sculpted straight and pale, with a flash of red hair hanging past her bottom. With a growl, he bit the sensitive area where back met buttocks before rising to kiss a path along her spine. Her knees buckled, and he caught her in his arms, turning her to face him. "I am the Giver. Do you take what I offer?"

"I am the Given." Aria's voice was low and filled with awe. "I accept with all my being." She touched his mouth.

Her fingers kissed him in disbelief.

He groaned, and Aria smiled with the satisfaction of a woman who has found her power.

He wanted her to use it. He wanted to lose himself in that part of her that was stronger than him, the part that loved, and maybe for a moment, he could love as well.

It was a heady, frightening thought, but she deserved no less. Here, in this Temple, for a night, he could prove his own worthiness.

"I have no sword for my hands, my Given." He nuzzled her neck. "But know that I would bleed for you."

"This is all the sword I need or desire." She gripped him in response.

Talon brought his mouth down on hers. She opened to him, and it became a sensuous battle, as they tasted each other, each becoming greedier with each breath.

The air grew heavy as Aria's Trancer talent took over, touching him, tasting his thoughts, and leaving her own open to him.

He reveled in it. Welcomed the intimacy.

She was exquisite, both life and death. He picked her up, and in one silken movement, she wrapped her legs around his hips, and impaled herself on him, completing the joining.

Buried in her, touching her mind, he knew this was all the life he needed or wanted.

She moved against him, guiding herself. Her pleasure mingled with his until he neither knew which was his nor which was hers.

The exquisite torture climbed out of control. How could she stand it?

How can you?

He opened his eyes, and for a moment, he saw himself through her eyes. Raw power, tanned skin twined with pale. A mighty Warrior. He did not deserve her praise.

But you do, Aria assured him.

I will try.

He crushed her against him, and she screamed her desire, a primitive sound that spoke of complete release, as she arched against his body.

The sound echoed through the empty temple and was answered in a deeper tone.

Talon realized it was his own voice that shouted, as his desire peaked, and he and Aria became one and the same—joined.

Twelve

The morning sun woke Aria, and unlike the day before, she welcomed it. Raising her arms over her head, she stretched with a sigh of contentment. Her muscles ached, but it was a sweet reminder of last night.

Talon mumbled in his sleep. Settling next to him, Aria watched him while listening to him breathe and wondering what he dreamed. In the time she had known him, this morning was the first she had woken before him and had had the pleasure of such speculation.

Deep in slumber, he lay on his back with one arm flung over his head and the other limp at this side. Pulled free from the leather ties that usually constrained it, his hair lay scattered across the blankets that served as their bed.

He was a handsome man. She had not thought about his looks, his sheer masculinity, since the Given ceremony. So much had stood in the way.

Talon stirred and brushed his hand against the scar that ran the length of his jaw.

Aria remembered how she had done the same on the morning after the Given ceremony. She had meant to ask him what had happened, but she had never had the chance.

Maybe she would this morning. Now that they were lovers again. Now that he was willingly joined with her.

Tentatively, she reached out and traced the length of the scar with a fingertip—

And found herself thrown flat on her back with the breath knocked out of her.

Talon loomed over her, one hand drawn back with his short knife in it, and the other wrapped around her neck. His eyes were wide. They did not see her. They saw an enemy, a demon from his dreams. He was not awake. Not yet.

She faced death with her eyes wide open.

The final blow did not come.

"Aria?"

She nodded.

He released his hold, and she clutched her throat. What

was wrong? All she had done was touch him.

He sat back on his heels, his expression confused. "Aria?" He hesitated, his eyes still unfocused. He rubbed them with his free hand. When he finally looked up, they were free from the grip of dreams.

He reached out to her, but his hand stopped short when he saw he still held the knife. With a groan, he let it fall from his grip, and it clattered to the floor. Neither spoke nor looked at the weapon.

After a moment, he took her hand and pulled her to him, clutching her to his chest. He stroked her hair. "You surprised me. Did I hurt you?"

She took a deep breath. "No. I am shaken but unharmed." What darkness kept his vigilance so high that he was ready to kill—even in his sleep? Even in this place of peace?

"Are you sure?" He turned her head with a delicate touch and traced what she was sure were the red marks left on her throat.

His expression changed from tender to savage as he slammed a clenched fist on his naked thigh. "It will never happen again."

"It was an accident."

"Accident or not, you are not safe when I am around."

The pain in his eyes broke her heart. She took his hand in hers and unbent his rigid fingers. "Do all Warriors attack so readily?"

"It is part of our training, but that is no excuse."

She nodded in understanding. He could not stop his well-honed reactions any more than she could stop being a Trancer. She would not want him to. "I shall simply be more careful in the future and wake you with a stick." She smiled, hoping her humor would diffuse his guilt.

Her smile was not returned.

"Yes, that would be best." He fell back onto the thin pallet.

"It was but a joke," she murmured. He did not hear her, and she knew that even if he had, it was no joke to him.

Instead, he stared at the ceiling. He looked so alone. So contrite and guilty at something that was as natural to him as breathing. Pulling a blanket back over them, more for comfort than warmth, Aria lay down beside him.

He pulled her close, holding her. "I swear I will never harm you."

She nodded, knowing it to be the truth. He was her protector, just as she was his, and he meant to keep his word. "Do not let it worry you so. There was no harm done." Even as she said the words, she knew he did not listen.

She would never fully understand him. Never truly know his past or what drove him. Even to her Trancer senses, there was too much shrouded. He carried so much pain within, and to let him carry this new guilt was unacceptable.

She kissed his broad chest. His muscles twitched at the contact. She kissed him again, enjoying his reaction as she worked her way across his body. Leaning over him, she tickled him with her hair.

Parting her hair, he tilted her chin up. "What are you doing?"

"Whatever I want." Sitting up, she slid a leg over him, straddling his waist. "And right now, I want you."

He shut his eyes with a groan, but his hands skated a path up her back.

She shivered at the caress, but did not let it sway her. For once, she was in control. She was the Giver, not the Given. Placing her hands on his bare chest, she felt his heart beat beneath her palms. She leaned forward and gently bit his nipple, holding it in her teeth. His breath caught, and his heartbeat raced beneath her palm.

"Aria..."

Enjoying her power, she moved on, kissing her way up to his shoulder and onward to his ear. "What?"

"You should not be doing this." Even as he spoke, his hands ran down her sides and over her thighs, urging her onward.

She ground her hips against him, taunting him. "Why not?"

"I am supposed to pleasure you."

"You are." She laughed and kissed his forehead, letting her breast graze his mouth. "Your every reaction pleasures me."

He gazed at her with half-lidded hunger. "Besides—"

She stopped his protest with a kiss, rubbing her lips over his. "Shh."

"We need to leave."

She ran her hands through his hair, knowing he did not mean it. His voice, his body gave him away. He wanted her as much as she wanted him. "Your quest will wait," she murmured. "Mako will wait."

He went rigid beneath her. "Do you really think that?"

Inwardly, Aria cursed her careless tongue. Mentioning Mako was a mistake. She should have simply kissed Talon harder.

She traced the line of his jaw with her nail. "Can we forget him? Just until the sun reaches its peak?"

"How can either of us forget the man who butchered our son? Your people?" Talon countered. "How can we make love knowing he could be taking the same joy from another?"

Tentatively, she bit his ear, hoping to make him forget the present. Nothing. He gave no indication of any emotion other than stoic tolerance. The moment of joy was gone like a shadow in the sun. She sat up and slid off him. Silent, scared of what she would say, she cursed her stupidity. She only wanted to give Talon the same joy he gave her, and she had ruined it with her careless words.

But why did the words have to be careless? Why did she have to be watchful of every sentence she spoke? A thin line of anger made its way through her psyche, poking at her, prodding her with its hot tip. She raised her head, her gaze meeting his dark one. "Can you not forget the world just for one morning?" she asked, her voice tight. "The Goddess gave us a reprieve from duty, and I do not want to walk away from it. Not yet. I think you feel the same."

Rising to his feet, Talon walked over to the edge of the pool and retrieved his damp leggings, yanking them on. "What I feel does not matter. There is never a reprieve from duty. One might forget for a night, but it always returns with the light of dawn."

Aria covered herself with the blanket. The thin line of anger grew into a ribbon. "Is what I feel for you not as clear as duty? Is what I want to give less important than the revenge you seek?"

Reaching down, he took her chin between thumb and forefinger, and tilted her head up to him. "I appreciate what you offer, but now is not the time."

What she offered? Could he not see there was more to her—more to them—than a moment of lovemaking? She resisted the urge to jerk her head away and instead stared at him, trying to read his expression. His stony gaze told her nothing. He was as closed as a tomb and as secretive as a thief. The ribbon of anger grew into a stream. "What do you see, Talon? Passion? Lust? Or do you see more?"

He did not answer, but released her.

She shut her eyes, holding in the hot tears that threatened to spill. His dismissal of her question told her more than words.

Duty came before her. Death came before her. Everything came before her. He saw her as a vessel for his needs, and now that his needs were met, he turned away without a second thought. She thought she knew him. *Knew his heart.* Last night, she had been so sure.

Please, my Goddess, do not abandon me now. Help me understand.

There was no answer. She held back a cry of disappointment.

Not sure of anything—not Talon, not her talents, and surely not herself—she stood. Letting the blanket drop, she found her clothes and pulled them on. Grabbing the discarded covering, she wadded it up and shoved it into her pack.

"You should fold that to make more room," Talon commented as he filled their other satchel.

She glared at him. "I will do as I please, and right now, it pleases me to do this."

For a moment, he looked taken aback, then he dismissed her with a shrug and continued packing.

The blood rushed to Aria's face. "Do you not even care that you hurt me?" She tried to shove another blanket into the bag.

He stopped. "My words are not meant to hurt. I simply want to get on with what we came to do. Afterwards, we will talk."

"If there is an afterwards," she muttered, still struggling to fit the second blanket in. It would not fit. He was right about folding the first one, which only served to irk her. She pulled both back out.

Talon walked over. "Let me help you." He took a corner of the blanket.

"I do not need your help." The stream of anger surged into a river and consumed her. She jerked the blanket from his hands. "I will not be a whore for you, Talon, and I do not need your help. In anything."

He took a step back. "A whore? I never called you a whore."

"No, but you would treat me as one."

"I never—"

"Yes, you do. When you turn away from me with no words and no explanation. When your duty is more important than my feelings. When only *you* are allowed to give pleasure and I am only permitted to take it." She stumbled over the words, her tongue tripping over the jumble of thoughts. "All of it lessens me."

"It is not meant to."

"But it does." Her voice echoed in the empty room. "Sometimes I think you are more like a Reaper than a Warrior. You take what you want and only give when it suits your purpose or desire."

He flushed crimson. "You think of me as a Reaper?"

What had she said?

"You would compare me to Mako?" His quiet, controlled voice barely made it the few feet to Aria's ears, frightening her more than if he shouted and yelled. "You think me akin to the man who killed our son and left you lying in a pool of blood?"

She shook her head, tangled hair flying. "I did not mean it like that."

He opened his mouth to speak, but stopped and turned away.

Trembling, she reached out to him. He did not see the gesture. She let her hand drop. He stood only a few footsteps from her, but it felt like a chasm as both anger and shame warred inside her heart.

***

Talon tied Aria's pack onto Cam's leather saddle, swearing under his breath. As if sensing his master's anger, Cam craned his neck around and nudged Talon, knocking him sideways.

"Not now." Talon pushed the *rohha's* nose away with a firm hand.

The animal sidestepped. Talon grabbed Cam's reins, stopping him. "I said, not now."

The *rohha* tossed his head.

"It is not his fault. Gentle words will go farther than a harsh tone."

Aria stood in the Temple's door way. One hand held her pack, and the other toyed with the end of her plaited hair.

"You would know about gentle words, would you not?"

She flushed and flung her braided hair backwards. The end of it brushed the top of her thighs as it swung behind her. Flinging a bundle over her shoulder, she walked down the white stone steps towards him, her leather clad feet silent. "What I said was cruel and wrong, and even I do not believe it."

"Why did you say it?"

"I was angry and wanted to hurt you as you had hurt me." She took a step towards him. "Please forgive my careless tongue."

Was she so careless, or did she know more than she realized? He was angry at Aria. Her words had cut him deeper than any blade, but overshadowing the anger was the dreaded thought that perhaps she was right. He had tried to forget his past, but maybe it was a part of him. He shuddered at the bitter thought, but he held out a leather-clad hand. "There is nothing to forgive. I, too, spoke carelessly. I would never consider you a whore, and I am sorry for making you think such a thing. I am the one who should beg forgiveness."

She smiled and took his hand in hers, and for a moment, all was forgiven. He was redeemed. But then he remembered what his future held, and hers, if he did not do his duty. He let her go and turned to finish readying Cam.

"Let me help." Aria interrupted him with both gentle words and hands as she reached to tie a knot.

He slid past and let her finish. If she knew his past, she would not be offering help but running away.

In a few moments, they were ready to depart the

temple.

Aria stepped back and looked at Talon with a hopeful smile on her lips. "So, where do we go next?"

Talon stroked his chin. With all that had happened— her weariness, last night's lovemaking and the fight this morning—he had not told her they were going to her hometown of Laini. He still remembered her words from the Given ceremony when he asked about her people, *They do not suffer Trancers to live among them.* Returning to those who had abandoned her would be an unpleasant experience at best. At worst...

His hand automatically reached for his blade. He would make sure nobody harmed her.

If only he could say the same about himself. He had promised he would not harm her, and yet he did so with every word, every action. He would choose his vows more carefully in the future. "I was told there is a man that was captured by the Reapers and escaped. We go to him in hopes he can either lead us to their camp or tell us the path." Silently, he willed her to let the subject go. Aria would taste the bitterness of reality soon enough.

"What is his name?"

"Guar."

Her look of recognition at the name drove Talon to silence.

The silence grew, taking on a life of its own. "Where is Guar from?" Aria broke the painful quiet.

"A small village at the base of the Broken Mountains." Talon sighed, knowing she would not give up until she had the full truth.

"Do we travel to Laini?" She asked the question as if dreading the answer. Her eyes pleaded with him to lie. To tell her Guar was just another man from another village. She begged him to not betray her.

"Yes," Talon whispered, hating himself for what he was doing to her.

Aria paled and stumbled towards the temple, almost falling onto the steps as she sat down. Talon remained next to Cam. He did not deserve to hold her or offer comfort. He deserved to be whipped.

"Why did you not tell me?" she asked after a few moments.

"I wanted to."

"Yet, you did not."

"There was never an appropriate moment. Yesterday, I had hoped to leave you at the Tower or even Barias'. You would never have known of this if you had not been so persistent. Last night—"

She gave a short harsh laugh, cutting him off. "Yes, last night you were busy."

"It was not like that." Talon took a step towards her, willing her to hear the truth of his words.

She turned away, hiding her face in her hands. When she turned back, he saw something in her eyes he had never seen before—distance, alienation, and an aloneness sharper than a blade.

Her eyes filled, but no tears fell. "Do you know what they did to me? How they made me feel? They shunned me, feared me. I left with nothing but some food and not one..." Her voice rose. "...not one person watched me walk away. Instead, they remained in their homes, cowering in fear. My father even kept my brother and sister from me. I never got to say good-bye." Resting her head on her knees, she wrapped her arms around her legs, holding on as if the pain were too much to bear.

To know he helped contribute to that pain overwhelmed Talon. No matter that he was not worthy of her, he sat next to her, wrapping his arm around her shoulders.

She scooted away.

Her pain was unbearable, but there was nothing he could do to mend her past. All he could offer was an alternative for the future. "You do not have to go. I can take you back to Barias', and you can wait for me there. I will come back."

Her head snapped up, and she glared at him, green eyes narrowed. "No. I will not be left behind. Not again."

"As you wish." He had not thought she would accept, not his Aria. Pride at her courage surged through him. If she were a man, she would be a Warrior. "If it were not important, you know I would not take you to Laini."

"Does it matter? You spurn me, treat me like a child, only telling me what I want to hear. Then, you do what you want to anyway. Why should my feelings matter?"

She scooted farther, stopping at the edge of the stairs.

He knew she argued because of the pain, but there was little he could do. His course was set not by desire, but by necessity. "I do not travel to Laini because I want to," he replied, and like a dying man wanted the sweet mercy of the Goddess, he wanted to quell her pain and tell her that her thoughts and feelings did matter to him.

Instead, he closed his eyes and held his feelings tight within his chest. If he revealed his innermost thoughts, then more would follow, and he would be as lost in her as he was last night. To confess his feelings would make them real, and he could ill afford such a sweet existence. Not while Mako lived. To love was to care. To care was to give Mako power. Only after the Reaper leader's death could he indulge in such a weakness.

He willed her to believe him. To realize he had no choice, not if Mako were to be brought to justice.

Aria wiped her eyes before any tears fell. "You once said they were a superstitious people, and you were right. They live in fear and trust no one, especially strangers and their Trancer daughters. Do not expect much help from a Laini citizen."

Talon sat in silence. He could neither refute her words nor lessen her pain—or change his course.

She continued, "I can seek Tarik's life force. If I can find him then there will be no need to travel—" Her voice broke. "Home."

If it were only that simple, but how could she find that which did not exist? He pressed his lips together. "Do what you must, but I do not see how that will lead us to the Reapers."

"It led me to you, did it not?"

"Yes." *But I am alive.*

As if privy to his thoughts, Aria shot him a defiant look and rose to her feet. Pulling her cloak from her shoulders, she spread it on the ground and sat in Trancer position. Taking a deep breath, she closed her eyes.

Talon sat on the stairs and watched her. How long would it take before she came back? Before she realized their son was dead? He waited, watching her face. Placid, she looked asleep as she searched.

He should have made her stay at the Tower, then she

would not be here, worn and hurt, looking for their dead child. He wished he could blame Lore for falling for her deception and letting her escape, but he could not. It was his fault. He should have kept quiet about his plans, been more secretive about his desire for revenge. She only came because she feared for him, and because she believed the impossible.

He did not deserve her. She was right, he was more Reaper than Warrior. But for now, it was what he needed to be, even if it meant pushing Aria away for her own good.

Aria's eyes flew open. She clutched her throat as if to catch her breath.

Fear surged through him, and Talon raced to her side. "Are you all right?"

She pushed him away. "I am fine."

"What happened?" he asked, already knowing the answer.

She shook her head, the sorrow in her eyes telling him more than words. "What you hoped would happen. I did not feel him."

Talon shook his head. "No. That is not my wish."

"Either way, the result is the same. But that does not mean I am wrong. It does not mean that Tarik is not out there alive and waiting for rescue."

"But you found nothing."

"No, that is not correct. I found something. A wall. It hinders me. It will not let me close to Tarik. When I try to breach it, I am thrown back into my body."

He had never heard of such a thing. "What does it mean?"

She stood and gathered her cloak in her arms. "Nothing other than I need to practice my skills."

Her explanation did not surprise him. She was stubborn and would cling to her dream that Tarik lived for as long as possible, even if it meant rationalizing, perhaps even creating, a reason for her inability to find him. "I know you want to believe—"

"If he were dead, I would know it in my heart," Aria interrupted, words tumbling from her lips. "What I feel is a place in my soul that only Tarik can fill. I cannot lose faith, not now. If I believed my son were truly dead, I would crumple and die."

More frightening than the vehemence of her words was the expression on her face. Anguish and pure fear twisted her features into a mask of sorrow. Then, just as quickly, the look was gone, and in its place was the same distant look he had seen but moments earlier. He was losing her as she built a shell around her heart to contain the pain.

He wanted to weep for the loss. Aria cutting herself off from life, from her inner self, was not what he wanted. He went to help her rise. She accepted with a cool grace. Once, a woman's emotions would have served to simply annoy him. Now, he would give anything to see Aria rage, to make her laugh, or to make her cry. Anything but this cold mask of indifference

Even worse was the knowledge that it was his fault, and he could do nothing about it.

Not while Mako lived.

***

Aria watched through narrowed eyes as Talon finished readying Cam. He did not believe her. He thought Tarik was dead.

She gave a small snort of disdain at his narrow-mindedness. He saw only his reality. He only believed in what he could touch with his hands, see with his eyes, taste with his tongue, and hear with his ears. He could not surf the currents and know that there was another world, one of color and texture and thought, which meshed and flowed through the world in which they lived.

Let him believe what he wanted. She knew what needed to be done. She had to shatter the wall that blocked her. Like a Warrior, she would have to break it down if she wanted to rescue those who dwelt on the other side, whether or not Talon helped her.

Wrapping her cloak around her shoulders, she walked over to Cam and looked at Talon over her shoulder. "Are you ready?"

Flipping his cloak behind him, it fluttered like a cheerless banner. Wrapping his large hands around her waist, he lifted Aria on to the *rohha's* back and mounted behind her.

Although the morning was almost gone, the air in the forest was damp and cool. She resisted the urge to snuggle against him for warmth.

"Are you sure you want to do this?" Talon whispered the question like an unspeakable name.

She was not, but she had little other choice. "Yes."

Talon acknowledged her answer with a slow nod.

Aria was grateful he neither pressed her to stay nor showed concern for her going. The chill inside her heart was but a thin covering for the anger, pain, and hurt that pulsed beneath it. If he had pushed, she feared she would break apart.

With a nudge of Talon's knees, Cam moved beneath them, walking with careful steps through the trees. Turning partway, Aria looked at the temple, silently apologizing to the Goddess for them both. She was sure they had failed. The Goddess had given them time to learn and love. A night to remember what they were and join forces.

Instead, the distance between their hearts was farther than before. Farther than even she would have ever imagined.

The temple shimmered as sunlight reflected off its white stone, and the greenery that surrounded it seemed to move closer, blurring its smooth lines. Aria blinked, and the temple wavered in the rising heat of the day.

Another blink, and like a dream upon awakening, it disappeared.

Thirteen

Iliana rocked Tarik in her arms and sat in the small room the Reaper leader allowed her, contemplating the many ways he might kill her. Perhaps he would do as he once vowed and cut off her head.

If he did, it was her own fault. Just this morning, he asked her to bring him a plate of bread, and she shot back she was not a serving girl.

She had said it in front of his men. *Stupid.*

For that she would surely be punished.

Would he hurt Tarik? She hugged the babe closer. It would be easy to think Mako would never harm a child, that no one would, but she knew better. She remembered the Tower. If it served Mako's interest, Tarik was not above harm or even death.

She would have to watch her tongue, or Aria's child would not have a future.

Tarik started to cry. Stroking his cheek, she noticed his head turned towards her, and he made snuffling noises. "Hungry, little one?" she murmured. Settling him into the pillows, she poured *rohha* milk into a tightly woven cloth tube. "I know it is not what you want, but it is all I have. She tickled his lower lip with its tapered tip.

Tarik latched onto the cloth and sucked vigorously, his tiny hands clenched into fists as they waved in the air.

She settled him on her lap and watched him eat, enjoying a moment of peace.

The door squeaked open, and Iliana looked up, annoyed at the intrusion. A boy stood on the threshold. Perhaps seven cycles, maybe a bit more. His dun colored hair was long and unkempt, and only a Reaper child would wear his combination of ragged, filthy leggings and fine cloth tunic.

The lad planted his grubby hands on his hips. "Mako would see you."

Time for her punishment. Her hands started to shake. Mako would not kill her, not yet, she reminded herself. She had not used her Trancer abilities to help him. She took a deep breath. Surely, he would wait a while longer to see the value of the prize before he destroyed it. Another breath and the shaking stopped. She eyed the boy who waited for her response. "Come here."

The lad walked over, his steps tentative, as one might approach a wild animal.

"Do you think I will eat you, boy?" Part of her wanted to taunt the lad, to make him feel the fear that consumed her. The other part of her felt only pity that one so young had already acquired the necessary trait of wariness.

He glared at her with contempt. "No."

He also had acquired the Reaper arrogance. "Then think again, because I might." She gave a wicked laugh.

The lad paled.

Enough taunting. She crooked a finger. "Come here. I was teasing. I do not eat small boys for my meals."

He gave her a guarded look, but shuffled over.

"Have you worked with babes before?"

He nodded. "Yes, but I'm too old for that now."

"Too old?" He had not even begun the change into a man.

The lad's brows knitted together in thought. "Yes. Besides, that's woman's work."

She did not have time to debate child-care and a woman's place with a boy. She thrust Tarik into his arms along with the feeding tube. "No matter. Mako has summoned me."

The boy clutched the babe in an awkward hold. Iliana held in a sigh of exasperation.

"Sit," she commanded.

The boy perched on the edge of her bed.

"Feed him, and make sure he is comfortable. Can you do this?"

He eyed the small child with a frown.

"If you do, I will tell Mako how pleased I am with you." Iliana offered, knowing that Mako had told all his men to treat her as a guest.

The lad tilted his head in thought for a brief moment, then nodded. "I will watch him."

"Good. Now I will go see my *benefactor.*"

Before shutting the door behind her, she took one last, quick look behind her. The boy and babe were a sweet tableau. She let a smile soften her lips, unable to help liking the lad. It was not his fault he was a Reaper. For some, there was little else.

Quickly, she paced down a hallway lined with paintings, anxious to be done with her penance.

The oversized wooden door to the main room was shut. With a groan, Iliana pushed it open and stumbled in.

The room before her was a paradox of beauty and pain. Bright tapestries covered cold stone walls stained with blood. Candles lent their warm glow to animal's heads mounted above the windows.

Still, at the center, at the focus of all the tragedy and brilliance was Mako. Like a fallen hero, he sat on the far side of the room, his broad shoulders spanning the width of the chair.

The door swung shut behind her. The few men in the room grew silent. She waited.

"Come here." Mako's deep voice washed over her.

Iliana took a few steps toward him, hoping it was enough. He chilled her both inside and out. Instinct told her to stay as far away from him as possible.

"Closer still."

Another few steps forward. She knew her reluctance was obvious, but could not help it. He was both everything she hated and the person she was sworn to assist. She reminded herself of whom she protected and forced her legs forward until she stood in front of him.

"Iliana?"

"Yes, Lord Mako?"

Pulling his feet off a footstool, he waved toward it with his hand. "Sit."

She turned her head away. What did he want? "Thank you, but I prefer to stand."

Mako laughed, and patted the stool with his palm. "Either here or on my lap, fair Trancer. The choice is yours."

Heat flushed through her, and she sat as far back on the small stool as possible.

Mako stroked his short, well-groomed beard.

All waited. The silence grew. Her heart pounded in her chest. She could stand it no longer. "Why have you called me? Do you have need of my services?"

"Services?" He leaned forward and traced her jaw with a rough hand, letting his fingers glide down her neck and linger for a moment against her beating heart. "What do you mean by services? Do you offer your Trancing abilities or something more?"

Ominous chuckles ran through the crowd.

Mako raised his hand, and they all stopped.

She bit her lip, remembering Tarik and her promise to keep him safe. "My Trancing abilities, of course," was her cautious answer. But she knew Mako wanted her. She saw it in the way he looked at her with half-lidded desire, heard it in the way his breath deepened when she was near.

Mako sighed and ran a hand over his short hair, smoothing it. "What a pity."

A guard snickered.

He played with her. Iliana's skin burned in embarrassment. "A pity to disappoint you, Lord Mako, but that was the bargain, was it not?"

Mako leaned forward, all teasing gone.

She wished she had held her tongue.

"Do you know why I summoned you?" he asked.

"No."

He leaned closer. Iliana leaned backwards.

With a quickness that belied his size, he grabbed the front of her dressing gown and pulled her to him. His face was inches from hers.

Her mouth opened, but no sound came out.

Her lower lip trembled. Reaching up with his other hand, he ran his thumb over it. "If I wish it, I can make you do more than tremble, sweet Trancer. It would not be a bad thing. What more could a girl want than the attention of a powerful man?"

She shut her eyes. "Freedom."

"Freedom is what you make it." He ran his thumb over her cheekbone. "There is a greater freedom that comes with doing what you want. Taking what you want. Like I could take you here and now, if I chose."

He tried to seduce her with words. Was he mad? Did he think she would willingly offer her body? She could not deny that he was an attractive man. His body was honed by hard life, and he resonated an aura of power that appealed to her baser instincts.

There was also the stench of blood and death. She

could not do this. Not even for Tarik.

"If I bedded you, do you think you would hate me or desire me?"

Her eyes shot open.

He buried his hand in her short hair. "Or both?" He pulled her closer until their lips almost touched.

Her stomach flipped, and she swallowed, hard. "You presume much, Lord Mako," she whispered against his lips. "I would feel nothing. Nothing at all."

"Are you so sure?" He thrust her away with a laugh. "Always the defiant one, are you not?"

She smoothed her hair away from her face and took a deep breath. Her heart still pounded, but it was over. He would not force her. At least for now.

He laughed again. "Thank you for reminding me why I summoned you."

She waited.

"Your attitude. I dislike it."

"I swore I would help you if you spared my son. I did not say I would make it easy." Iliana prayed his own twisted code held enough honor to make him keep his own oath.

"That was the bargain," Mako agreed.

Iliana let a sigh of relief pass her lips.

Leaning back in his chair, Mako continued. "And I suppose it would be a good one if Tarik were, of course, your son."

Fourteen

"You cannot take me with you, Talon. My presence would only hinder your attempt to gather information on the Reapers."

With both longing and loathing warring for her attention, Aria peered through the forests leaves at the small village that was once her home. Once, she had hoped to return, and now that she was here, she wanted nothing more than to ride far away.

"I know your presence will make my task more difficult," Talon motioned towards the ground. "But look."

She glanced down at the forest floor. Among the leaves and dirt were prints made by animals that were better left alone. By creatures whose appetites demanded flesh.

"I cannot leave you unprotected. Not here." With a kick of his heels, Talon set Cam into motion.

The *rohha* stepped from the forest onto the hard-packed dirt road, and Aria's heart pounded as trepidation consumed her. "I would rather take my chance with the wild beasts."

"And I did not offer you a choice." He motioned Cam to move faster. "So let us finish this as quickly as possible."

Aria swallowed hard and gave a curt nod of acceptance. Talon was as stubborn as a *rohha* when it came to her safety.

She only hoped his decision did not prove to be the wrong one.

The village loomed closer. Within moments, they passed the small altar that marked its border, and her every fear became realized as the village turned silent in their wake.

For what seemed a sun, the only sound was the muffled thud of Cam's hooves on the dirt road. Then, the whispering began. Murmurs of distress as mothers ushered their young children into the house and small protests of curiosity from the children who wanted to see the strangers.

"*She's* back. Somebody find Martus." The hushed order floated through the air to Aria's ears as she sat perched in front of Talon.

Martus would arrive in a moment. A shiver of apprehension chilled Aria, despite the warmth of the day. She pressed her lips together and straightened her shoulders, beating the panic back. Let him come. When she last saw him, she was but a girl. Now, she was a woman tempered by life and unmoved by his wrath.

"Hold stranger."

Cam came to an abrupt halt. A man in a simple robe the color of a sunless day stood in front of them. He held a wooden staff in his right hand, and a scowl furrowed his brow.

It was Martus. Her father.

"Explain your presence." He held the staff upright and forward, like a shield, as he circled to stand beside the *rohha*.

Aria frowned at the absurd display. How like him to expect the worst. She spoke first. "Hello, Father."

"Quiet, girl," Martus commanded. "You bring malevolence to our village by returning. Do not compound the issue by behaving in an unseemly manner."

He still expected her to keep silent like her mother and all the *righteous* women of the village. Aria opened her mouth to make a sharp retort, but Talon interrupted her. "I apologize for the intrusion, but we come on a mission of great importance."

Dismissing Aria with a scathing glance, Martus looked past her, almost through her, as he addressed Talon. "What mission is so crucial that you bring this witch into our village?"

"Our mission is best discussed in private," Talon replied. His voice sounded calm, but Aria saw his hands tighten on Cam's reins until the knuckles whitened. Was it because of the delay or because her father called her a witch? It was difficult to tell with Talon. He kept much from her now.

Probably the delay. Aria tucked a stray strand of hair behind her ear. Did her father's accusations bother Talon? He had cared little for her feelings on the road as they journeyed to her home. In the past few suns, she had tried to talk to him and had failed at every turn. He rarely spoke when she addressed him, and when he bothered to reply, the answers were clipped and curt. He treated Cam with more affection, as they journeyed over streams and through the mountain pass.

So, why would he care that another treated her poorly?

"Why not speak? Do you hide something?" Martus insisted.

Aria straightened and glared at the man she once called 'Father'.

"No," Talon answered for them both. "But the information we seek is sensitive, and I have no desire to risk any of your people."

For the first time, Aria noticed a crowd of men had surrounded them, watching the conversation with great interest.

"You risk their souls by bringing *her* here." Martus shook his staff at Aria.

"My name is Aria, *Father*. You gave it to me." She glared at him, past caring what anyone thought. They had banished her with their fear. Their twisted morality no longer applied.

Martus ignored her words, treating her like she did not exist and spoke to Talon once again. "Follow me to my home. We can talk in private and remove her from the streets before she taints anyone with her evil ways."

"Thank you. We accept your offer," Talon answered. In a quieter voice, he whispered in Aria's ear, "Hush. He treats you poorly, but we need information. He seems to be the one to go to."

Aria bit her tongue. At present, it was not Talon who angered her most. "I suppose you are right."

"He is your father?" With a knee, Talon motioned Cam to follow the dour man in front of them.

"You did hear me call him such, did you not?" she snapped.

"Yes, but I find it unimaginable that a father treats his child, his blood, with such heartlessness."

"I am his daughter no longer."

"I am sorry to have brought you here," Talon said, "You understand there was little choice."

"I know," she said through gritted teeth. "Since I failed to locate Tarik, there was no other option." Over the past few days, she had tried to find their son using her Trancer abilities, but she was always flung back into her body by the black wall. Either the phenomenon was stronger than she first thought, or her abilities were weaker. Neither thought pleased her, and her mood darkened.

"Do not blame yourself. You tried."

"Trying is not enough," she whispered over her shoulder. "If I had succeeded, we would be suns closer to our child instead of here."

"Every talent, every strength, has a limitation. Do not blame yourself because your talent is not what you want it to be."

"Spare me the platitudes. I failed, and now I pay the price."

Talon touched her shoulder for but a moment before he snatched his hand back.

Did she mean so little to him that even a gesture of comfort was beneath him? She bit her lip again and refused to let a single tear form. Instead, she looked around as they rode through the silent village.

The swing of a window cover caught her eye, and the hairs on her arms rose. She sensed the women and children who watched their passage, peeking through coarse, dull cloth, but when she returned the stare, the faces disappeared.

She did not need to be a Trancer to taste their fear. It permeated the air like a heavy cloak, keeping their hearts and minds closed to her both as a Trancer and as a friend.

She squeezed her eyes shut, fighting the pain, not wanting to see any more of what she had lost. If her abilities had not ever emerged, she would be living here still. She would have a family. Friends.

Maybe even a father.

He was not much of a father before my change, she reminded herself. Aria opened her eyes. Besides, the only real regrets were her sister and brother. She had come so far. Would Martus let her see them, or would he hide them away from her?

Her home came into view. Its stone walls were washed white, and the wooden fence surrounding the garden needed to be replaced.

"Hold," Martus commanded. "You." He pointed at them with his staff, "Remain here."

"Not friendly, is he?" Talon commented as the door closed behind her father.

Aria turned partway in the saddle. Talon's eyes were narrowed and his expression heated. "No, but he never was."

"Not even before your abilities emerged?"

She shook her head. "Never. He ruled our household with the staff he carries, using it to correct any lapse in morality. We all learned, even mother, to keep our council to ourselves for fear of a beating."

Talon's lips turned downward. "I pray he does not consider it his duty to still correct you."

"Why? Would you protect me?" Aria baited him but did not expect an answer.

"You are my Given, and even if you were not, nobody deserves a beating for voicing an opinion. Especially a woman."

A woman and *his* Given. That was all he saw. Someone who needed protection. He never saw her as a Trancer capable of taking care of herself. Aria opened her mouth to retort and stopped herself. She had asked the question and should not berate his honesty. Perhaps he felt the need to protect anyone smaller than himself, which included all woman she knew and most men.

Or, perhaps he cared more for her than he wanted to admit.

Either way, if she challenged him, a fight would ensue, and she needed her emotional and mental strength to deal with Martus. She frowned at the absurdity of the situation.

"Do you have something to say?" Talon asked.

"No, nothing, other than to warn you to be wary. Martus may be unkind, and he may be superstitious, but he is neither ignorant nor dimwitted."

Talon shrugged. "I plan on finding our information and leaving as quickly as possible. Any unknown agenda should not be a problem."

Aria bristled. "Let me finish. When you ask to speak to Gaur, he will deny your request."

"Why? What we do is for the good of all."

"Because there will be nothing in it for him."

"If need be, I will find Gaur and speak to him myself."

Aria rubbed her eyes with upturned palms. He did

not understand. His strength would not help him here. Only intelligence and the ability to outwit Martus would bring success. "Listen to my words. No one in the village will speak to you unless Martus allows them to. No one. He is the religious council and the law. When my abilities emerged and I was banished, he lost pride. Now that I have returned, he will make us both pay the price for his humiliation."

Talon gave a thoughtful nod. "Then we must give him a reason to help us."

A sigh of relief slipped past her lips. "I see you begin to understand."

"A Warrior does more than wield a sword. He also plans strategy. This is a small battle, but I think it is one we can win."

"Let us hope so, or Tarik is lost."

The creak of the door drew both their attention away before Talon replied.

"You may enter." Martus pointed his staff at Talon.

Dismounting, Talon placed his massive hands around Aria's waist and lifted her from Cam's back.

"Not her." Martus stopped them at the door.

"Where I go, she goes." Talon's tone threatened a fight if denied.

But Martus barred the door with his staff. "No. Not into this house. No witch will corrupt *my* family."

Talon took a step forward. Aria stopped him with a hand on his arm and drew him aside. "Remember what I told you."

He nodded. "I do."

"Then know that my presence will not help our cause. Do what needs to be done, and let us leave this place."

Cupping her face in his hands, he grazed her ear with his lips. "I will not let him treat you in such a manner."

Aria smiled to herself, somewhat pleased he cared enough to protect her feelings, if not from himself, then from others. "Thank you," she replied. "But if belittling me mends his wounded pride, I must endure it. We need his help."

"I do not like this."

"Neither do I, but we have little choice."

He nodded agreement, but his expression remained

pensive.

"When you and Martus finish talking, walk behind the house. Beyond the trees there is a stream." Impulsively, she stood on her toes and kissed Talon's cheek. "Cam and I will wait for you there."

Talon nodded and turned on his heel, his sword banging against his thigh.

Without a word or a glance towards Aria, Martus opened the door, ushered Talon in, and shut it behind them

Leading Cam by the reins, she walked away. The thud of wood against wood reached her ears. She knew her father barred the door with a short wooden plank, locking her out and the others in.

She refused to let it hurt her. In her heart, she knew Trancing was a gift, but why did she feel so evil and unclean whenever her father called her a witch?

Reaching the small brook, she tied Cam's reins loosely behind his neck so they did not drag. Sitting under one of the many trees lining the stream, she watched as the *rohha* walked into the icy brook, seemingly oblivious to the cold. "Cam, you do not think me a witch, do you?"

The *rohha* did not answer but dipped his head and drank.

Aria leaned back against the rough bark. "I can see you do not, because of the fearless way you turn your back to me." She joked, but it was more for her benefit than Cam's.

A soft, feminine voice interrupted the silence. "Neither do I."

Aria turned her head. Her visitor was a young woman with pale green eyes and nervous hands. Her hair was red, but unlike Aria's fire bright curls, her hair was deep and dark like berry wine. Aria's heart pounded. "Kisa?"

The girl nodded and held her arms open. "Yes, Aria. It is me."

Aria jumped up and ran to embrace her sister.

***

Talon watched, his anger barely held at bay, as Martus barred the door. Aria was his daughter, and this man treated her like a raging *katah'* that threatened to enter and maul him.

Perhaps the man knew nothing of Trancers and their oath to do no harm, but surely he knew his own daughter. She was incapable of evil. To suspect otherwise was beyond Talon's comprehension.

"Now, tell me why you are here, Warrior." Martus said, turning back.

Talon paused at the comment made so offhandedly. "Why do you call me Warrior?" he asked.

"You tie your hair with a Warrior cord, do you not?" Martus answered.

Talon reached back and fingered the tanned leather cord that held his hair back. Aria had warned him that Martus was not dim.

"Let us speak plainly." Martus gestured with his staff as he spoke. "But know it is your status as a Warrior that allows you in my house. Any other man would be driven away for bringing *her* here."

"You mean your daughter?"

Martus whacked the tabletop with his staff. The sharp sound reverberated through the small room. "She is my daughter no longer. Say so again and not even you will be beyond my wrath."

Talon burned within. This petty man and his warped principles were wearing thin. He wanted nothing more than to wipe the self-righteous expression from Martus' face.

Then he heard Aria's voice, reminding him that her father was the key to information. Strategy, not brutality, would get them what they needed.

"As you wish." Talon forced himself to relax.

"Sit, and tell me why you journey to our small village."

Talon sat on a short wooden bench next to the fireplace, the wood groaning under his large frame. He noticed Martus remained standing. "We seek information about the Reapers."

"We know nothing of them. It seems your journey was a waste of time." Hurrying over to the door, Martus raised the bar.

"Hold." Talon commanded.

Martus stopped. The bar fell back into place.

"I was told a man named Gaur lives here. He was once a prisoner of the Reapers but managed to escape."

Aria's father did not reply but stared at Talon as if waiting for him to continue.

Talon obliged him. "I need to speak with him to find where the Reapers hide."

"Why?"

Perhaps the old man would soften towards Aria if he knew she bore, and lost, a child, but Talon doubted it. Looking at Martus, he saw only bitter lines flanked his mouth, and his eyes were bright with power and hatred. No, this man would not feel pity. He would feel pleasure at Aria's loss. Talon would not give him the power to hurt her in such a deep way.

"They destroyed Aria's Tower—"

"Good for them. The only good witch is a dead one."

Talon continued, ignoring the callous remark. "The Council wants us to seek them out and report their whereabouts."

"You still give me no reason to help you."

"They may come here. The safety of you people should be motive enough to assist us."

Martus laughed, a creaky, stilted sound, as if it was something he rarely did. "We have nothing they want. Besides, they live far and away from here." He paused. "Or so I hear."

Talon turned away, his mind racing, searching to find what might motivate this man who understood nothing but control. His gaze fell on a pot of stew. Hung over the flames, it simmered in its black metal pot. It seemed he and Aria interrupted the midday meal.

He hoped it burned.

"It sounds as if you know more than you care to divulge. How can I convince you to help us?" Talon asked. The low timbre of his voice was more threatening than words, although he thought he knew the answer. A man like Martus responded to few things—power, money, and threats. But strategy, not threats, Aria had said.

Why not use both?

"What do you offer?" Martus asked, his face eager.

Talon shrugged. "Your life."

Martus went from tanned to pale, as the color drained from his face. "You w-w-wouldn't," Martus stammered. "You are a Warrior. A protector."

Talon shrugged his shoulders again. "Things are not always what they seem. You noticed the Warrior's cord and assumed my status. What you did not see was this." Reveling in the building tension, Talon slowly drew his sword from its worn leather sheath. Then, he turned it to show the single blood red stone that adorned the dull metal hilt.

Martus went from pale to the color of gray ash, confirming, to Talon, his knowledge of the Reapers.

"You carry a R-R-Reaper sword," Martus stammered again.

Talon nodded. Once.

"Why do you carry a Reaper's weapon?"

Talon tried not to enjoy the man's fear too much, but it was almost impossible. He knew others like Martus, and they all were similar. Petty and small. Cruel to those weaker than themselves when there was no need. Beating their families, their daughters, when they should be cherishing every moment spent with them.

Martus had no idea what loss was. He knew only power, and that was the answer. Talon would have to show himself more powerful to gain his assistance. "Why? Because I was once a Reaper."

Martus clutched the tabletop with crablike hands as he stumbled to sit on a chair. "You. A Reaper?"

Talon ran a gloved hand along the nicked edge of his blade. "Yes."

Martus pointed towards a closed door. "My other daughter, Kisa, is in there. Take her if you want. She is young and pretty. You can sell her and make a good profit—"

"No." Talon cut him off in disgust. "You do not seem to understand, little man. I do not want your daughter. I want information. Now talk, or I will make you talk."

With a cry, Martus slid to the ground, prostrate in front of Talon. The sounds of his harsh breathing, punctuated with mumblings, broke the silence as Talon waited for him to speak.

Talking to his god, Talon supposed. A man this cruel did not follow the way of the Goddess.

After a few minutes, the mumbling stopped, cut off abruptly. Martus rose to his knees. He looked straight at

Talon. The fear had vanished, replaced with a crafty glint.

It seemed as if his god had spoken.

"You said *once* a Reaper?" Martus asked, settling into a chair.

"Yes."

"And now you are a Warrior." The man talked aloud but did not address Talon. "You might carry the Reaper's sword, but you will not use it," he crowed, his voice shrill with victory. "It was a bluff. You would never hurt me."

Reaching towards the ground, he picked up his staff. "So, Warrior, it seems your ploy failed. Now what will you offer me for information?"

Talon shook his head. "The payment is the same. Your life."

Martus shook his staff at Talon. "You would never harm me. However, you will pay extra for your lie."

"You assume much based on little." Talon rose to his feet and sheathed his sword. Each step deliberate, he walked to stand behind Martus. The old man waited, his confidence apparent in the careless way he rested his hands upon the tabletop and the arrogant tilt to his head.

The old man chuckled, his glees overflowing. Talon leaned forward. His large hands flanked Martus' as he spoke. "I was once a Reaper. I was once a Warrior. Now, I am neither. That, in itself, should tell you what kind of man I am. I follow my own rules. I can slay you, or I can let you be."

Martus' chuckling ceased.

Talon leaned farther until he spoke directly in the old man's ear. "I can use this sword to make you talk, and believe me when I say that towards the end you would beg to speak. You are a small, bitter man. You took a daughter's love and twisted it until only pain and anger remained. For that cruelty alone, I would enjoy making you talk. So please, do not help me. I want to use the sword. She deserves any retribution I can give her."

He did not move, but waited for the old man to break under the pressure. Out of the corner of his eyes, he saw Martus's hands begin to shake. The rank smell of fear permeated the air, overpowering all else.

Talon straightened and crossed his arms, waiting for the words he knew would come.

"What do you need from me?"

He smiled at the victory. "That is better. I would speak with Gaur. Aria tells me that nobody will talk to me without your permission."

Martus nodded, broken. "I am their spiritual leader."

Talon's lips curled into a sneer, but he did not say what he thought of Martus' example of spirituality. There was too much to do. He did not want to be sidetracked. "When can I speak with this man?"

"Tomorrow. Perhaps the next sun."

Talon fingered the hilt of his sword. "I lose patience, old man. Do not put me off, thinking it will be to your advantage."

"I do not," Martus babbled. "I swear by the God Thoth. Gaur caught an ill wind and has been asleep for over five suns."

"When do you expect him to awaken?"

"No one knows," Martus said cowering.

"Have you no Healer?"

Martus shook his head, his robe quivering as his trembling increased.

There was no time to wait. If word of Talon's quest had reached Mako's ears, each lost moment gave his enemy the advantage of preparation. "I will give Gaur until tomorrow, and then Aria and I will speak with him."

A banging on the heavy wooden door interrupted Martus's reply. The old man looked to Talon for permission. Talon nodded.

Rising from the bench, Martus grabbed his staff and skittered to the door. Lifting the wooden bar, he opened the portal. Martus blocked most of the view, but Talon managed to catch a glimpse of the visitor. It was another man. He wore a robe similar to Martus's, with the hood pulled over his head, obscuring his face.

Talon strained his ears. Nothing other than mumbling reached him. After a moment, Martus turned back. The hairs on the back of Talon's neck rose. Gone was the fear from Martus' eyes, and in its place was a righteous anger.

Something had happened.

Martus bowed low. "Duty calls me, with your permission..."

Better to let the old man go and follow, Talon decided.

He waved his acquiescence, and the old man shut the door behind him as he left.

Within moments, Talon followed, each step as light and silent as a *katah's*.

***

Aria pulled away from her sister and held her at arm's length. "You have grown." She marveled at Kisa, amazed at how much she had changed. Gone was the shy little sister who had followed her around like a pet, and in her place was a confident, beautiful young woman. "When I left, you were but a child on the verge of womanhood."

Kisa blushed, and a smile quirked her lips. "It is amazing what time can do."

Aria laughed and hugged her sister again. "I know I babble, but it is so good to see you. I thought I never would."

Her sister gripped her in return, their arms tight about each other, and the two stood silent for a few more moments.

This time, Kisa pulled away. "I knew something was wrong when Father made us go into the back room and lock the door. He told us we were not to make a sound."

Aria nodded, knowing their father and his commands.

"I figured it must be someone interesting. I hoped it was you, but I never dreamed...If Father found out..."

"Hush." Aria laid her hand gently over her sister's mouth. "We have little time here. Let us not talk of Martus."

Kisa nodded and wiped her damp eyes. "You are right." Sitting, she pulled Aria down beside her. "Tell me what you have been doing since Father sent you away."

Facing her sister, Aria crossed her legs at the knees. "Training at a Tower."

"To be a Trancer?" Kisa asked, her eyes bright with curiosity.

"Yes."

"Why are you here?"

Aria sighed. "It is a long story, but I shall keep it short." She folded her hands in her lap. "I had a son by a Warrior named Talon. Our child was taken when my Tower was destroyed by Reapers. Now, we go in search of him."

Kisa's jaw dropped. "I...I do not know what to say."

"Say nothing other than you have missed me. Your

voice is all I need to hear."

Kisa reached over and took Aria's hand in hers. "You know that is true, but you have been through much, and words are meaningless."

"Not from you. Not when I thought I would never hear your voice again." Aria's voice broke as she remembered her first nights at the Tower. She would have given the entire world to hear Kisa's laugh. "I missed you so much."

"I missed you, also. Both Anok and I have."

"Anok." She had forgotten about her young brother in the thrill of seeing her sister again. "Where is he? Is he all right?"

Kisa laughed. "He is fine. He is in the back room waiting for me to return. He is still young and has not found the pleasure in defying Father."

Aria nodded in understanding. "He still seeks father's love?" They all had at one time, until he beat the hope from them both physically and emotionally.

"Yes. He does not yet understand that Father has no love to give."

Fingers intertwined, Aria squeezed her sister's hand. "But you know, do you not?"

Kisa squeezed back. "All too well. When you left, I thought he banished you for our protection. I was young. I wanted to believe. Then, one day, I gave up trying to gain his approval, and that is when I started to question."

"Question what?"

"You. Why you left. Was Father right? Everything. He has never been a good man, so I questioned it all."

Aria nodded in understanding. Her own evolution into adulthood was much the same. "What did you discover?"

"I knew the answers all along. Especially when I remembered you. You were always kind. Always patient. Do you remember when we snuck out because we wanted to see the silver maiden?"

Aria gave a low chuckle at the memory. "We thought that if we waited she would show herself to us. Instead, all we got were sore eyes from staring too long at her moon."

Kisa did not laugh. "You received a sore back when father found us. You took my punishment because you were the eldest."

Aria shrugged. "It was not a bad beating."

"You were bedridden for two suns."

"It was long ago, and I have since healed. Let us not speak of the past. It is gone and done and father cannot hurt me again."

Kisa nodded. "I suppose you are right." She leaned forward. "Tell me of your Warrior. Is he handsome?"

Aria laughed in delight. It had been so long since she had spoken with another woman about such things. Not since she lost Iliana. Her heart gave a little cry at the loss, but she pushed it aside. "His name is Talon, and I suppose he is handsome. He is a large man, but most Warriors are." Thinking back to the first day she met him, Aria added, "His hair is as dark as *katah'* fur, and his hands are both gentle and strong."

"Is he kind to you?"

Aria knew her sister thought of their father and his cruel nature and hoped she had found better. She fingered the end of her braid, brushing the ends across her palm as she thought about all Talon did and said. Was he kind? He had angered her, deserted her, loved her, and saved her life. He mourned his son and sought to kill the killers. He was both harsh and tender. Kind was not the word to describe her Giver, but neither was cruel.

He was a mystery hidden in a puzzle.

"The night of the Given ceremony, he treated me with unexpected gentleness, but since we lost Tarik, he has changed."

"How?"

"His gentle words are fewer. His gentle touches even less. He is obsessed with finding Mako, the Reaper who destroyed my Tower and took Tarik."

"Does he hurt you?" Kisa questioned, jumping to her feet.

Aria laid a hand on her sister's arm and drew her back down to sit beside her. "No, he would never harm me willingly, but he does not understand that his refusal to open to me is as harmful as words of hate."

"Have you told him? If he is as kind as you say he should understand."

Aria plucked a blade of grass and twirled it between her fingers as she spoke. "I try, but his mind is so clouded by the desire for revenge I fear there is little room for kindness."

"Why go with him?"

There were so many reasons. "Because we are joined, and I would not lose him to revenge. My duty is not just to save my son but also to save his father. I can only pray to the Goddess that—"

"Witch!"

The shout, the screech of treachery, interrupted Aria. Both girls jumped to their feet.

Martus marched towards them, his hair wild and his robe flapping about his thin legs as he shook his staff at them. Memories of cowering in the corner as the hated stick came down upon her shoulders flooded Aria. She wanted to shout. To run. To scream for help. Only a whispered "No" emerged.

Despite the ingrained fear, the instinct to protect Kisa overwhelmed her. Aria's legs shook, but she stepped in front of her sister, shielding her. The blade of grass fell from her fingers.

Martus reached them and raised the staff above his head. "Witch! You brought Kisa out here and tried to corrupt her mind with your lies!"

Shoving her way past Aria, Kisa gripped her father's arm. "She did nothing, Father. It is my fault. I snuck out to see her."

He shook her off and took another menacing step towards Aria.

She took a step back. The cold water of the stream licked the heels of her boots.

He followed. Kisa grabbed at him, and he pushed her away. She fell with a cry.

"Stay down," Aria called as she backed into the stream. The water sloshed over the tops of her boots, chilling her feet. "We were just talking, Martus. I swear it."

He followed her into the water, heedless of the cold. "Liar! You shall pay for your crimes."

Like a great wave, panic overwhelmed Aria, drowning her in its murky waters. "No, please, Father. We were just talking." She took another hurried step back and slipped, landing on her bottom. Her jaw clicked shut, and she bit her tongue, the taste of blood in her mouth familiar as she stared at the man who had fathered her.

He lifted the staff above his head. "Trancer whore."

With no thought other than that of survival, Aria raised her arms over her head for protection and shut her eyes.

Fifteen

The blow never came. Aria peeked up through her fingers. It was as if time stopped. The staff drew her eye. It was still in her father's hand, raised above his head, but Talon gripped it in the upswing, his knuckles white against the dark wood.

Her eyes darted back to her father. His face was contorted in rage as he stared down at her. He meant to do more than beat her. She saw it in the way his upper lip curled and by the hatred in his eyes. The sweat of the self-righteous dotted his brow. Yes, he had planned to do much more than beat her.

He could not. Talon had saved her.

She let out the breath she had not realized she held.

Sound and time crested into being.

Her father whirled to face his antagonist. "Let go." He struggled to pull the heavy staff from Talon's grip. "She must be stopped."

"No." In a single, powerful movement, Talon tugged on the staff. His strength broke Martus' grip, and with a low growl, Talon shoved Aria's father backward into the stream. Martus fell, howling in shock as the cold mountain water enveloped him past his waist.

Talon stood over the man, unmoved by the chill water that swirled about his calves. "You will never hurt her again." He poked Martus in the chest with the staff.

"Give it back." Martus' bony hands reached for the staff, clawing the air.

Talon weighed the heavy, carved stick in his hands. "That which you love so well shall be your undoing."

Talon's hushed vow carried to Aria, and she gasped as she realized his intentions. "Talon, no." She rose to her knees, Talon's well-being now a greater concern than her own. She stretched a hand out, praying she could break through the haze of his rage.

She tried to stand and slipped on the rocks again, falling backwards. She sputtered as she rose back to the surface and saw the stick poised above Talon's head. She met his dark eyes. *No.* She mouthed the words, a silent plea for undeserved mercy. Neither spoke. She saw the hesitation, his desire for revenge struggling to overcome her request.

He broke her gaze. The decision was made.

In a single movement, he brought his other hand up to grasp the opposite end of the rod, raised his knee, and brought the staff down with enough force to break stone. The crack of the wood rent the air like a scream. He let the pieces drop from his hands and into the water.

"What have you done?" Martus cried. Flailing in the water, he retrieved the broken pieces of wood and cradled them in his arms like a babe. "This was sacred. A symbol of guidance passed down from the first leader of our village."

Talon merely scowled, put his fingers in his mouth, and whistled. The sound of splashing water reached Aria's ears, and Cam galloped from around a bend in the stream, water spraying through the air as he headed towards them. The *rohha* came to a dead stop in front of his master, his ears perked forward.

"You were supposed to guard her," Talon snarled.

The *rohha* pawed at the water, and Aria swore Cam looked both sheepish and ashamed.

"Watch him," Talon commanded, glancing at Martus. "If he tries anything, kill him." Cam tossed his head and positioned himself beside the fallen man, his lips curled back to reveal large, solid teeth.

Nodding in satisfaction, Talon stepped around the pair and offered his hand to Aria, helping her to her feet. Water streamed from her sodden cloak.

She leaned her head against his shoulder as they walked to the shore, and a sense of peace settled over her like a warm blanket. Martus could not hurt her anymore. Not with words or deed. Martus was as broken as his beloved symbol.

Kneeling in front of Aria, Talon ran his firm hands over her scalp and worked his way across her body. "Did he harm you?"

"I am fine." Aria wriggled against the attention. "What are you doing?"

"Making sure." He ran his hands up and down her legs, his fingers kneading her muscles and testing her flesh. "Are you sure you are not hurt. If he hit you, tell me now."

Aria shook her head, pulled her braid around, and wrung the water from her hair. Droplets spattered to the ground. "I am cold, but otherwise unharmed."

"Aria."

Kisa's voice, sounding small and alone, caught her attention. She had forgotten her young sibling in the panic of the moment. Still on the ground where their father had pushed her, Kisa's eyes were wide with fear.

Kisa hiccupped, and her eyes welled with tears. "This is my fault. I should never have snuck out. I am sorry."

Aria ran to her. Falling to her knees, she wrapped her arms around Kisa's trembling shoulders. "No, do not apologize for this. It is Martus' fault and no other."

"If I had done what he said, you would be safe."

"You followed your heart. Do not apologize for that." Leaning back, she wiped away Kisa's tears. "I am only a bit wet. See?" Standing, she held her arms out and turned in a circle to show the truth of her words.

"He tried to beat you." Kisa covered her face with her hands.

"He tried, but failed." Aria stopped her slow turn and wished, for a moment, that her sister were a Trancer. If she were, then she could see the depth of Aria's love and the pain that she endured everyday they were apart. The sisters from the Tower had been good to her, but blood was blood, and Kisa knew her from her days of skinned knees to the awful day of banishment.

Just as she knew her sister. "Kisa, I would endure a hundred beatings to see you again."

Kisa raised her tear-streaked face. "And I would endure them for you."

It was true. Gone was the woman-child who thought mocking her father was a game. In her place was a strong young woman who understood his shortcomings all too well. "I know." Offering her sister her hand, Aria pulled her to her feet.

Kisa sobbed on her shoulder, clutching her.

"It is all right," Aria murmured, stroking Kisa's hair. She looked over her sister's shoulder to see Talon watching them. "Thanks to Talon."

He accepted her comment with a tilt of his head and

walked back to a still stunned Martus. Grabbing him by the robe, he pulled him to his feet and dragged him to the shore, with Cam following. Water dripped from Martus' robes in rivulets and puddled onto the dirt at the edge of the stream.

The old man jerked his wet robe out of Talon's grasp. "Do not touch me, *Warrior.*" He spat the title like a curse.

Aria untangled herself from her sister and kissed Kisa's pale cheek. "Wait here," she said and went to take her place beside Talon.

"A witch and a fallen Warrior. How fitting you found each other," Martus sneered.

Aria grasped Talon's arm. His muscles flexed and stiffened beneath her fingers. She squeezed his forearm, stopping him with a touch. "Has he agreed to help us?" She addressed Talon, ignoring Martus' comment.

"I agreed, but it was under duress."

She waited for Talon to answer.

"Yes, as you said, strategy worked best."

"He threatened to kill me," Martus spat.

Talon shrugged his broad shoulders. "Strategy comes in many forms."

Aria accepted the answer with a repressed grin. Martus was the village leader, never challenged or questioned. The threat of bodily harm probably encouraged him more than all the money in Zaraza. "When do we speak with Gaur?" She looked at Talon. His face was unreadable.

"Tomorrow. Martus says he is ill and will not waken."

"Tomorrow?" She did not relish the idea of spending the night in so inhospitable a town.

"Do not worry." Talon laid his hand on the hilt of his sword. "We bed down in the woods. Cam will keep watch through the night as penance for leaving you alone."

It would have to do. Still, suspicion reared its head— especially where Martus was concerned. "Do you truly believe that Gaur is ill? That this is not a ploy to delay us or cause us harm?" She knew how convincing Martus could be.

"In this, yes. He is too cowardly to lie under threats."

Her father. A coward. Once, she had thought him as strong as the staff he carried. Now, she saw the broken staff was a shield. A false cover for the fear he carried in his heart.

The fear he would have to live with.

It was a fitting sentence for one so cruel.

***

"This is it." Martus stopped in front of a small house. Immediately, Talon recognized that this small hut was different from the others. The flowerbeds were untended, and the small wooden porch was dusty and littered with bits of grass.

Leaving Martus to wait, Talon and Aria stepped through the doorway and into the dimly lit room. The air was thick with the stench of unwashed linen and the stink of infection. Talon wrinkled his nose.

"What do you think happened?" Putting her hand over her mouth and nose, Aria coughed in the foul air.

"I did not ask," Talon replied as he walked over and squatted at the bedside. Its occupant was pale, and his breath rattled in his chest. "But the air is rank with illness." He flipped the covers back, and his hope of waking the sick man fell. Every rib showed, and his skin was so thin it looked as if it would tear. Martus had said he had been asleep for only five suns, but it appeared as if Gaur had been ill for much longer. This was a man more dead than alive.

Talon did not see Aria, but he heard her ragged breath as she came to stand near him.

What had he thought to bring her in here? He stood, blocking her view. The sight of death distressed her, and she had already been through too much. "There is no need for you to be here." He pointed her towards the door. "It will be better if you wait outside."

She shook him off. "I am not as delicate as you believe. Just give me a moment to become used to the smell." She coughed again and wiped the sweat from her brow.

Again, she proved much stronger than he thought— stronger than he sometimes wished. "If you so desire, but I will not think worse of you if you decide to wait outside."

She shook her head.

Talon crouched by the bedside, shook Gaur by the shoulder, and called his name. "Gaur, awaken. We need your help."

The bedridden man offered no hint of awareness.

"What if he does not open his eyes?" Aria stood by Talon's side. "How will we find our son?"

Or Mako? Talon straightened. The wooden floorboards creaked, slat rubbing against slat, as he paced the length of the room and back again. "Is there a healer in the next village? Someone who could use a medicine to bring him around?"

"As I told you before, there is no one to help."

Talon stopped in the middle of the floor. Martus stood in the doorway, watching them.

Glaring, the old man sauntered into the room, his lips curled in disdain. "I suppose you must leave here without the information you need."

Talon's sword hand twitched in response as he contained the urge to shake Aria's father senseless. "No, old man," he replied. "We will wake him. Somehow."

With his staff broken, Martus waved his arms in front of him in a useless, agitated gesture. "How? By shouting his name? You will wake the village before Gaur opens his eyes again."

As much as Talon hated the thought, the old man had a point. Gaur was past life, past speech, and past answering any questions. Unless the Goddess granted them a miracle, they would have to seek their answers elsewhere.

"We do not need to shout for our answers, Martus," Aria said, interrupting the pair. "I shall use my gift to obtain the answers we need."

The air thickened with sudden tension.

Martus stepped towards Aria, one fist raised and shaking. "You will not taint his soul with your evil ways, witch."

Unsheathing his sword in a single movement, Talon pointed the tip towards Aria's father. "Touch her and die."

Martus shot Talon a lethal glance, but he stopped mid-step.

"If you fear for Gaur's soul, you may wait there and watch the ceremony." Using his sword, Talon pointed towards a chair that rested under the window at the opposite end of the room. It was far enough where he could stop Martus if he attempted to hurt Aria or leave, but close enough, hopefully, to appease Aria's father and keep him quiet. As much as he detested the old man, he might still be useful. "If you approach her again, you shall pay in blood."

"It is all right." Aria placed her small hand on the hilt of his sword and lowered it to a less threatening position. "He cannot hurt me with his words, and with you close, he dare not harm me physically."

"Still, he waits over there."

Martus sat with a grunt and scowl. Talon watched him out of the corner of his eye. He did not trust Martus. Beneath the gray hair was a brain as rotten as an overripe melon. He was cruel as a father and worse as the virtuous destroyer.

"I have no issue with that," Aria said. Walking over to Gaur's bed, she sat on the edge and brushed his unkempt hair away from his face.

"We banished her to keep her from performing such ill-gotten tasks," Martus hissed from his forced position.

Talon sheathed his weapon, confident he could pull it faster than the old man could move. "You are a fool," he shot back. "Her gifts are from the Goddess, the mother of us all."

"Bah, the Goddess is a harlot. A whore whose worshippers are blasphemers to Thoth, the true god."

Talon's hand went back to the hilt of his sword. "Watch your words, old man. I allow you to live because of Aria and the teachings of the Goddess. Blaspheme against either again, and I will not be able to hold my temper."

Martus did not reply, but his lips twitched as he mumbled to himself.

Talon went back to the bed and laid a hand on Aria's shoulder.

She looked up, her eyes deep with sorrow. "Once, when I was young and Gaur's hair was not yet gray, he brought me home. I was gathering herbs and strayed too far to return before sundown."

Talon tucked a strand of Aria's hair behind her ear, savoring the texture between his fingers. "He was a friend?"

She shook her head. "He spent the season of cold in the woods, hunting animals. In the season of life, he traveled, selling the pelts to other villages. I found his chosen profession distasteful, but it breaks my heart to see anyone in such a state."

"Even one who agreed in your banishment?"

"I do not know that he did. He was not here. Perhaps he would have. Perhaps not."

"He felt no sorrow for you, witch," Martus mumbled from his chair.

Both ignored him. Aria took Gaur's hand in her. "Fear makes people do senseless, stupid things. It makes them irrational and blind to the good in front of them."

Talon knew she spoke not of Gaur but of Martus and the entire town of Laini. He gave her shoulder a comforting squeeze, hating that he had brought her here to relive the pain of separation. "Can you use your powers to see if he will recover?"

"It does not take a Trancer to see he will not. His heart is but a whisper beating in his chest."

"Then you will enter his mind?"

Aria nodded. "Yes." She glanced at her father and motioned Talon to move closer. "Make sure he does not call for help. If my body is hurt while I am away, it could cause complications."

Talon crossed his arms over his chest. "What kind of complications?"

"I could become lost in the currents and be unable to return."

The blood drained from Talon's face at her words, and for a moment, he was back in the Tower holding a seemingly lifeless Aria in his arms. All the pain and rage and loss overwhelmed his senses once again.

He could not survive the loss a second time—not even to find Mako. "Why have you never told me this before?" His voice sounded harsh, too harsh, in his ears, as he held in his anger and fear.

She shrugged. "Why would I? It is a rare occurrence, and a Trancer is seldom in a situation where such an accident could happen." She glanced towards Martus. "Given the circumstances, I think it a risk, but if you keep Martus here it is one I am willing to take."

"I am not." He could not let her Trance, not if it put her at risk.

She pressed her lips together. "You cannot stop me. Even if we did not need the information, I must help Gaur.

It is obvious he needs assistance to reach the other side, and it is my duty to provide it."

"No." Talon uncrossed his arms and pulled her from the bedside and to her feet. "I cannot allow it."

"Do you fear my gifts?" Aria asked. "Is that what this is about?"

"No, I do not fear you." He stroked a strand of hair away from her cheek. "I fear *for* you."

She smiled. "I am pleased to hear you say so."

The smile both jarred and annoyed him. "This is not a game. There is a real danger, and I promised to keep you safe. If I had known before of the risk, I would never have let you Trance." His stomach lurched as he thought of all the times he could have lost her. She searched for a dead son and could have died herself.

She rested a soft hand against his cheek. "I am a Trancer. This is not what I do. It is what I am."

"I will not have it." She might be a Trancer, but he was a Warrior bound to keep her from harm's way.

Her smile disappeared. She jerked her hand away and sat on the wooden floor next to the bed, her legs crossed. " I will enter Trancer state." She flashed him a defiant stare. "Guard me."

Talon took a deep breath. "It is too dangerous."

She rested her head in her hands for a few moments, drumming her fingers against her scalp. Finally, she looked up, her eyes still flashing. "How can I make you understand my need to do this?"

"Understanding is not the issue. I do understand, apparently better than you. I understand you could die, and I would be left with another body to bury."

Another life to mourn.

"I will be fine with you watching over me," Aria insisted.

"Can you guarantee you will come back to me unharmed?" Talon knew the answer, but he hoped the question would make her see reason.

"No." Her tone was clipped. "There are no guarantees. There never are. You know that."

"Then this discussion is over. I cannot let you risk your life for a stranger."

"What of Tarik? Can you say that our son is not worth the risk?"

"Our son is dead, Aria. I know you do not want to believe it, but it is true."

Her eyes narrowed, but no tears appeared. Perhaps it was perverse, but her strength of heart and hope impressed him, even if she was wrong.

She turned away. "Revenge blinds you. Faith would clear your vision, if you would let it."

Why did she not listen? He shook his head at her stubbornness. "Common sense gives me the wisdom to know Mako would not take a Trancer and a newborn babe with him on a journey through the mountains. His world is made of blood and screams. There is no room for mercy, and no amount of wishing and hoping will make that true."

"Perhaps there is room. Can you not even consider another option?"

"He killed your people, Aria. How can you think such a thing?"

"Because he let my son and best friend live."

A scrape sounded, and Talon turned to see Martus rising from his chair. The old man had heard everything.

Talon pulled his sword again and strode over to him. "You. Wait." He pointed towards the chair with the flat of his weapon. It looked as if the old man wanted to say something, but Talon shot him a lethal glance. Martus' jaw snapped shut, and he sat back down in the chair.

Talon sheathed his sword. By the Goddess, he had thought Aria was getting better, coming back to reality. He saw now that he had deluded himself as surely as she did. She wanted her son so badly she created a world where he lived.

Still, he could put tragedy off for another day. Right now, he needed to keep her alive and safe, and that meant no Trancing. They would simply find another way to find Mako. They would return to Zaraza, and he could talk to Ciella again. Perhaps more information had come to her since their departure. It was unlikely, but it was an option, unlike Aria's idea.

It was time to end this conversation. He turned on his heel. "No matter your desires, I cannot allow you to do this."

She still sat on the floor, but her eyes were rolled back in her head. Only the whites showed.

He was too late. She had already left.

***

Aria swam through the currents, searching for the light that was Gaur. Finally, in what felt like a turn, but was merely a moment in time, she spotted him through streams of color. Faint and pulsing, his life spark glowed with a yellow light. She called with her mind, her thoughts.

Gaur.

She saw the life spark flicker and felt the response in her head. His tone sounded young, not old and ill like the body in the bed.

Have you come to take me to the other side, oh bright one?

No. She had only a moment to wonder how he saw her before his being hit her like a fist, making all thought impossible. So much emotion and all at once. He mourned. He cried. He was frightened and relieved. His desire to cross over was mirrored by the fear that he would. His desperation engulfed her.

With a mental cry, she pulled away before he overwhelmed her. *Please, I cannot stay if you do not control yourself.* She forced her thoughts past his fear to make him understand.

Do not leave me alone. Take me with you. His mournful wail ripped through her, and she wavered with the intensity

If she were in her physical form, she would have sighed. Unable to waken and unable to cross over, he was desperate. His very essence oozed fear. She could not blame him.

Listen to me, she called again. *I come asking a favor. Help me, and perhaps I can help you.* Using all her power, she forced her need, her sense of urgency through him.

It seemed to work. She felt him calm in the face of a need more vital than his own.

How can I help? I am dead.

No, you are not dead, Aria answered

Then why can I not wake? I am blind in this void. His life spark flickered, not understanding.

His sense of distress rose again.

You see me, she reminded him, forcing him to concentrate on something other than his predicament.

Yes, but your light is as bright as a sun, a seraph's glory come to take me to Thoth's temple.

Aria gave another mental sigh. *I am neither a seraph nor a god's emissary. You are not dead, but neither do you live. You are stuck. Unable to enter the other side. Unable to waken.*

Then, who are you? What are you?

Aria heard caution in the thought. *A friend,* she replied, hiding her inner self behind a tight shield. She did not know his feelings about her banishment and had no time to look. Her strength was limited in this realm, and conversing with Gaur was using most of it.

Help me awaken if friend you are.

She wished she could. *It is not in my power.* A current, deep blue in feeling, slid through her.

You are neither seraph nor healer. What use are you to me? Gaur asked. His light dimmed, heavy with disappointment, and moved away, forcing her to follow.

Gaur, believe what you like, but I am a friend. I cannot heal you, but I can help you. But first you must help me. You felt my need. How can you ignore it? Aria held a mental breath.

Gaur's life force stopped moving and shimmered with color. *Tell me what you wish.*

The Reapers. I would know where they are.

Fear. Blind fear. Gaur's panic crashed over her. *No. I cannot. They will kill me.*

You are already dead, Aria answered.

You said I lived.

Your body does. Aria tried to bury her frustration at his lack of understanding, but knew some of it showed in her tone of thought. *Only because you hang onto it like a child clutches a favorite toy. Show me the Reapers, and I will help you release that which no longer matters, and you can cross to the other side.*

Taking a mental breath, she calmed herself and tried to emanate tranquil thoughts in an effort to calm the stricken man.

One heartbeat, then another passed.

Why do you want to find the Reapers?

She sent him one simple thought. *They have my son,* and then, she showed him. She gave him the agony of

Tarik's birth, the thrill of holding the new life, and then the inimitable sorrow at losing that which she pushed forth from her own body. Opening herself, she shared all the pain and loss, and all the joy and love, that went with having, and losing, a child.

No more. Gaur's cry halted her projection, his spark overwhelmed by sorrow. *Please, Aria. No more. I will give you what you want.*

You know me?

Yes.

You will still help?

Witch, Trancer, or woman, I cannot turn my back on your pain. Not when I can help.

Within a heartbeat, a breath, a flicker of time, he opened his mind to her, and she knew. She saw it all. She knew where the Reapers hid. She saw their Keep, high in the mountains and below it the village of Mardid.

He showed her more, more than she wanted to see. She saw how Gaur went to Mardid to sell his skins and was taken by the Reapers for an imagined affront. She felt his constant fear of being beaten and killed.

She tried to pull away, but he held her close in his thoughts. *I bore your pain, Aria. Now bear mine and understand.*

He was right. She stopped struggling and let the flashes of emotion and life flow through her. Another slave. Warner. He helped Gaur. Brought him food and showed him the best places to rest. The places where the vermin of the earth were fewer.

Warner, escaping with Gaur and then falling from a great height. Gaur, helpless as his friend died in his arms. Gaur running. No prayers and no parting promise, he left Warner unburied, lest he lie next to him in the endless sleep.

This was what haunted his life-spark. This was the act left undone, and in Gaur's eyes, unpunished. It was why he did not, could not, cross.

You did what was necessary. You survived. Aria touched Gaur with the gentle thought.

How can I believe that when I left him in the mud? Not a word passed my lips in parting. I ran like a coward.

If you had stayed, you would have died.

Better death than this void.

He was right in that matter. The currents were a force of life and of nature. Aria navigated them, but even she carried an enormous respect for their savage beauty. To be stuck in them would be unbearable. Even a Trancer's time was limited, not just by necessity, but also by choice.

And her time was almost up. Gaur had helped her, now it was time to return the favor. *What can I do? Your friend is undoubtedly already buried.*

When you find the Reapers, do what I could not and say the proper words. Let him find the path to the afterlife with your prayers.

I will do as you ask. Taking the burden from Gaur's shoulders, she placed it on her own.

Thanks and acceptance passed from Gaur to her. His life-force glowed like the sun upon the fields, and bliss filled her, a gift from Gaur as he passed. His light went out like a flame in the wind.

He crossed.

Sixteen

The midday sun passed its zenith, and Aria still sat in Trancer state. Talon paced, waiting for her to awaken. He glanced at Martus. The old man still sat in the chair, his eyes half closed in the heat, head tilted back.

It surprised him that Aria's father was not more agitated and eager for her to either waken or fail in her quest, but if he caught any of their previous conversation, he probably thought her lost.

Talon prayed the old man was wrong.

A loud gasp punctured the silence, and Talon turned on his heel to see Aria's eyes roll forward, returning to normal. For a moment, she stared vacant-eyed and confused, like a dreamer woken in mid-sleep. His heart pounded. Then, she focused on him, and awareness crept back into her eyes, bringing her back. The tension drained from his body. *Praise the Goddess.* He had not lost her to the currents.

His concerns about Martus disappeared as he rushed to her side and pulled her up. With one hand clenched in her hair and the other wrapped around her slim waist, he held her close as "what ifs" crowded his thoughts.

"Talon, I cannot breathe," Aria said, her voice muffled by his shoulder.

He relaxed his grip.

She leaned back in his arms and traced his scar, from brow to jaw, with the pad of her thumb. "Were you worried?"

Worried? She acted as if she had done nothing more than take a midday nap, not as if she had just risked her life—and his peace of mind—for a slim chance at information. "There would be no need to ask if you had listened to me and not taken such a foolish chance."

She glanced down at Gaur. He lay still, unmoving. She looked back at Talon, her jaw set. "I did what I was born to do—trained to do."

Talon frowned. She was not oblivious to the danger she had put herself in. She simply chose to ignore it.

And him. "The next time I make a decision, I expect you to abide by it."

"Even if it is a foolish decision?" She asked, her voice tight.

"If I make a decision, it is for a reason, and not a foolish one. Generally, it is to protect you from harm."

Her eyes narrowed, and she stepped back from his arms. "As you can see, I am fine. I did the right thing. I made the right decision."

"You are lucky," he countered.

"I am skilled."

"There was another option. You did not have to risk yourself."

"What would you have proposed?"

"We could have traveled back to Zaraza."

"And wasted more time?" Aria stared at him in disgust. "You brought me here to find the Reapers, and that is what I did. I know where they are."

She had done it! Despite his anger, hope flared.

Aria continued, "I want my child back as soon as possible, and you want to find your revenge. I do not understand why you are so willing to keep me from helping both of us to gain our desire."

Before Talon could reply for either good or ill, a man's hoarse shout caught his attention. Both he and Aria turned. Martus. Talon had forgotten him in the heat of their argument, but it seemed the old man had not forgotten them.

Or Gaur.

Martus stood at the end of the bed. Shaking, he straightened and pointed a finger at Aria. He opened his mouth, but only a strangled cry emerged, as he picked up his robes and ran for the door.

Talon swore under his breath and pulled his sword. The old man would be the death of them. A delicate hand stopped his from unsheathing it completely.

"Let him go," she said.

Even though the villagers were untrained, they were many, and such a crowd could prove dangerous. "I cannot have him incite the others to harm you."

The pressure of her hand on his remained steady. "He will not, at least not for a while. Most of the villagers are as much a coward as Martus. They will not attack until nighttime, when they would hope to catch us unawares."

Even if she were correct, he could not risk her life for a second time today. "Then we should leave, be well away before…"

Even as he voiced the words, he knew she did not hear them. Instead, she turned away to tend to Guar. Crossing his hands over his chest, she pulled the thin blanket around his equally thin frame and closed his sightless eyes. And though the dead man had not been a friend, Talon knew Aria mourned him.

A trickle of guilt threaded its way through his psyche. He should have been kinder when she emerged. He did not want to fight with her. He wanted to keep her safe, stroke her hair, and tell her that he would always take care of her.

Mostly, he wanted her to understand that whenever she took a chance with her life, part of him died while he waited to see if she would emerge victorious.

But he could not say the words. To say them would bring her closer to his heart, and closer meant weakness—at least where he was going. He could not have that. Not now. Not when they were getting nearer to Mako by the day.

Aria straightened, tugging on her wrinkled tunic. "We should give him to the ground."

There was no time for such niceties. Talon shook his head. "That is for the villagers to do."

She bit her lip, and even through her sorrow, he saw the defiance in her eyes. "I entered his mind. They will not help him now. It is our duty to send him to the Goddess and sing his spirit."

She was right, it was their duty, but he had a higher calling. "No. You have taken enough chances today, and you can see what that has wrought."

Hands on her hips, Aria raised a scarlet brow. "I do what I think best and will continue to do so."

"By the Goddess," Talon growled, his tolerance at an end. "You are as stubborn as that *rohha* that dumped you in the river. I will not let you do what you want if it means sacrificing yourself."

She stormed to the other side of the room and yanked the pale window coverings down, ripping them from the nails that kept them in place. The afternoon sun caught her through the window, setting her hair afire in its light. She looked like a defiant, powerful Goddess—one he wanted to both worship and protect. "You cannot stop me. We are not bonded in the holy ceremony. You have no say in what I can and cannot do."

She stormed back, shoved past him and began wrapping the body.

Whether she was as beautiful as the Goddess or not, she was as mortal as he. Gripping her shoulders, he pulled her to him. "Perhaps we are not bonded in ritual, but we are joined. Moreover, I am the leader of this quest, and you come with me only on the promise that you do as I ask, or do you forget?" If she would not agree with him, she would obey him.

"Then I will stay here." She shook him off. "You are free to continue on without me."

"That is not an option."

"Then you can wait."

"I cannot protect you from so many people, and you cannot handle a sword."

Chest to chest, she glared up at him, her breath heavy with anger. "I may not be able to handle a blade, but do not make the mistake of equating inexperience with incompetence. I am your equal. I may not have a Warrior's courage or skill, but I possess a Trancer's talent. It may not mean much to you, but it means everything to me, and I will not have you interfering with my duty."

"It is not your courage or ability that is in question," Talon said through gritted teeth.

"You lie." Aria's voice rose. "You balk in letting me face the same possibilities, the same sacrifices, that you do. You deny me that which you freely claim. So, do not stand here and tell me of your confidence in me. Your very reluctance tells me more than words."

She turned away, only to sag against the wall. "Why can you not believe in me like I believe in you?" Her voice was quiet now.

Too quiet.

Still, he could not say the words that would erase her uncertainties. He could not tell her that the doubt was not in her. It was in him. She held his life, his happiness, in the palm of her small hand, and he feared that to speak his faith in her would only give her another excuse to risk herself.

He sighed. "Aria, we do not have the time to do this."

"We will make time." The sadness in her voice stirred him, and any remaining anger vanished in the face of her pain. Besides, he knew he was the loser in this argument. The more time he wasted trying to make her see reason, the more he put her in danger. "It will be as you wish, but we must hurry."

Relaxing, she sat on the bed to finish the task of wrapping Guar. "Thank you." She wound the cloth over the dead man's face. "He gave me what we needed. I owe him a peaceful afterlife."

What they needed? She had mentioned it before, but he had lost the thought as they argued. "What did he tell you?"

"The Reapers take refuge in an abandoned Keep that lies just above the village of Mardid."

"On the other side of Mard's pass?" He remembered the village well. Known for its remarkable wine and even more remarkable women, as a Reaper, he had been there on numerous occasions to sample both.

She glanced up from her task and gave him a curious look. "You have been to Mardid? From Gaur's memories it seemed to be quite distant."

Talon hesitated. Perhaps it was time to tell her of his past. He owed her that much of an explanation.

No. There would be time for the truth afterwards. "I have heard of it, that is all."

With a shrug, she turned to finish preparing Gaur.

Talon walked outside and began digging Guar's grave in one of the flowerbeds that decorated the small area.

After Mako was dead, he vowed he would tell Aria of his past. Then, if she left, he could face it. If he died, the truth would not matter.

***

Aria stood outside her family's home and waited to see if either her mother or siblings would answer her call of farewell. She needed to say her good-byes, but did not want to enter Martus' domain. It held too many bad memories, too many beatings, and too much fear.

Even more painful were the good memories—playing

in the garden with Kisa and Anok, helping Mother gather herbs, or simply laying in the grass and watching the sky with her brother and sister by her side. She had never thought it would end.

Then, in a moment, it all changed, and she was banished as a witch. She sighed and leaned against the fence to wait.

"The sun nears the horizon. We must leave." Talon squeezed her shoulder.

She nodded. "I know." She turned into him, not caring if he was reluctant to hold her—only knowing she needed comfort.

His arms tightened around her.

The squeal of a door carried through the cooling air, and Aria turned, hopes rising in a surge.

Kisa. Only Kisa.

Aria's hope fell, knowing that her mother and Anok waited inside for her to depart. She took a deep breath, reminding herself that Anok was still young, and Mother's fear ran deep. *Not of me,* she thought, *but of Martus.*

If her father found Mother speaking with Aria, the consequences would be severe, and Mother was older now. Broken.

And at least she could speak her farewell to Kisa.

Pulling the heavy door shut, her sister ran towards them. Aria let a smile play on her lips even though their good-byes would be short.

Her sister reached her and grabbed her in an embrace. "Must you leave?"

Aria nodded and clutched her tightly, knowing she would probably never hold her again. "Yes."

Cam snorted, drawing Aria's attention. Talon was already mounted. "I will wait over here." He pointed the *rohha* towards the dirt road that passed by the cottage.

Kisa pulled away. "When will you return?"

Aria reached out and twirled one of her sister's deep red curls around her finger. How did you tell your blood, your heart, that you would never return? That you would never laugh with her again. That you would not be there on her day of bonding ceremony.

You just did it. It was like pulling a thorn. You did it fast and quick. Otherwise, you would lose the courage needed. She let the curl slip from her fingers. "I cannot come back."

Her sister's smile disappeared. "You mean that you cannot come back soon."

Aria took a deep breath. Kisa was not making this easy, but then, even as a child, she had always wanted her own way. At least it was honest. "No. I mean never." She smoothed her sister's hair back with her free hand. "If I come back, it will only makes things harder for you, Anok, and Mother. Besides, Father will never allow me to see you again."

Kisa waved the comment away with a blithe flourish. "I can handle Father, and he dare not harm you with Talon to protect you."

Aria gave a sad smile. "I wish it were so simple."

"It is, if you want it to be."

"No. It is not. Even now, Father speaks with the village, trying to rally them against me."

"It does not matter. They will do nothing. Fear rules them. Come back after you find Tarik. Bring your son for me to see."

Aria hung her head and rubbed her eyes with the heels of her palms, wishing Kisa would not make this harder.

"You can always sneak back," Kisa suggested. "I will leave a big stone by the tree where we last sat, and you can leave a note under it. Then, we can meet and—"

It was time to end the pretense. "No."

Kisa's jaw snapped shut. "What do you mean? No rock or no tree?"

"I mean no note."

"Why not? Why deny me this?"

Aria squeezed back the tears. She could not cry. Not now. If she let the tears come, she feared they would never stop. "I cannot promise to return, because I do not know what is going to happen. Talon could die. I could die."

Kisa took a step back, her eyes wide. "Do not say such things. You have Talon. He will not let anything happen to you."

"I did not say I would give him a choice," Aria replied, knowing even as she spoke the words it would be better if she kept silent. But there was little she did not tell her sister, and old habits died hard.

Kisa did not reply, but her alarm grew and washed over Aria in a thick wave.

Aria bit her lip, not wanting to explain, but knowing she had too. "Talon is so full of anger that all he can see is death. I cannot gain our son, only to lose his father. I do not know how, but I must save them both, even if it means confronting the Reapers without him."

"You cannot do this. He is trained in war. Let him do what he must to save your son."

Aria's temper flared. "I may be a Trancer, but do not ask me to sit idly by while Talon pays in blood." She took a deep breath, trying to rein in her anger. "I am trained in people. I know their desires. My skills can save both Talon and lives if he would just let me help." She grabbed Kisa's hands in hers. "Promise me that you will not tell Talon what I have said."

"You are my sister." Kisa glanced over her shoulder, towards the spot where Talon and Cam waited.

"Promise me," Aria demanded.

The tension swelled in the silence. Finally, Kisa hung her head. "I will do as you ask, but only if you swear that you will not do anything foolish."

It was enough. "I swear."

Kisa looked up. "By the Goddess?"

Aria nodded, grateful to offer some hope.

They stared at each other for a moment, and then Kisa chuckled, breaking the tension. "I see that Talon is skilled and worldly and assumed he should take care of you, not you of him. I did not know that women could do such things."

"I would rather we take care of each other," Aria murmured. Her sister was young and only knew the village. She did not know that women could be so much more than a man's slave, or that some men did not hit. They caressed.

Then again, neither had she seen death in its hideous glory, nor lost an entire way of life to a band of murderers.

Kisa nodded knowingly. "If it is any consolation, I think it is his caring, not duty, that drives him to protect you."

She knew what her sister meant. Their father and mother's bonding had been arranged, and all knew he took the vow out of duty, not love.

Kisa continued. "I see it in the way he watches you. When you are busy, he stares at you like a thirsty man stares at a pool of water."

Aria paused. "Truly?"

Her sister's mouth gaped open at the comment. "How could you not see this? He thirsts for you, sister. It makes me wish I were you, just so I could know that deep a love."

Aria shook her head. "I think he cares for me and even desires me, but I do not think he loves me."

"Then why does he keep you by his side?"

"My own stubbornness," Aria said with a short laugh, remembering his face when she refused to leave. He had been so frustrated his brow burned red.

Kisa squeezed her hand. "For a Trancer, you are dense. He could have forced you to a Tower, under guard, if he so chose."

Aria gave a snort of disbelief. "I would have escaped. I did the first time."

"Perhaps, but he would have been more cautious the second." Kisa pulled her close and whispered in her ear. "He does love you, Aria. He may not know it, and you may not believe it, but he does. And what's more, you love him."

Could it be true? Did Kisa see what she could not?

"Aria." Talon called her name.

Cam danced impatiently, wanting to leave as if he sensed the tension in the air.

It was time to depart. "Kisa, I do not know what will happen, but I do hope you are right."

"I want you to promise me that you will live so you can tell me I was." She squeezed Aria to her.

"I cannot come back, but I will send word." Aria said and backed slowly away, her arms sliding down Kisa's until only their fingertips touched.

Then, that too, was gone.

Seventeen

"Why should I help you?" The young man's brown hair, cut short, revealed a face far too old for one barely past the bonding years.

Talon breathed deeply. With over ten suns of hard travel behind him, it felt good to sit on something besides Cam, but the pleasure was short-lived. The tavern was full this evening, the air thick with pipe smoke as men of all ages sat on long benches, their elbows resting on wobbly wooden tables. The setting was the same as Barias' and countless other alehouses, except that suspicion and muttering replaced the friendly banter and gaming.

He supposed living in fear did that to a people.

"Well?" The young man stared, waiting.

Talon rolled his half-empty mug between his palms and gave the only answer he could. "Freedom."

"I am no slave," was the terse reply, followed by a snort of disbelief as the lad raised his tankard and threw back a mouthful of ale.

Talon glanced around the tavern and hoped not all people in Mardid wore similar blinders. If so, his and Aria's quest would be impossible to complete. He wondered how she fared outside, and if she were still angry that she watched Cam while he gathered information. Talon smiled to himself. His Given was a doer, not a watcher.

He loved that about her.

It was also why she waited outside.

"Are you done with your questions?"

The lad finished his ale and made to rise.

Talon stopped him with a firm hand on his forearm. "You claim no master, but I say different. You are as much a slave to the Reapers as the women they steal."

The lad sat back down, his lips pressed tight.

Talon let go. "You let the Reapers do as they please for fear they will kill either you or your loved ones. You give your crops to a lord who gives back neither protection nor money nor help in the fields."

Talon took a swig of his drink. The icy coldness of the liquid calmed him, and he wiped his mouth with the back of his hand. "You are a slave. Not bought and paid for, but a slave just the same."

"Why do you care?" The lad's voice carried no farther than the distance between them. He glanced down at Talon's side. "You carry a Reaper's sword. You might be one of them, trying to lure me into a fight, or you might have killed one. Either way, I'm a dead man if I follow you."

Despite his wary words, the lad was intrigued. Talon saw the hope in his eyes, and it was greater than the suspicion in his voice. "If I were a Reaper, I would not need a reason to fight. I would challenge you, and you would defend yourself or die. As for taking my sword from another, it is how all Reapers earn their weapons. We take our enemies honor and add the blood stone." His leather-clad hand fell to rest on the hilt of his sword. "My weapon has a sordid history. I cannot deny it."

"You *are* a Reaper." The young man's eyes grew large as hope died and fear filled the void.

"I *was.*" Talon hoped his story would not frighten the young man further away, but he deserved to know truth if he was going to fight, and maybe die, for Talon's cause. "It was a long time ago, before I found the path to honor. It is something I would prefer to forget, something I tried to forget, but I cannot. Not until Mako lies on a burial pyre."

The young man still eyed Talon with a wary gaze. "I hear the Reapers never let one of their own go."

"They did not let me go. I went on a scouting mission and never returned."

The young man leaned forward and stared at Talon, searching his face as if he read his thoughts. Talon met his gaze straight on. If the lad wanted to see the truth of his words, then let him.

The silence went on as the people around them talked. The sound of a tankard shattering on the hard floor cut through the air.

Finally, the young man nodded and settled back into his seat. "Why did you leave?"

He believed him. Relief draped over Talon like a dry cloak on a rainy day, but the story was not over yet. "The senselessness. The lack of purpose other than the day's bounty. There had to be more to life than slaughter."

"What did you do after you left?"

"I joined the Warrior clan."

"The Warriors?" The lad raised a dark brow. "That's a far cry from the Reapers, is it not?"

It was the exact opposite in belief and reason. His first days with the Clan flashed through Talon's mind. They distrusted him, and with reason, but he proved himself by passing the Ritual of Acceptance and later, in honorable battle. "They took my skills, honed them, and gave me discipline. They brought honor and reason into my life."

"So why come back? Returning to Reaper country does not sound reasonable to me." He shook his head. "In fact, it sounds mad."

"Mako killed my son." The words tasted bitter in his mouth. "I seek revenge."

"Revenge? Is that not contrary to the teaching of the Warriors?"

"Yes, but I am no longer a Warrior." Talon waited, listening to the alehouse conversations and arguments carry on around them. Would the lad help, and if so, would others follow as well?

The boy across from him leaned forward, hands clasped in front of him. "Why should I trust a man without allegiance?"

"Better a man who fights for what he believes in than a man who remains untrue to himself out of blind loyalty."

He nodded. "Point taken." Raising his hand, he signaled the barkeep for another tankard. Both men sat in silence until the serving wench left. The lad raised his mug and took a long drink. "Why me?"

Talon let the ale remain untouched. "What do you mean?"

The lad gestured with the mug. "You could have told your story to anyone here. I will not deny your story—your request—intrigues me, but you should watch your words. Not all here fear the Reapers. In fact, some are paid to give them information on men such as you."

"Thank you for the warning, but I knew you were safe to speak with."

"How?"

Talon leaned forward. He had trusted the lad this far, now to tell him the rest. "I travel with a Trancer—"

"A Trancer?" The surprise in the lad's voice made the words carry farther than Talon liked.

Talon grabbed the front of the boy's shirt, jerking him forward. "Shut up." The command was deliberate and harsh. "Or you will give us away."

The lad struggled to dislodge Talon's hands, but he could not move them. "Did she read my thoughts?"

"No. She is true to her calling and would never read another's thoughts except in healing or with consent."

"Then how did she pick me from the others?"

"She scanned the area for emotions, not thoughts. She touched on your dislike of the Reapers and something more." Talon leaned forward, pulling the lad until they were head to head. "She felt resistance." His whisper of truth barely stirred the air.

The lad dropped his hands. "Forgive me. You surprised me."

"Understandable." Talon released his grip, and the lad fell back into his seat.

Glancing about, it did not surprise Talon that the rest of the patrons ignored them. When living in fear, one learned not to become involved in anything.

The young man tilted his head in acquiescence. "She was right, but she did miss one fact."

"That is?"

"There are others."

A surge of victory shot through Talon. He tamped it down. He had gained the lad's trust, but it was only the first win in what would probably be a bloody fight. One did not celebrate the battle; one celebrated the war. "The others, do they feel the same way?"

"Some do. Others are more timid in their hate." He shrugged, his nonchalant exterior a lie when compared with the fire in his eyes. "The old men fear death, but for many of the young ones, this life is death. We can do nothing without fearing the Reapers. They take our food, and our children starve. They take our women and turn them into whores."

The lad's eyes glittered. "I have a sister. She will soon be a woman, and I will not have her taken against her will."

Aria was right. Talon smiled grimly. This young man

was ready to fight. "If oppression is what you claim it to
be, what has kept you from attacking your oppressors?"

"We can wield weapons, but we know little of battle or
strategy. Even if we managed to get into the Keep, we
would all be dead within a breath."

It was what he had hoped to hear. They had desire,
but no leader to shape it, focus it, and forge them into a
fighting unit.

They needed him.

"There are more ways to conquer than by the sword."

"What do you suggest? We are but a few men."

"There is the cover of darkness and stealth. Sometimes
a war is not won with battle cries and waving weapons.
Instead, it is won with quiet footsteps and a dagger in the
ribs." Would they follow?

The young man smiled. "My name is Orrin."

"I am Talon." If he did not believe, Orrin would not
have given his name, and if he believed, then so would
others.

***

Standing next to Cam, Aria shifted from one foot to
the other, watching the townspeople bustle about her.
Across the hard-packed dirt street, a produce vendor
haggled with a woman wearing a red scarf on her head.

"Four coins for eggs? You must be mad." The woman
in the scarf made as if to leave.

"Three. Three coins, and you are breaking me." The
vendor wiped the back of his meaty hand over his sweaty
forehead, emphasizing his troubles.

The woman turned back. "One coin."

"One?" The vendor's shriek rose above the general din.

The red-scarfed woman shrugged her shoulders. "It is
the offer."

"Two, and I will be a poor man by the time you leave."

"One and a half."

The vendor hesitated, and Aria sighed. He was going
to take the money. This was all part of the dance. She had
been watching him since Talon left her outside to wait,
and his act never changed. Sometimes the amount
changed, but never the act. The red-scarfed woman was
not making as good a bargain as she thought. Earlier, a
man bought the same amount for less than a single coin.

"She should have held firm," Aria muttered, reaching out to stroke Cam's nose.

The *rohha* pulled away, but he tossed his head as if in uneasy agreement.

Aria turned her attention to the merchant just down from the produce vendor, but it was the same conversation. Only about wine.

A sigh escaped her lips. She would give her boots for the simple entertainment of a juggler.

What was taking Talon so long?

The door to the tavern opened, and the squeal of rusty hinges caught Aria's attention. A short figure, face hidden by a heavy brown cloak, emerged from the tavern.

It was not Talon. Aria's boredom and irritation grew. She had hoped, after their trip, that Talon's fear for her safety would dwindle. After all, no mishaps had occurred, and neither man nor animal had threatened them.

Instead, his heart grew more distant the closer they got to Mako. As foolish as it was, she had hoped the uneventful journey would make him rethink his vow of revenge, but in her soul, she knew his hate for Mako was stronger than any words she spoke or example she set.

Now, after going against her own judgment and helping Talon find a possible ally, she was left to wait while he set his plans into motion.

It would have been nice to be included in the planning, but perhaps it was better Talon separated from her. It would make what she was going to do easier for both of them to accept.

"Mistress." A hushed voice called to her from the side of the tavern.

In reflex, Aria turned. It was the hooded figure that had emerged from the tavern only moments ago.

She took a step back.

"Do not be alarmed." The figure threw the hood back to reveal the delicate face of a young woman. Her hair, as black as a starless sky, curled and framed her high cheekbones. "I am a friend."

Her voice, although barely audible above the sounds of the street, was as beautiful as her features. A tinge of envy shot through Aria. She fingered the end of her braid, the grit from the road thick in her hair and coarse under her fingertips. "A friend?" Those were bold words for a stranger. She let her braid swing back behind her. "I know nobody here."

The woman smiled, revealing even, white teeth. "My name is Medea."

The name felt familiar. Aria slid over the memories in her mind and came up blank. "I still do not—"

"Please. Let me finish. We have never met, but we fight for the same cause."

"How do you know my cause?" Aria stepped closer to Cam, ready to vault into his saddle if need be.

"I heard your man talking."

A spy. Aria sent her thoughts out and touched the woman. Not enough to enter her mind, but a surface glance.

This woman told the truth, at least about hearing Talon, but the only other emotion Aria felt was desperation. Medea wanted to be believed more than she wanted air to breathe or water to drink.

Medea's desire was so great, so powerful, that Aria wanted to believe her, but still she hesitated. "Why broach my help? Why not Talon's? After all, it was his words that spoke to you, not mine."

Medea's smile broadened. "For the same reason you wait outside with his *rohha*. Men see us as fragile. Useless. They fear for our lives. If I offered my help, he would ignore me. However, you are a woman. A sister. You understand that we are strong. I thought we could work together."

Aria could not argue with Medea's reasoning, but neither could she accept her assistance. "I appreciate the offer, but I do not want your help."

"I have no one else to turn to. I will do anything."

"Even die?" The threat of death would scare her away, if nothing else.

"I do not care. Death is a small sacrifice."

Easy words, and ones Aria did not want to put to the test. "You should care. You are a beautiful young woman, and I am sure any man would be happy to take you from here if you but asked."

"My beauty? It is why I ask your favor." Medea held her chin high. Tears pooled in her bright blue eyes.

Tears that Aria ignored under peril of betrayal. "Cry

or not, it will change nothing."

"You do not understand." Oblivious to Aria's rebuff, Medea wiped away the tears that slid down her face. "You would if you lived here, growing up in the Reaper's shadow. It is because of my beauty that I offer my help. It is because of my beauty that I am cursed."

"I do not understand," Aria said, intrigued despite her own objections.

"You will." Medea reached out, a slim hand sculpting the air. "You are also a beautiful woman, and when they catch you they will do to you what they did to me."

"What was that?"

Not breaking her eye contact with Aria, Medea unwound the decorated cloth that wrapped her wrist and held up her arm for Aria to see.

Scars. Scars as wide as a thick branch wrapped her wrist like a tragic bracelet. Without thinking, Aria stepped into the shadows where Medea waited and took the damaged hand in hers. "Why?"

Medea chin tilted up another notch. "I was not willing to lie in their beds so they forced my *cooperation.*"

By the Goddess, they were animals! Impulsively, Aria pulled Medea to her and hugged her in silent sympathy.

"It is all right. I escaped." Medea pushed away and rewrapped the scars with her cloth bracelet. "That is what I wanted to tell you."

"That you escaped?"

"No, not exactly. More like *how* I escaped."

Aria's ears perked up. What did this girl know that poor Gaur and his friend never knew? Shaking inside at the horror Medea must have endured, Aria focused on the issue at hand. "Tell me."

Medea looked around, and Aria followed her gaze. The street grew busier as evening approached, and people shopped for supplies for the evening meal.

In quiet agreement, Aria followed Medea behind the building. A murmur of conversation as they passed under the tavern's window caught Aria's ear, but no raucous laughter or shouts broke the silence. When compared with Barias's tavern, it was out of character. The hairs rose on the back of Aria's neck.

Medea stopped when they reached the far corner.

"First, tell me what you plan to do."

Aria hesitated. Medea asked for much, but if she could provide the information she suggested, her assistance would be invaluable. She touched the girl's mind again and still found nothing but the desperation. The temptation to delve further, to find the inner truth, overwhelmed her, but she stopped herself. Medea had not given permission for such a thing, and if she took advantage of her Trancer powers, she would truly be the witch her father claimed her to be.

And she did not want to ask for permission. If Medea did not know she was a Trancer, Aria did not want to tell her. Knowledge was a powerful thing, and she could not chance losing any advantage she might have.

She would have to trust the girl—for now. After seeing what the Reapers had done to her, it was not hard to do.

"I plan on sneaking in, finding my son and friend, and getting them out."

"That is it?" Medea expression was incredulous. "I thought you wanted to hurt the Reapers."

Aria shook her head. "No, that is Talon's plan. He thinks our son dead and plans revenge."

"You think your son lives?"

"I know he does."

Medea hesitated and apparently reached her conclusion as to Aria's story. "I must admit, I had hoped for revenge, but I cannot force you to that which is against your nature. What I can do is show you how to sneak in."

"How?"

"There is a secret tunnel leading to the cells. I found it when I was imprisoned, and I used it to escape."

"Why have you not used it to find the revenge you seek?"

"One day, I might. For now, it will be enough to have them hurt. To make them know they are vulnerable and to not know why."

Medea's need for justice coursed over Aria, and she hoped what Medea said was true, that hurting them would be enough. The true question was, would it be enough for Talon? Would he forget his vow of vengeance when he held his son in his arms?

He would have to. Aria leaned towards her companion.

"Tell me about the tunnel."

"I will do better. Meet me at the stables tonight, after your man has gone to sleep, and I will show you where it is."

Perfect. "Tonight it is."

Cam's shrill cry sounded.

Both women's heads jerked up at the sound. The *rohha* was in trouble, and Aria had left him alone.

"Tonight," Medea whispered furiously and ran down the path that followed the back of the tavern.

Whirling on her heel, Aria followed the sound of Cam's cry and ran around the corner, ready to do battle for the beast.

There was no need. She groaned aloud.

Cam was fine. His cry was not one of battle or terror. It was a cry of greeting.

Next to him, another *rohha* shuffled restlessly, his pale coat and mane a sharp contrast to Cam's dark coloring.

"Hello, Aria." Lore smiled down at her.

***

"How did you find us?" Talon stood in the doorway, arms crossed in front of him as he surveyed the pair. How could Lore have been so foolish? The Council would not take his desertion lightly, and neither would he.

"You left a trail that a blind, deaf, and half dead *katah*` could follow." Lore dismounted and walked up the wooden steps.

Talon glared at his friend. "I told you this was a personal matter. I do not want you involved."

"I know." Lore grinned and thrust his hand out. "And you should be angry, but you are not."

As much as Talon hated to admit it, Lore was right. He should be angry. To be disavowed was a nightmare. To have Lore lose status and title was worse. But, instead of anger, a sense of gratitude flowed over him. He needed a friend at this crossroad. Someone he trusted to guard his back. Letting a smile curve his lips, Talon grasped Lore's forearm in his hand. "It seems you know me better than I know myself."

"Do not judge me too good a reader of character." Lore let go of Talon and glanced over his shoulder towards Aria. "I thought she was simply a pretty face. Did she tell you that she drugged me?"

Aria's blush was visible even in the dimming light.

Talon chuckled. "Yes. You underestimated her."

I will never do so again." Lore bowed low to Aria. "Mistress, you have my admiration."

The smile she blessed Lore with squeezed Talon's heart for but a moment before he pushed it back. Jealousy of Lore was unbecoming.

Lore turned back to Talon, his charm, melting like shadows in the sun, was replaced with the serious countenance of a trained Warrior. "I have brought news of the Council."

"What do they want?"

"Nothing, but I thought you should know their decision to excommunicate you caused restlessness among the clan."

"How so?"

Hurrying up the steps, Aria completed the circle of three. "Talon, you are a great Warrior. To lose you was a blow they could ill afford."

Lore nodded in agreement. "She is correct. You are much admired for both your skills at strategy and your ability to command."

"The Council's decision was justified."

Lore shrugged again. "Perhaps, but after seeing the total destruction of a Tower, many of the younger Warriors agreed with your actions."

Talon hid his surprise. While he had joined the clan after his bonding years, most Warriors came to the Clan as children. They were saturated in the Clan's beliefs, and for them to go against the teachings was unheard of.

To ally themselves with him was unthinkable. "I am sure their displeasure did not please the Council."

"No, but it displeased them more when we left to follow you."

Talon cocked is head. "We?"

"Yes, we." Lore's hushed voice traveled no farther than their ears. "Warriors wait in the woods, ready to follow you and destroy the Reapers."

"How many?"

"Your contingent and more," Lore advised.

Involuntarily, Talon took a step back. *All* his men were

here? It was an honor, and the last thing he expected. It was also the best news he could hear. No matter what he had told Orrin about stealth, some Reapers would escape their blades and make their way to the village to exact their revenge on Madrid's more helpless residents.

He wanted Mako dead and the villagers freed from the tyranny of the Reapers, but he did not want the villagers destroyed in the battle to come. Now that he had Warriors to assist him, he would have enough men to help raid the Reapers as well as guard the village.

It could work.

Aria coughed, drawing his attention. He did not want her to hear anymore. He had not missed the circles under her eyes that grew darker every day, and the weariness in her step. At night, when she slept, she tossed, sometimes calling out for Tarik and sometimes for him.

Now with Lore's help, and his men's steel, Aria's nightmares would soon be over.

Eighteen

The door to the tavern swung shut behind him as Talon walked across the dirt road. It had been a long evening, but worth the effort. With Lore and Orrin's help, they had managed to formulate a plan to assault and win the Reapers' Keep.

Now, he wanted a night's sleep in a soft bed. A small comfort, but those were the most important.

Making his way in the dark, he went to the house where Aria waited. Orrin had vouched for the old couple, saying they were sympathetic to the cause. Still, he insisted Aria take a room with a window that latched.

Quietly, he knocked on the rough wooden door and waited. No one answered. He knocked again. A voice spoke, muffled by the heavy structure. "What do you want?"

"Orrin sent me. I am meeting a friend."

The door squeaked open a few inches. Talon held his hands out, palm up, to show his good intentions. "Her name is Aria."

A short woman, her dressing gown pulled tightly about her, poked her head through the gap. "She said you would come. This way." The door opened further, and she ushered him in. He followed her down the short, dim hallway. They stopped at the end in front of a large wooden door. "I gave your woman dinner. The food's probably gone cold, but it should be good."

"My thanks."

"You should have come earlier, you could have had a bath."

Talon smiled at the motherly reprimand. "I apologize if I kept you up."

She left, taking what little light there was with her. Her voice carried in the dark. "Ha. Apologize to your woman. She waited as long as she could."

Talon thumbed the latch. Heavy, but well oiled, the door swung open without a sound. With a Warrior's training, he hesitated, listening and looking, before he stepped through the portal. The fireplace lit the room, creating shadows, pockets of darkness where anything, or anyone, could hide, but nothing and no one did. Only the familiar sound of Aria as she breathed deep in her dreams, and the crackle of the dying fire, broke the night's silence.

The room was safe. They were alone. He shut the door behind him.

A small murmur caught his attention. Aria. She called for Tarik as she dreamed.

Taking off his boots, Talon set them by the fireplace and walked over to her. Murmurs changed to pitiful cries, breaking his Warrior's heart. Since the Temple, he had denied them both the simple warmth of touch when all he wanted to do was draw her close and ease her torment.

It was not to be.

He unbuckled his scabbard and laid it on the small table next to the bed. Aria called for Tarik again, pushing restlessly at the covers.

He rested his head in his hands. It was torture wanting her and denying her. Just for a night, he wanted to keep her demons at bay. To let her know she was safe, would always be safe, as long as he breathed.

Her hands grasped at the air, searching for her lost son.

Was it so wrong to want to hold her on the last eve they might have together? He pulled his shirt over his head and tossed it to the end of the bed. Unlacing his leggings, he threw them to lie with his shirt. Clad in only his breechclout, Talon pulled the heavy covers back and slid into bed beside Aria, pulling her to his side. The tossing stopped, and she snuggled into his warmth.

He relaxed, her innocence and pain touching the place in his soul he denied so passionately. He nuzzled her hair. It was still damp from her bath and fragrant with the scent of a flower he did not recognize. After the battle, he wanted her to have this every night. Safety. A warm bed. All the comforts she deserved. And he would give them to her.

If he lived.

A future with Aria? It was a heady thought, and one he indulged for but a heartbeat.

He let the vision go. The thought of life, of living with Aria, was one he could ill afford. To desire life was to fear death. If he worried about death, he would put those who had pledged their lives to him at risk. Still, it did not keep him from hoping to walk away from the fight and into Aria's arms.

If he lived, he would devote his life to making her happy. To loving her and making sure she knew it in both deed and word. He buried his face into her hair, inhaling her, memorizing her, and burning her into his brain as a token he could carry into battle with him.

Would you devote your life to me? Aria tilted her head up, her eyes still closed. Was Talon real or a dream? Either way, she prayed his thoughts were true. He kissed her hair. His lips were firm and warm and sent a jolt of pleasure from her scalp to her heels.

He was real. Thank the Goddess. This moment was real. He was in her bed, holding her, his bare flesh pressed against her. His hands kneaded her back as he rubbed his cheek against her skin.

The desire she had worked to deny blazed into life, and she kissed his neck.

His arms stiffened.

"Aria?"

"Yes." She opened her eyes.

"I thought you were asleep." His arms slid away from her as he moved to the other side of the bed.

"I know." She should have remained silent, pretended to be asleep, until he was unable to deny his heart and body.

Now he was the cold and distant Talon she had traveled with from Laini.

He pulled the covers over them and lay back, looking into the flickering light. "I apologize. I did not mean to take advantage of you."

Lying on her side, Aria propped her head up on one hand. "There is no need to apologize for offering comfort to another."

"Perhaps not, but it was not comfort I thought of."

Aria grinned at the admission, knowing how difficult it was for him to admit his carnal vulnerabilities. "I know."

"It was wrong of me to force myself upon you." His body tightened, muscles constricting as he fought for control, but still, she saw the truth of his desire.

Her Giver was a both a brilliant strategist and a magnificent Warrior, but he was inexperienced when it came to expressing his heart. She scooted across the expanse of bed until she lay next to him. He did not move away, but neither did he move to acknowledge her. "There would have been no force involved." She raked a nail down his chest.

He stiffened and pulled away.

A trickle of anger cleaved her passion in two. He was as stubborn and single-minded as the *rohha* he called friend. She moved to return to her side of the bed, but his sigh, deep and lonely, stopped her. Perhaps he was hardheaded, but that did not mean she had to behave in the same manner. She would not let tonight end like this. Not with careless words and love unspoken.

Not when she might die.

Leaning forward, she kissed his shoulder.

"What are you doing?" His expressionless tone clashed with the passion that radiated from his soul, touching her Trancer senses.

She shivered despite the room's heat. "I am kissing you."

"Why?"

She smiled. "Because you are letting me."

"I am not worthy."

She kissed his shoulder again, tasting the salt of his skin as she slid the kiss towards his mouth. She stopped but a breath away. "I say you are."

His breath, sweet with wine, caressed her cheek as he gazed at her. She felt his conflict within as his need to make love to her warred with his need to remain apart and aloof.

Which would win?

Breaths mingling, she spoke the words of her heart. "Make love to me." Her request was a whisper in the dim light of the fire.

It was all he needed. Aria moaned as Talon rolled her onto her back, covering her with his large frame. His desire blinded her. It was primitive. Urgent. He wanted her like a *katah'* wanted its mate. She writhed against him in response, and their lips met in a hard kiss, each seeking to devour the other.

Hands frantically moved over flesh, kneading, stroking, as each pulled the other closer. Reaching between them, she pulled his breechclout away, freeing him to her waiting hands. He throbbed and strained as she grasped him, guiding him towards her waiting depths.

He tried to pull away. "Let me ready you." His voice broke as he fought for control of himself.

She would have none of that. No control. No thought. Only action. Only need.

Wrapping her slim legs around his hips, she guided him again until he was at her entrance. She thrust upwards, burying him in her.

He groaned in surrender.

Aria shut her eyes. Skin slid against skin, lips kissed, hands grasped. It was a maelstrom of sensation. A war of pleasure as each tried to satisfy the other.

Aria wanted to win. Pressing against Talon's shoulder and using her legs as leverage, she pushed him onto his back and went with him.

Talon throbbed hard inside her as she sat astride him. She smiled, looking down at him through half-lidded eyes.

She rolled her hips, and Talon's breath hissed through his teeth. "Now you are mine."

His large hands slid along her calves, over her knees and thighs, stopping to squeeze her. "As you are mine."

His reply was everything she wanted. No denial, just acceptance of what was.

Leaning forward, her hair cascading over her shoulder, she rested her hands on his chest and raised her hips. When she lowered them back, Talon used his hands to guide her, pressing her against him.

It was exquisite.

"Again," Talon begged. She raised her eyes to see him lost in the moment, creating a memory that would sustain them both through the battle ahead.

She closed her eyes and focused on the sensations that coursed through her—Talon's eagerness, stroking her like his hands stroked her thighs, his yearning to take and give pleasure, and his solid muscular body, giving her what his heart desired and his mind denied.

She rose again and again. His hips thrust upwards to meet her, grinding against her.

The fire in her body grew higher, hotter. In the distance, she heard Talon cry her name as his release drew close.

Her love surrounded them like a cocoon, and his desire blended with hers, taking them both to a new height. A new place.

In a great shout, they merged, as release took them both away in a maelstrom of currents and color.

***

Sated and content, Talon slept a deep sleep for the first time in many moons. Aria smiled. It was what she wanted, what she needed if she were to meet Medea at the stables. Still, she wished she could see his eyes before she left.

What if she never saw them again?

She gasped at the thought, then quickly banished it before it grew. Now was not the time to think of defeat but of the goal. Sneak into the Keep, find Tarik and Iliana, and leave before the Reapers had a chance to know what happened.

She hoped it would be as simple as it sounded.

First, she had to leave without waking Talon, and with the way his arms were wrapped around her, that was going to be a difficult task. She slid downwards. He moaned. She stopped. Her heart pounded. *Breathe*, she reminded herself. *You must breathe and relax.*

Another heartbeat later, she moved, but at a slower pace, until she was free of his hold.

Talon turned over, pulling the covers with him.

Did he wake?

No. She breathed a soft sigh of relief. Slowly, she slid her feet over the edge of the bed, being careful not to disturb the mattress, and followed with her legs, hips, and torso until she was kneeling naked on the floor. She glanced over her shoulder. His back was to her, and his breathing was deep and even.

She stood up and gathered her clothes. Naked and padding on bare feet, she opened the door and paused, turning to take one last look at her lover. "I love you, Talon. No matter what happens, know this to be true."

The silence of sleep was his reply.

Stepping into the hall, Aria shut the door behind her, dressed in the dark, and moments later, was out of the house and on the way to the stables.

Would Medea still be waiting? If not, she would simply

have to find her own route into the Keep. Aria walked faster.

Rounding the corner, the stables loomed in front of her. The light of the moons illuminated the wooden shack, giving it an almost otherworldly air. The sound of a stomping *rohha* greeted her as she entered. It was Cam. Leaving the door ajar for light, she walked over and patted his nose. "You must be quiet," she told the beast. "I do this for Talon."

Cam nuzzled her palm.

"I am glad to see we finally agree on something," Aria murmured.

"I thought, perhaps, you had changed your mind."

Aria jumped and spun about. "Medea?"

A figure emerged from the shadows. "Of course." She came close and laid a smooth hand on Aria's arm. "Are you ready?"

Aria placed her hand over Medea's. "Yes, and thank you for waiting."

Medea accepted the thanks with a nod. "You left with no trouble? Your man does not suspect?"

"No," Aria replied. "He suspects nothing and is oblivious to all except his dreams."

"Good. We must go. Quickly, before the morning comes."

Medea's overwhelming urgency to leave tugged at Aria's mind. And there was more. Disliking her own suspicions, Aria scanned Medea's thoughts one last time.

Excitement. Vindication. Uneasiness

All the emotions of a woman bent on revenge. If only she felt the same, then perhaps her stomach would stop rolling.

She pulled away, fighting the temptation to delve deeper.

It was time to leave, time to prove her convictions. Letting go of Medea, Aria hugged Cam around the neck. "Watch over Talon," she whispered in his ear. "Keep him safe until I return."

The *rohha* tossed his head. Aria left, following Medea out the door and onto the deserted street. Walking away from the village, the trees engulfed them in moments.

"Is it far?" Aria asked her guide who walked gracefully

ahead. Even with moonlight, it was dim within the forest
as they trudged up the mountain trail. Aria stumbled over
a root.

"No. Not as far as some of the villagers would wish,
but far enough to hide from the children who used to play
in these woods."

"They do not anymore?"

"Not since the Reapers came. It is feared they will be
taken as slaves or hostages if they wander too far."

"Better to curb their play than—"

"Silent, my friend." Medea interrupted. "The walk is
still a distance, and you are not used to our thinner air.
Conserve your strength."

Medea was right. Aria focused on breathing and
keeping up with her guide. When the sun shed its first
light through the trees, Medea stopped. "We are here."

Aria shaded her eyes from the sun's beams that slanted
towards them. *Here* was a cliff. Impossibly high, it ran
past her length of vision. An appropriate place for a secret
entrance, and a well-kept secret it was. The cliff's face
was smooth with no large outcroppings that could hide a
tunnel.

"You wonder where it is, do you not." Medea ran her
palms over the rocky surface before them.

Aria squinted, still searching. Where could it be? How
did they manage to hide a door in solid stone? "I must say
I am surprised at the Reaper ingenuity. I did not know
they were such clever builders to hide the entrance in a
sheer wall."

Medea laughed, the sound surprisingly sinister in such
a ethereal creature. "They are not clever, merely strong. I
doubt they built the tunnel."

Aria paused in surprise. "Then who?"

Medea shrugged. "I do not know. Perhaps the
Builders."

"The Builders?"

"A local legend. It is said they flew, and that their ships
traveled both over the water and under it."

"What happened to them?" Aria asked, curious despite
the gravity of their situation.

"No one knows." Medea waved the musings away.
"Anyway, the tunnel is right..." she pressed against a large

rock. It slid away. "Here." She finished with a flourish.

Aria's heart skipped a beat.

Medea stepped into the opening and pulled a small handmade torch from a pocket on her robe. "I will lead."

Aria ducked to enter the tunnel behind her. Once inside, the size surprised her. She stood erect with no problem. She held her arms out towards the smooth walls, but they were out of her reach as was the earthen ceiling above her head.

In front of her, Medea pressed a lever, and the rock closed behind them with a dull thud. Darkness engulfed them. The sound of a tinderbox opening broke the silence. A single scratch, a beat of time, and the torch burned, giving just enough light for them to walk without stumbling. Medea reached back and took Aria's hand. "Do not be afraid. Soon, we will both get what we want."

Aria squeezed her hand, grateful for the touch. "As long as I have a friend for company, I will be fine."

Medea squeezed back, and they set off down the tunnel.

***

Talon woke to the sound of someone knocking on his door. "Wake up, Aria," he muttered, hoping to convince her to answer it.

The only answer was more knocking.

He opened his eyes. Except for him, the bed was empty. He bolted upright. Where was Aria? A flash of dread, tangible and real, settled over him like the blanket that covered his body.

The knocking continued.

He jumped from the bed and took his sword in hand. Naked, he faced the door and crouched into a fighting stance. "Enter."

The latch moved, and Lore stepped through, his long blond hair pulled back with a Warrior's leather cord. His eyes surveyed Talon's naked form. "I see you spent a most interesting, or should I say intimate, evening."

Talon glared at the comment and tossed his sword onto the empty bed. Now was not the time for jest.

"Where is the beautiful Mistress Aria?" Lore sat in one of the high-backed wooden chairs with a grand gesture.

Talon pulled his leggings on. "I do not know."

The laughter in Lore's eyes vanished, and he leaned forward. "What do you mean?"

Talon strapped his scabbard and blade to his hip. "Just that. I woke when you knocked, and she was gone."

Lore leaned back, his hand tapping the table as he thought. "Perhaps she is simply doing whatever it is that women do in the morning."

"I do not think so." Her nature and singular ability to find trouble dictated a more complex reason. That, and the feeling of dread that refused to depart.

"How could she leave without you knowing it?"

Talon flushed, grabbed his shirt off the floor, and tossed it on. "I do not know." Nevertheless, he knew exactly what had happened. For a night, he had let his heart rule, and now Aria was gone.

"Did she drug you? She is capable you know," Lore commented.

She had drugged him, but not with wine or medicine. She had drugged him with her love and her body. She had taken away his edge with the promise of unspoken possibilities.

Then, she used it to leave. But to where?

Taking a moment to shove his boots on, he pushed past his friend. He would find her if he had to search every house and every building. He could not take on the Reapers not knowing if she were safe.

Was that what she was doing? Did she hide, hoping to prevent the battle? He would not put it past her. If that were her plan, he would have strong words with her once he found her.

Slamming the door open, Talon strode out of the house with Lore at his side.

"Sir!" The shout came from behind. He stopped. A coarse brown robe swaddled about her, the owner of the house, caught up to him.

"What do you want?" he growled, waving her away.

"Are you looking for the young girl? The redhead?"

Talon stopped and grabbed her arm in one smooth motion. "What do you know? Is she all right? Where has she gone?"

The pudgy woman pulled her arm away, dusting his touch off. "I do not know where she went, but I saw her go towards the stables before the sun rose."

"Why did you not stop her?"

She frowned. "In this town, you don't pry."

"Why tell me now?"

She motioned Talon closer and raised herself up on pudgy toes. Her whisper carried no farther than his ears. "As courtesy to the cause. I see your anger and will not have you barging around town asking questions and getting us all killed with your ignorance."

She was right. Talon wrestled his anger under control. Stealth over brawn would gain more in a situation like this. He would start at the stables, and if he found nothing, he would go from there, but he would go with stealth and secrecy in mind.

"My thanks, madam." He turned on his heel.

"Why the stables?" Lore asked as they strode through the already crowded streets. "Do you think she took a *rohha?*"

"Not likely," Talon answered, thinking of Aria's limited experience with the beasts. She knew only Cam, and he was battle trained. The others would most likely be like the first *rohha* she rode, ill tempered and trained for menial tasks.

The wide door was already open, and the stable master was sweeping the stalls. A *rohha's* head poked itself out and stared at him. Cam. He was still here. Aria had not taken him. So where was she? Why had she come here?

"Warrior?"

The stable master tossed a folded piece of parchment to them. "I found this stuck to your *rohha's* stall this morning."

Talon caught it in the air. Perhaps Aria had left him an explanation, and his fears were not as tangible as they felt.

 He unfolded the small square.

"Is it from Mistress Aria?" Lore's expression remained grim.

Talon read the words. His heart sank. "No, but it does say where she is." He folded the scrap carefully back up and put it in the leather pouch at his waist. "She has been betrayed."

***

The tunnel is getting smaller. Aria shoved the thought from her mind. It wormed its way back. She took a deep breath. Tighter and tighter, the walls grew closer with each step. She spread her arms like a *bykla* in flight. She touched nothing but air. The walls were the same distance as when she and Medea entered this empty, dark, realm. It was her perception that had changed. She was losing focus. Losing control.

Remember the goal, she reminded herself. *The dark is but a moment in time. An uncomfortable stretch that will be banished by the light of Talon's smile when he holds his son in his arms.* She let thoughts of Tarik, Talon, and their reunion soothe her. A bit of soil trickled from above, dusting her face. She coughed.

"Are you all right?" Medea's voice echoed past Aria and returned.

The small flame from her torch cast eerie shadows over her delicate features, and for a moment, Aria saw a demon. A spirit. Not Medea. The illusion disappeared. Relieved, Aria coughed again and waved Medea forward. "Yes. Just a bit of dirt."

The girl laughed, the sound carrying in the silence. "I suppose there is enough of that around here."

Silently, Aria thanked the Goddess for her new friend. Such a brave woman. So delicate, yet so tough to have survived the Reaper's cruelty. When this was over, she would ask Medea to go with her and Talon. Offer her a new life away from those who judged her.

The ground started to rise.

"Almost there," Medea called over her shoulder.

Aria took a deep breath. Tarik. She lightly touched the currents, hoping to feel him. The same wall blocked her. A tangible shield that allowed no access to the Keep. Had the Builders constructed a spiritual wall to keep out even Trancers? It would be an impressive feat. No matter. Soon she would hold her son. Kiss his tiny hands. Touch his soft skin. Tears filled her eyes, but she wiped them away. There would be time for tears when they were all safe.

The tunnel stopped, ending in a wooden wall. Dusty and dry, it was clearly once in better condition. "This is it," Medea pronounced, resting her free hand on a large lever. "Wait here. I will check to make sure our passage is clear."

Aria stopped Medea with a hand on her shoulder. Her guide had been through enough. "I will not have you risk yourself for me."

Medea shook her off. "I understand your desire, but please understand that you could kill us both with lack of knowledge. The entrance opens into a sheltered cove, so there is little danger there. The peril comes in what lays beyond the shadows. I know the Reapers. I know their ways. I will know what to look for. Do not let your pride kill us both."

Aria bit her lower lip. She hated to admit it, but Medea was right. To insist otherwise was nothing other than conceit.

"You agree?" her guide prompted.

"I suppose," Aria said, although letting Medea take such a chance left a troubled feeling in the pit of her stomach. "But come back if there is any sign of danger."

"I promise." Medea pulled the lever. The panel slid aside, gliding as if on a sheen of oil.

"Be careful," Aria whispered.

Her guide nodded and stepped away.

Aria waited. Time crawled. She shifted nervously. A footstep approached. She held her breath. It went past. Nothing. Her knees weakened in relief, and she leaned against a wall. Where was Medea? Had they captured her? Did they torture her even now? Panic rose. Aria stepped towards the panel and stopped. *Patience.* She forced her runaway imagination under control. *It just feels like forever.*

A woman's scream rent the air.

All hesitation gone, Aria ran through the door. The room opened before her. It was occupied by a small group of unwashed men. Reapers. Medea stood in the middle of them, unchained and unhampered, her hands on her hips, and screaming.

Aria stopped mid-step.

Medea's shouts died. She doubled over, and a different sound emerged. Laughter.

What was going on? Ready to bolt, Aria stepped backwards.

Still laughing, Medea nodded to the men. From the shadows, two stepped forward and grabbed Aria's arms, their thick fingers digging into her flesh.

The Reapers joined in Medea's mirth.

The scene became clear. A cry of betrayal sounded through the room. Aria realized the hoarse shout was her own.

By the Goddess, how could she have been so wrong? She had trusted Medea. Cared for her. Still in shock, Aria did not struggle as the Reapers dragged her forward and threw her to the ground at Medea's feet.

"Help me, my Goddess." Aria's whispered prayer was lost in the jeers and hoots of the Reapers. An early lesson flashed through her mind. The Goddess only showed the path, it was up to the person to walk it. What path was the Goddess showing her? Death? A test of faith?

The road before her remained unseen. Instead, she saw Talon. He searched for her. He worried for her. He believed in her.

She would not let him down. Fury at the betrayal, and fury at her own naiveté, engulfed her. If Medea planned to kill her, she would not die like an animal. She would be strong like her Warrior.

She would die on her feet.

Legs wobbling, she stood to face her betrayer.

Gone was the beauty. Silent was the friendship. Medea reached out with a delicate finger. "Welcome to my home." She raked a nail along Aria's jaw, drawing blood. *"Trancer."*

Nineteen

"If you ride up to the Keep in daylight they will kill you before you can make it past the gate."

Talon ignored the remark as he readied Cam for battle. Lore and Orrin stood on each side of him, each man urging him to reason. They did not understand. Medea had taken Aria.

Medea. As sweet as a crystalline morning and deadly as a viper's bite, her laughter echoed through his memories. She had wanted him once and begged him to kill her lover, Mako. He had refused and escorted her from his room. She had screamed at him, ranting that he would pay.

Laughing, he had thrown her shoes to her.

Now, years later, she had made good her promise. He squeezed his hands into tight fists, his leather gloves creaking in protest.

"Talon, you cannot do this. It is suicide."

"Perhaps, but I see no other choice. They knew about Aria. They knew where to find Cam. Imagine how much more they know, or worse, imagine what they will do to Aria to find out."

"I cannot let you go." Lore rested his hand on the hilt of his sword.

"You would use that," Talon followed the movement, "to stop me?"

Lore's hand fell away from the weapon. "Of course not, I would simply remind you of what is at stake here."

"Aria's life."

"And the village. Would you storm the Keep and put others at risk?" Lore gestured towards Orrin. "He has a plan if you will but hear him out."

Talon yanked Cam's reins from his pack. "The time for planning is over. The Reapers know we come and will be waiting for an attack to be mounted."

"Then we wait," Orrin countered.

"For what? Aria to die—or worse?" He remembered what Reapers did to women, misusing them in the worst way a man could misuse a woman. His mind went back to Medea. She had liked the pain and domination. She claimed it gave her power, and it did. As much as he was capable, Mako loved her. It was he who scarred her, branding her wrists to show her who her master was.

Medea wore the scars with pride.

Talon shuddered. What would Mako do to his Aria?

He would not give the Reaper lord enough time to harm her. He made to vault onto Cam's back.

Orrin laid a hand on his shoulder, stopping him.

"Take your hand off me before I do it myself." Talon forced the words through gritted teeth. Orrin was a good man, and he did not want to hurt him, but he would.

Orrin removed his hand. "Please, listen to what I have to say. We can wait a while longer. Aria will neither die nor be hurt. Not today."

"How would you know that?"

Nervously, Orrin glanced around and drew closer to Talon, motioning Lore to listen. "I have a man in the Keep. He has managed to get word to me. She is captured, but safe for now."

"How can your man guarantee her safety? Mako is as unpredictable as a water starved *volen.*"

"He plans a feast for tonight to display his newest prize."

Talon tightened. "Aria is no trophy to be displayed."

"A Trancer is a great prize to Mako."

"They know she is a Trancer?" The news was not the shock it should have been. The Reapers seemed to know everything else, why not this last bit of information?

"It is why they want her. They plan to use her skills."

The same fear, that she would enter Trancer consciousness and never emerge, consumed Talon. To lose her to the currents was unthinkable. To let her perish while enslaved was unforgivable. By the Goddess, he would not let that happen. Mako would die by his hands. "Feast or no, our plan will not work if Mako knows about it, and I promise you, he almost certainly does."

"I know he does. I made sure of it," Orrin said.

"You did what?" Talon's hand instinctively went to the hilt of his sword, and he took a step forward.

"I made sure he found out. I needed him to if I wanted our new idea to work."

"New idea?"

Lore explained. "Orrin's men were nervous about your Reaper's sword, so he held back some information from you."

Talon curled his lip. "Yet he told you?"

"Only just this morning."

Orrin continued. "There is a tunnel. A secret passage that leads into the lower part of the Keep. Tonight, my men attack the gates, distracting the Reapers and drawing them away from the tunnel—."

"While we take the Keep from behind?" Talon finished.

Orrin nodded. "Exactly."

"Why have you not used this passage before?" It seemed suspicious to him to have such an advantage and to have not used it.

"We did not have enough men to mount both a frontal assault as well as a rear one. With the Reaper's numbers, one assault by itself would fail, as both the gates and tunnel are sure to be guarded. We need both assaults if we are to stand any chance of success."

The explanation was sound, and although the plan was a simple one, sometimes those were the best. Even with the arrival of the Warriors, they barely had enough for a two-part attack, but it was something Mako might not suspect. If he knew of Talon's arrival, and Medea would make sure of it, then he would only remember the Talon from long ago. The Talon of Mako's memory was headstrong and often let passion overcome judgment. The Talon of the Reapers would have stormed the Keep alone.

Alone, much like he had planned to do before Orrin and Lore spoke to him. He eyed the reins still clenched in his fist. Was being near Mako changing him? Influencing him to behave like the man he used to be? Not the man he had become?

He could not let passion rule him. He had to hold onto the Warrior within—the man who ruled with his mind, not his heart. It was the only way to save Aria. The only way to outwit Mako in his own element. Anything else would get them all killed. His friends were right about that.

He took a deep breath, held it, and released his anger, driving it away in the same breath. The reins fell from his fingers.

A question came to mind. "What makes you think that Mako is not herding us towards such a plan?"

"My man assures me otherwise."

"How well do you know this man who claims to be helping us?" Talon asked. "How do we know that it was not he that informed on us?"

Orrin's lips curved down. "He is my brother. I would trust him with my life. Mako is quite pleased with himself and the capture of your woman. He plans the feast, but he has no idea of how many we are or how strong. He knows nothing of Lore and your men. He knows only of the resistance and that you lead it."

Interesting. Mako did not know of the Warriors arrival? His mind searched through the events of yesterday. Whoever had informed on them, probably Medea, must have overheard the initial conversation he had at the alehouse with Orrin because Lore arrived afterwards. A surge of guilt rushed through him.

He had caused Aria's capture.

***

How long had she been in the cell? A day? A night? A season?

It seemed like forever.

Sitting on the dirt floor, Aria wrapped her arms around her legs. She glanced up. A high vertical slit on the outer wall, too slim to call a window, offered little light and even less hope.

She rested her head against her knees. How could she have been so blind? She had asked herself the same question again and again. Medea had seemed so friendly. So truthful.

For once, she wished she had ignored righteousness and delved the woman's mind to find her true intentions.

But she had not. Now, she waited for rescue, death, or opportunity. Death seemed the most likely. The thought of rescue both thrilled and appalled her. Did Talon search for her, or had he figured out where she was? If so, he would most definitely storm the Keep in hopes of rescuing her.

And she had wanted so badly to rescue him.

Now, all she could do was wait and hope.

It would be tolerable if she could see her son and Iliana,

but Medea denied her even that comfort. It was not a surprise. Once she revealed her true self, her guide had emerged as a vindictive, small-hearted, and evil woman.

"Aria?"

She raised her head, peering into the dimness. Someone kneeled on the dusty ground, calling to her. Iliana? No, the shorthaired vision was outside the bars and dressed in a clean gown of a rich red color. Aria rested her head back on her knees. What would Medea not do?

"Aria, please. It is I, Iliana."

Aria covered her head with her hands.

"Please, listen to me."

The girl sounded so much like her best friend that Aria almost looked up. She stopped herself. She would not give Medea the satisfaction. "Go away. You are not Iliana. Tell Medea that her plan failed."

"I am Iliana. I can prove it. I called out the name of your Given on the beach."

The information was too common. All knew of the ceremony, but the small truth had to come from somewhere. What had they done to her friend to get that bit of knowledge? Bile rose in Aria's throat.

The girl kept talking. "The day after the Given ceremony, you gave me a necklace of *isi* flowers. You said we were sisters of the heart."

The memory touched her. It was a piece of life so minor that only her friend would know or care about it. Aria raised her head. "Iliana?"

"Yes." The figure stretched her arm through the bars, imploring Aria to come to her.

Aria wanted to believe her. Was it really her closest friend calling to her, or was her mind gone? Cautiously, Aria scooted over on hands and knees, just out of reach of the hand that beckoned her.

"Please," the figure implored.

Before she thought any farther, Aria reached out. Fingers met and held. Familiar warmth flooded her.

Iliana. It was true.

The hand pulled her closer. Another joined it, embracing her through the bars. Tears wet Aria's cheeks. Hers or her friends, it did not matter.

"How touching."

Both turned. Medea stood at the entrance to the chamber, leaning against the wall. "It is always so uplifting to see two friends reunited."

The women parted. Iliana stood, brushing the dust off her dress. "What are you doing here?"

"Watching you and Aria. Who knows, I may learn something."

Iliana laughed.

Aria's brows knit together at the sound. It was not the sound she remembered. This was a mocking laugh. Cruel.

"The day a *rohha* learns to speak is the day you learn something beside how to be a thieving, sadistic, stupid whore." Hands clenched at her sides, Iliana stepped towards Medea. "Leave us, *whore*."

Medea raised her hand and closed the gap until the two women were only a breath away from each other.

Using the bars to pull herself up, Aria watched the conflict with shock. The woman in red spoke with Iliana's voice and moved with her womanly grace, but the Iliana she remembered would never threaten another in such a manner. What would this new person do if Medea hit her?

Probably hit back.

"Lay a hand on me, and I will tell your master."

Even in the dim light, Medea's scowl was visible. "I do not care."

"You should. You know the rules. He no longer beds you, so do not think you are above them." Iliana tucked a short curl behind her ear. The silence grew, lengthening as Iliana and Aria waited to see what Medea would do.

Finally, Medea shot Iliana a look of pure loathing and dropped her hand. Turning in a swirl of skirts, she stomped from the room.

Iliana laughed again. The sound followed Medea.

"What are the rules?" Aria asked, both curious and concerned as to what her friend, this woman she no longer knew, would say in return.

The laughter stopped. Weariness passed over Iliana's face. "The rules? No man, no woman may touch me in anger or to do harm. They do, and they die."

"Mako has kept this promise?"

Iliana rested against the bars, forehead on her hands. "More than once."

Mako protected her. Why? Was she his newest lover? Was that why she roamed free? Aria shuddered. What had her friend done to survive?

Had that survival included Tarik?

She both craved and feared the answer. She let the words slip past her lips before apprehension stopped them. "Where is my son?"

Iliana raised her head. "Safe in my room."

Tarik lives. She had known it in her heart. Felt it in her soul. Still, to have it confirmed and her inner doubts banished made her want to shout. To cry. To laugh. She leaned into the bars. "When can I see him?"

"Tonight."

It was too long a wait. Her feet danced in impatience. "Not before? I know this is a joyless place, but please bring him to me. Just for a moment."

Iliana shook her head. "Mako has forbidden it."

Aria's heart crashed, and the dancing stopped. "You do what he says?"

Her friend turned away, bitterness covering her features like a mask. "Do you think I have a choice?"

"I do not know." Time with Mako and the Reapers had changed her friend, but Aria could not be sure of how much. Where did Iliana's loyalties lie?

Iliana gestured at the surroundings. "Do not let the fact that I am out here and you are behind the bars fool you. I am as much a prisoner as yourself, only my bars are the kind you cannot see." She squeezed her eyes shut. "Why have you not asked my about my hair?"

"What do you mean?" Iliana's hair was shortened, but it seemed of little importance in light of the danger that surrounded them.

"My hair." Iliana's voice rose a notch, and she grabbed a handful of the short strands between her fingers. "Can you not see that it is gone?"

Aria took a step back. "Of course."

"I disobeyed once, and he cut it off."

"But if he protects you and has not truly harmed—"

"Another slip and he warned it would be my throat. Or Tarik's, and he would do it. He always does what he says. Even if it means killing a man for talking to me in the wrong tone of voice." Iliana wrapped her arms around herself.

The heat of shame burned Aria's cheeks. Oh Goddess, what had she done? She had judged her best friend—the one who had saved her son by sacrificing not just the silky black strands that crowned her head, but also the light that lived within. The heat deepened. She did not deserve such a friendship. "I am sorry." Small words, but they were the only ones she managed to push past the lump in her throat.

"So am I." For a moment, Aria saw the untainted Iliana emerge. The woman she knew before the Tower was destroyed, along with their lives.

Then the friend of her memory disappeared, lost behind the hard countenance of the stranger who stood before her.

"No matter. Now, we have to save you and Tarik."

No noise broke the silence that separated them. Not another prisoner's cry, not the sound of movement above. Aria nodded. Once they were free, they could speak of what happened. Now, it was time to focus on gaining their freedom. "What do you propose we do?"

"Mako is having a feast to celebrate your capture. The acquisition of a Trancer."

Aria frowned. "He has you, why would another matter?"

"I am a Trancer no longer."

Aria knew her jaw dropped at Iliana's words, but she was unable to hide her shock. "What do you mean?"

Iliana wrapped her arms even tighter around herself, clinging to the only person she could. "I am unable to surf the currents."

It was not possible. One did not just stop being a Trancer. "H-how?"

Iliana shook her head. "I do not know. All I know is that the other side is closed to me."

"For how long?" It was so unbelievable.

Iliana shook her head again. "When I arrived here, I tried to reach you, and that was when I found out."

A stray thought popped into Aria's head. "Did you try to reach me before you arrived here?"

Iliana loosened her hold on herself. "No. I was too foolish, too scared, to even try."

"So it has only been since you entered these walls that your skills have disappeared?"

"Since I noticed, yes," Iliana answered, her voice tinged with impatience.

The stray thought blossomed into revelation. A gleam of hope she could offer her friend. "Perhaps it is not you."

"Then what?"

"This Keep."

"The Keep? Are you saying theses walls have powers to stop a Trancer?" Iliana scoffed.

"Hear me out. I have tried to touch you or Tarik more than once after you left. Each time something stopped me. Something not natural."

Iliana paused, her expression wary. "What do you mean?"

Aria reached through the bars and touched her friend's hand. Iliana flinched, but did not pull away. "There is a local legend of a group of Builders. It is said they made wondrous things. I think they made the wall that keeps us out."

"Where did you hear of this legend?"

"Medea told me—"

"Believe nothing that whore has to say," Iliana spat.

Aria understood Iliana's passion and could not disagree, but what was said about the Builders carried the taste of truth. "It does explain why I could not enter," she offered.

Iliana pulled away. "You were tired. Weak. Have you tried to trance now that you are in the Keep?"

"No."

"Then do it. Surf the currents and enter my thoughts. I bet a coin that you can."

Aria nodded with a smile. She would show Iliana that Trancing in the Builder's domain was impossible. Sitting in Trancer position, Aria closed her eyes, and breathed. *Focus.* The simple word spiraled through her thoughts. In with a breath, out with another. The gray void loomed, and then she was though it and in Iliana's mind. No longer bright blues, greens and white, her friend's mind reflected the bleak thoughts she carried within. Bitter red, deep purples and midnight blue.

And something different. A solid wall that lacked color.

Black as the deepest night, it surrounded most of Iliana's thoughts. The truth struck Aria like a physical blow. It was not the Builders that kept her away. It was not the Builders' wall that blocked her. It was her friend. Stronger than she thought, or perhaps made so by her capture, she kept out all who would be near her.

Including any who would help her.

She laid a mental hand on the dark slab, and a barrage of fear and pain overwhelmed her. With a sharp inhalation, she was back in her body. She opened her eyes. Iliana was on the floor, curled up in a ball.

What had happened?

"Get out of my mind. Get out of my mind." Sobbing, Iliana rocked back and forth.

Carefully, Aria rested her still throbbing head in her hands, shocked and disheartened by what she had seen. The Elders spoke of many things, but never something like this. "I am out."

The sobbing stopped. "It hurt. It never hurt before."

"I am sorry." But why had she been able to enter Iliana's mind at all? Why now and not before? Perhaps the proximity. Perhaps the flicker of hope in her friend's eyes. A tear of pain, distress for her friend who hid behind the darkness of her own mind, slid down Aria's cheek.

"You owe me a coin." Iliana's voice was hoarse.

"I will give you two."

"I do not want you to do that again."

"I know."

Iliana pushed the short strands of her hair away from her pale skin and stood. Dirt covered her red gown and stained her cheeks. She did not dust it off this time. "I told you the fault lay within me."

"There is no fault."

"No, I told you—"

"We will talk of this later." Aria cut her off. She knew the real Iliana lay trapped behind a wall made of anger, betrayal, self-loathing and a thousand other little hates. It was not a wall broken easily or in a single conversation.

Perhaps not at all. By the Goddess, what had Mako done?

Iliana paced in front of the cell, all traces of pain replaced by the inscrutable expression of one who knows what must be done. The rich cloth of her gown whipped her ankles as she walked. "I came to tell you what is going to happen and what you must do if you want to live."

Her friend was right, now was the time for action. Healing would wait. Aria drew closer.

"At the feast, Mako will want to show you off as his newest prize." Iliana continued to pace. "He will ask you to enter the minds of his enemies and find their vulnerable points."

She was not the first Trancer to be asked to do the forbidden, and she would not be the first to refuse. "He must know that I will not comply."

Iliana stopped and gripped the bars, her intensity as tangible as the wall that surrounded her soul. "He does. In fact, he is counting on it."

Aria's brow rose. "What do you mean?"

"You must understand that power is everything to Mako. Power over life. Power over death. Power over others. Even more important than information is his need to triumph over you. Once he has that, the rest will come."

"He cannot make a Trancer use her powers for ill."

"He can if he threatens your son."

The fact that Mako knew Tarik was her son was not the shock it should have been.

The anger in her blue eyes as bright as a flame, Iliana continued, "I think I found a way to beat him."

"How?"

"I overheard him talking to his first man. At the feast, he will bring in a prisoner for you to read. Refuse to do it as you normally would. He will insist and threaten Tarik. After much protest, you will give in and do as he asks, letting him win."

Aria gasped at the thought before she could stop herself.

Iliana continued. "What you do not understand is that it is not a prisoner you will Trance. It is one of his men. That is what he will want you to find out."

"Why the elaborate scheme? Why not a real prisoner?"

"I am not sure, but I have spent enough time with him to know that he trusts no one. I suppose it would be easier to see if you were being truthful if he knew the outcome ahead of time."

The test was Warrior-like in strategy, and so was Iliana's countermove and her own role. She sent a small prayer to the Goddess that she would live to tell Talon about it. "I will do as you ask, and with the help of the Goddess, we may yet walk away from here."

"Do not hope too hard. I did, and it came to naught."

Aria reached through the bars. "I am here now. Do not say hope is for naught."

Iliana did not take her hand. "You are in a cage. I am without the keys. Your son is used against you, and the Keep's whore wants you dead. How can you still hope?"

Through the currents, Aria felt Iliana's wall solidify and grow stronger. Keeping out all who would touch her heart.

Still, Aria had faith. Faith in Talon, faith in herself, and faith in her Goddess. "You have given me the only hope I have. How is it you cannot feel the same?"

Iliana's eyes brightened, then she blinked, and any emerging faith in their future was shuttered back behind her mask of indifference. "I will see you tonight. I must go before Mako begins to question what I am doing here." Turning on her heel, Iliana ran from the room.

***

Mako plugged the hole in the wall with its wooden stopper. The Builders of the Keep had been wondrous indeed, even building a listening device that went from the prison to the main bedchamber—a perfect place for a ruler to learn secrets without others knowing. The small opening, perfectly drilled, made the merest whisper audible. He pushed the plug until it was flush with the wall, and then let the heavy, deep-red curtain fall back into place. It would not do for others to know *his* advantages.

Satisfied, he strode across the vast stone room towards the bed. Retrieving a bottle of wine from the bedside table, he put the bottle to his lips and took a long pull, savoring the richness on his tongue. He had waited for the dark-haired Trancer, his Iliana, denying his own pleasure in the hope to gain her trust and thus, restore her Trancing abilities. Now the waiting was over. Aria had proven herself, and he could bed Iliana without the worry that he would further damage her abilities. After he exposed their little scheme, Iliana would be a submissive, if not willing, partner. The leather ties that graced each corner of the bed caught his eye. Hopefully not too submissive. He chuckled to himself.

As for the resistance, they were only a distraction. If Medea had not learned of their plan, it was possible their attack may have worked. Although few in numbers, few could do much when properly motivated. Now, their confidence was gone, fled with Aria's capture. They would attack because of her situation and their foolish sense of honor. And they would die. Not a simple death, either, but a slaughter.

Then, when the carnage was over and both Trancers were broken, he would take Iliana and make her his. Introduce her to the art of love in ways she had never imagined. Thank her with passion for the little demonstration that proved Aria was what she was not. "Tonight, my beauty, I will take you here, by this window, for all the world to see. For all to know that you are mine."

He took another long pull from the bottle. It was going to be a busy evening.

Twenty

Formidable.

It was the first word that came to mind as Talon visually measured the hand-cut ironrock that made up the walls of the Keep.

He waited at the edge of the trees and watched the daylight fade. Cam moved, restless beneath him. Soon, Mako would celebrate Aria's capture. The thought made Talon's stomach roll. He remembered some of the Reaper leader's parties. The Reapers dined and drank until they were numb. Mako arrived only after he had personally broken the prisoner.

What would the Reaper leader do to break Aria? What would he ask of her?

Something that would tear at her tender heart? Her mind? Her body? If she succumbed to him, it would prove his mastery, and he would demand more. If she refused, Talon feared Mako would kill her. Or worse.

There were things worse than death, and Mako knew them all.

"My Given, I am coming for you," Talon whispered into the night air, hoping her Trancer abilities would allow her to feel his presence if not hear his voice. "Be brave."

Cam tossed his head and shuffled from leg to leg. Talon patted the *rohha's* neck. Was his small group of men as restless? He peered over his shoulder and into the woods. If so, they gave no sign of it. Not a man was visible, but he knew they were there. Motionless, they waited for him to give the signal. Once given, they would loose arrows to hold the Reapers at bay while he scaled the wall to open the gate.

If all went as planned, their small band would occupy the enemy while Lore and the larger contingent of Warriors slipped in through the tunnel and took the Reapers by surprise. A risky plan, but it was all they had.

If it worked, Aria would be free before Mako could harm her.

The last rays of the sun disappeared, and the shadows grew into night. It was time to attack. Talon thrust his sword above his head, raised his face to the night sky, and screamed out Aria's name, the word falling from his lips like a Warrior's battle cry. Arrows flew over his head and towards the Keep.

Howls of outrage and pain sounded seconds later, and a single Reaper fell from the top of the wall. A return volley was fired.

Time to ride. Man and beast bolted forward, carrying both within range of the Reapers' returning shots. An arrow whistled past Talon, so close it grazed Cam. The *rohha* did not falter but continued onwards.

They reached the wall. Talon reined Cam in and slid from his back. More arrows flew above him and over the Keep's wall, keeping the Reapers occupied. Grimly, he smiled, grateful for the skill of the men who chose to walk this dangerous path with him.

Pulling a rope and hook from Cam's back, he wondered what would greet him when he reached the top of the wall. He slapped the *rohha* on the rump. "Go."

Cam pawed the ground and dashed back towards the trees.

Swinging the rope above his head, Talon let the momentum carry it up and over the wall. He tugged hard. The hook caught. Time to prove his worth.

Hand over hand, he scaled the wall, expecting to fall to his death when a Reaper cut the line. White knuckled, he grabbed the top of the parapet and pulled himself over. Twenty lengths away, one of the Reapers rained arrows down on the men in the woods, so intent on killing them that he never saw Talon.

"Shortsighted fool," Talon muttered.

As if hearing his words, the Reaper turned, his arrow notched.

In a singular swift motion, Talon dropped to one knee, pulled a short knife from his boot, and threw it.

The Reaper fell backwards onto the cold stone, Talon's knife protruding from his throat.

Still crouched on the ground, Talon made a quick reconnaissance. There were less than ten Reapers on the Keep's walkway. Their ploy seemed to have worked. Mako always had been arrogant. Now, it would be his demise as long as the missing Reapers were at the feast and not waiting by the tunnel.

Standing, Talon pulled his sword from its sheath. He spotted the entry to some stairs and headed towards it. Running down the spiraled stairway, his boot clad feet were as sure in the dark as they were in the light. He held his sword at the ready.

He stopped when he reached the bottom and the open entry to courtyard. To the left and just ahead, he spotted the wheel and pulley system that opened the gate.

He also saw the two men who guarded it. Their swords still sheathed, they talked to each other, paying no attention to either their comrades on the rampart or the attackers in the trees.

One was young. Probably a new recruit. The other he recognized from his time as a Reaper. The man, Karr by name, had been conceited, filthy, and fat. From the state of his matted blonde hair and generous gut, not much had changed. No matter. Their past relationship held little bearing now. The man would either stand down or die. They had been comrades, not friends.

Reapers had no friends.

Talon stepped through the doorway. The men spotted him and unsheathed their swords in unison.

With a dancer's grace, Talon whirled his sword in a circle, the blade cutting through the air with a soft swoosh. "Stand aside."

"We missed your sword, Talon," Karr replied. A lethal smile on his bearded face changed his expression from surprise to delight. "Perhaps after I kill you, I will claim it as my own."

"Brave words for a man who fights like a one-legged *kaffa*," Talon taunted.

The Reapers charged.

Talon met them head on. The sound of metal-on-metal rang through the air as he parried one sword and then the other. In unison, the trio moved backward, then forward, each trying to overcome the other.

The younger Reaper parried and left his side open to a thrust. Talon pressed towards him, taking the advantage. His sword found unguarded flesh, and the Reaper died.

Karr did not spare his fallen comrade a glance, but came at Talon in full force. He sliced his sword through the air. Talon stopped it with his own blade. For a moment, the men were face to face, jaw to jaw, as each fought to defeat the other. "I've always wondered what it would be like to fight you." Karr grunted the words, his bulk no match for Talon's well-muscled strength.

Talon did not reply to the taunt. He cleared his mind of everything but his training, assessed the situation, and knew what he had to do.

He stepped away and rolled to the right. Karr stumbled forward, his great bulk caught off-guard. Now on his knees, Talon thrust his sword up at his off-balance opponent.

When Karr regained his footing, he found Talon's sword in his ribs.

The Reaper did not utter a word as he fell to the ground, dead.

Talon pulled his sword from the body, and wiped it on Karr's tunic. He glanced at the dead men at his feet and shook his head. What he wanted was Mako, not a war.

He shook the brief regret off his psyche. Now was not the time for recrimination or hesitation. It was time to stop Mako from ever taking a woman against her will or killing a child. It was time for revenge.

Revenge against the monster who killed my son, Talon thought, reveling in the bloodlust that roiled up like a sudden fire in his veins. It rose higher with each breath, tainting his vision with its red veil and making regret something found only in the recesses of his mind.

His strength returned, he grabbed the wheel, and cranked it around. The gate rose as high as his knees. Another turn and the gap reached waist high.

Under a barrage of arrows, his men ran from the safety of the trees and dove under the gate.

All were present. He motioned with his sword.

It was time to find Mako.

***

Wrists tied together, Aria lurched down the hallway as a Reaper poked her in the small of her back. His Reaper status was not nearly as offensive as his unwashed state. A waft of old sweat and unclean teeth assaulted her nose. A revolting combination, and one that made her want to retch.

It was either that, or the fact she was finally going to

meet the Reaper leader, Mako. Her knees shook at the thought, and she stumbled, crashing into the wall with her shoulder.

The Reaper jabbed her in the small of her back again, pushing her forward. "Walk, Trancer or I'll drag you by your hair."

He said the word "Trancer" as if he spewed something foul from his mouth. Aria glanced over her shoulder and shot her tormentor a scathing glance.

"I said walk," he commanded.

"Where to?" The retort escaped before she could stop it.

Without hesitation, the Reaper gripped the back of her neck and turned her head until she faced a door to her left. "Thank your Goddess that I do not snap your pretty neck," he muttered in her ear. "But Mako seems to think we need another mind-reading witch in our midst." He released her, pushing her forward. Aria stumbled again, but regained her footing. She did not look back. Her tormentor sounded as if he wanted a reason to hurt her.

She stopped at the door. A huge wooden structure, it was big enough to ride a *rohha* through and solid enough to withstand an assault. *The room behind it must be huge,* she thought. *More than enough room for the Reapers and their feast.*

"Open it."

Her wrists still tied, she took a deep breath and pushed.

The chamber opened before her. Smaller than she had thought, it was as dim as an underground grotto, and just as empty. She cocked her head in confusion. Where were the Reapers?

"I am so glad you decided to join me for dinner." The comment boomed in the silence, and a torch flared to life.

She set her focus towards the source. No, not empty. A single table graced the end of the room. A shadowed figure sat at it, waiting. Mako.

"The decision was not mine to make." Aria glanced backwards.

With a growl, her jailer shoved her forward. "Walk." Behind her, the door slammed shut, leaving her alone with the Reaper leader.

Stiffening her resolve, she made her way across the room, her footfalls bouncing off the bare stone walls and back to her ears. She stopped a few feet from her captor and took him in through hooded eyes.

Indifferent, lethal and quite handsome. The unconscious assessment caught her by surprise. Rich black garb clung to a well-muscled body. His short hair was clean and neat. His brown eyes gazed at her fearlessly, but it was not his physical presence, that held her attention. He had an aura, a presence that commanded respect, but it was respect born of fear, not love.

He was everything Iliana had said and much she had not.

With slow deliberation, the Reaper leader stood, unfolding himself from the chair. He was as tall as Talon. He stared at Aria, capturing her eyes with his own, unnerving her. "Please. Sit." His gaze moved to the chair that graced the other side of the table.

Aria sat. *Calm of mind. Calm of body.* She recited the mantra in her thoughts, but it went no further. Her hands shook. She hid them under the table. If she did not find her center, she would never be able to do what was needed.

She shut her eyes and saw Talon. He battled. His sword swung like the hand of righteousness as he destroyed his foes. His strength and resolution shone like a holy light.

She watched her Giver win the fight and move on. Her focus wavered. She could not tell if the vision was present or future. It did not matter. If he were here, would he see the same strength in her? Or only her weakness?

If she could not gather herself, do as she had planned and make Mako believe her, she knew what the answer would be.

Calm of mind. Calm of body.

"Are you ill, Trancer?" Mako asked.

Aria jumped at the voice behind her and opened her eyes. Mako stood behind her now. His presence was solid and menacing.

"I said, are you ill?"

The concern in his tone, the warmth of the question, displaced her fear with anger, strengthening her. Did he think she was stupid? That she would fall victim to a handsome shell and false affection? "No, but eating could prove to be a problem." She held up her bound wrists.

Wielding a small knife, Mako reached over and around her.

She stiffened.

Instead of plunging the blade into her heart, he cut the rope that bound her. "Eat."

Aria tried not to flinch as his hot breath caressed her unprotected neck. "Are you dining as well?"

The air sucked away from her as he straightened and walked to the other side of the table. He did not sit, but smiled down at her. "Perhaps later. For now, I will watch you enjoy your meal."

Refusing to meet his gaze, Aria rubbed the raw welts and wished Iliana had mentioned that she would be alone with him. She poked at a platter of meat with her tong. She was not much of a flesh eater, and this looked as if it were just cut from the animal.

"Is there something wrong with the food. I can have something else brought if you want." Mako offered.

"It is fine." Selecting a slightly more cooked slab of flesh, Aria placed it on her plate and cut off a small piece.

It tasted like dust in her mouth.

Satisfied, Mako nodded. Tapping the flat of his knife against his palm, he began to pace. Tap. Step. Tap. Step. Then a turn, which brought him within a breath of Aria's unguarded back. She held in the need to shudder, the urge to pull away.

Tap. Step. He walked away from her. "After the meal, I will require your assistance. I have a prisoner who refuses to tell me the location of his followers."

A wave of relief swept over Aria. This was what she had expected, what she waited for. She did not say a word, but watched Mako out of the corner of her eyes. He turned back. Tap. Step. She swallowed the tasteless piece of flesh. *Let him make the first move.*

Tap. Step. He was behind her again. He stopped. "I want you to break his mind for me. Conventional torture has been, shall we say, unsuccessful."

Conventional torture? Mako spoke the phrase casually, as if torture were normal dinner conversation. Thank the Goddess this was all a game to test her. She raised an eyebrow, ready to play her part. "You know it is forbidden for a Trancer to delve the mind of an unwilling subject, much less break that mind."

She felt a tug as her braid lifted away from her neck. A flash of Mako's blade caught her eye, but did not connect with her flesh. In horror, she reached back. The waist length strands were still intact. What had he done?

He answered her question when she heard his knife slip back into its leather sheaf and felt her braid being undone. He had cut the leather thong that bound it.

"Yes, but under the circumstances, you will do as I bid." Now her hair was free and Mako buried his hands in the red mass, weighing it.

Aria shut her eyes and reminded herself this was but a game Mako played with her. To flinch from his touch would declare him the winner. "You cannot make me do the unthinkable," she managed to say.

He released her hair from his grasp with a laugh. "Now is not the time to discuss such matters." Walking back around the table, he returned to his chair. Sitting, he speared a piece of meat from the platter. "After you have eaten, we will see what it is you will and will not do."

Her captor played with her like a *katah'* played with its food. First smacking with the extended claw, and then pulling back to see what the prey would do. Would it run? Would it cower in fear?

She straightened. She would not be his prey.

The great door opened, and Mako looked up. The sounds of shouting accompanied the Reaper who entered. It sounded like a battle.

Her heart beat faster. Talon? A surge of determination—a Warrior's will and conviction—flooded her senses. Yes. She was sure it was him. Her vision was true. The attack raged.

The Reaper walked towards them, stopped in front of Mako, and stood at attention, waiting for his leader's acknowledgment.

Mako nodded. The man leaned forward to mutter something. Aria strained, but she could not hear their words.

She did not need to. Mako's change of expression told her more than words ever would. It was as dark as a nightmare, as deep as a well.

"Take a contingent." He spat the words, the fury beneath them barely contained.

The man nodded and walked away. The sounds of shouting halted with the closing of the door.

The strain was tangible as Mako continued the meal. He gestured for Aria to eat. She broke off a bit of bread and stared at it. What was happening?

Now, the sounds of shouting, so loud that they broached the thick walls, broke the silence. With each cry, Aria watched Mako's grip on his knife tighten. It did not matter. Now that she knew Talon had come for her, it was even more important for her to succeed in the charade. Perhaps she could buy enough time for Talon to reach her and Tarik.

The door opened again, and Aria's gaze jerked up. It was not Talon. Another Reaper entered and walked over. Disappointment nipped at her. She pushed it away.

"Speak. Are the rebels contained?"

The man shifted from one foot to another. "No, my Lord Mako."

"Why not?" Mako asked, the words forced from his clenched jaw and gritted teeth.

The messenger shifted again. "There were more than we thought, Lord Mako."

"How many more?"

"Two contingents of Warriors have joined them."

Mako rose to his feet. Gone was the rage. Vanished was the anger. In its place, calm descended. An unreadable mask that was far more frightening.

"What would you have us do?" The messenger stammered the question.

"Take the remaining intruders and kill them, of course. I want their heads on spears by morning."

The man backed away. "As you wish."

Mako smiled. "I will join you after I have finished with her."

Aria cringed as a wave of hate, black in its purity, rolled over her, touching her Trancer senses. She recognized it from the Tower and the night her people died. No matter that he attempted to play the gracious host, there was no mercy in this man. No caring. And there was something more, something beneath the blackness. She shut her eyes and focused, skimming his mind. Knowledge. Somehow, he knew everything she and Iliana had discussed. Another wave of hate rolled over her, through her. Her stomach fell. What had they been thinking, believing they could fool this man? No, not a man. A dark angel bent on destroying everything.

She opened her eyes to see him staring at her. Assessing her. Gazing at her as if he knew she searched his soul.

He said nothing, but pulled a rope. Within moments, Iliana appeared. She had to warn her. Tell her friend that Mako knew of their scheme. Tell her to take Tarik and run. Aria sank into her chair. Warn her how? Iliana was mind deaf and to shout would be to endanger them all further.

"Get the child, and bring him here." Mako barked the order. His eyes never left Aria's.

Iliana bowed her head in acknowledgment, and Aria's heart sank. *No*, she begged silently. *Keep him safe.*

Head still down, Iliana left, only to return moments later with Aria's son in her arms.

"Tarik." His name was like the first breath of life upon Aria's lips. She reached for him, and Iliana placed him in her arms. He wiggled and waved his arms. Her heart broke into a thousand pieces, and then mended, filling the hollow space that had been created with his loss. *So alive. So perfect.* Bending her head, Aria kissed his chubby hand as he tugged at her hair, and for a moment, there was no battle. No fear. There was only mother and child.

"Enough." Mako's command broke through the tiny flash of hope, and he took Tarik from Aria's arms.

She reached out. The loss, so soon after she had just found him, was worse than a blade. Worse than when she woke and found her people dead.

Mako ignored her and held the babe up and out, surveying the young life like one would look at a wounded *rohha*. Was it worth saving, or would it be better to put the poor thing out of its misery?

Aria let her hand drop, mentally burning with fear that Mako would do worse than just hold her child.

A heartbeat later, he handed Tarik back to Iliana. "You are dismissed."

Even though her friend was deaf to the currents, Aria sent out a mental plea for Iliana to keep Tarik safe.

With a nod, almost as if she heard the appeal, Iliana stepped back through the curtain, taking Tarik with her.

Aria let go a sigh of relief. For now, her son was safe. Iliana would continue to protect him, as she had been doing for so long.

Mako turned his chill gaze on Aria. "I had hoped to let you play your game of intrigue. It amuses me to watch those who think they can outwit me."

A shout of outrage sounded in the hallway. The fighting was close. Another heartbeat and their rescue would be at hand. "What do you mean, outwit you?"

Mako must have sensed the urgency as well. His hand shot out, grabbing Aria's upper arm, and pulling her to him. His fingers dug into her tender flesh, and she winced. "Do not play games with me, Trancer. That time is past. You will do as I say, and do it now, or shall I bring Tarik back to help encourage you. Is that what you want?"

Aria did not try to pull away. To let Tarik suffer at Mako's hand... She shuddered at the thought. "No."

"Good. No more games." He pushed Aria to the ground. She landed with a small "oomph." "Tell me how many attack. Tell me their vulnerabilities. Tell me everything."

She could not, *would not*, sacrifice either Talon or Tarik. Aria ran a hand over her tangled hair, dipping her head and hiding the fear in her eyes.

"Do it now, Trancer. Choose between your son and those whom you do not even know."

She glanced at the door, but it remained closed. Tarik's life was in her hands as well as Talon's and his men's. She could not sacrifice any of them. She could not ask them to die. She could not ask them to kill.

Not if she refused to do the same.

The path opened before her. She would kill Mako. Not with a blade, but with her mind and a mental grip as tight as a gauntlet. Bile rose in her throat. She swallowed hard.

It was the ultimate betrayal to the Trancer oath, and if the act of taking a life did not kill her, her people would. Still, to save her family and her friends, she would do anything. Even become the very thing that her father accused her of being. A witch.

Crossing her legs in the Trancer position, she looked up at Mako. "I choose my son."

"I thought as much." A smug grin distorted his face.

His conceited smirk rankled, but it would be gone soon enough. She closed her eyes. *Forgive me my Goddess. Forgive me Talon. I never wanted it to come to this. I wanted better for us both.* She sent the plea to ride on the currents, using all her love, all her hope to force it along, before she gathered the darker forces within.

***

"I thought I told you Trancing was too dangerous."

Standing in the doorway, Talon could not take his gaze off Aria. Smudged, tangled, and very much alive, she was a vision to behold.

Aria opened her eyes, her surprise and relief obvious even in the dim torchlight. "Talon." Her voice carried across the room, breaking the spell of shock. In a flash, she rose and moved towards him.

She ran only a step before Mako's hand shot out and grabbed her by the hair, jerking her back. Just as fast, his other hand produced a knife to hold at her throat.

Sure that Mako preferred a live hostage to a dead Trancer, Talon waited for the Reaper's reaction as opposed to charging blindly forward. One did not attack when the advantage clearly belonged to the opposition. Instead, one waited for change, because with change came opportunity.

He did not have to wait long.

"Medea told me you had returned, but I must admit I thought she lied."

"Why?" Talon's eyes narrowed. "Did you think me a coward?" He slid a step closer to Mako. A step closer to Aria.

"No. I know your bravery. I never thought my own blood would be so foolish."

Talon stopped. Silence descended on the room. Of all the words Mako could have said, these were the ones he had prayed Aria would never hear.

"Your blood?" Aria repeated, her tone stunned.

Her question pierced Talon's heart like a blade.

The silence lengthened, growing in enormity, until Mako shattered it with a laugh. Head thrown back, he howled. "You did not tell her?" He laughed harder.

Despite all of his training, Talon faltered. Did Aria hate him, now that she knew the truth of his lineage? The thought cracked the armor around his heart. "How could I tell her that the Reaper Leader, the slaughterer of innocents, is my brother?"

Despite the knife at her throat, Aria slouched in Mako's arms.

The crack around Talon's heart widened into a gulf, exposing emotions he thought he had banished long ago. He inhaled sharply at the unfamiliar pain.

"Did you neglect to tell her you were a Reaper as well? A commander in my army?" Mako asked.

"Yes, he did." Aria answered for Talon. Her voice broke with a sob.

She no longer loved him. He saw it in her eyes and heard it in her silent accusation. Her love had seemed almost an inconvenience before. It made her do foolish things. Made her act in ways that brought her harm. Now, he would give his life to see that look in her eyes again. The armor shattered, releasing his raw emotions. Pain of loss washed over him, drowning him in its deep waters, dragging him under.

Talon staggered forward a step before righting himself. His pain could wait. Now, only one thing mattered. Saving Aria.

"Let her go." Talon raised his sword and pointed it towards his brother.

"And do what? Fight you?"

"Yes. Let us end this rivalry."

"Stand up, Trancer." Mako jerked Aria closer to him.

Slowly, she straightened. She said not a word, but her look of betrayal spoke volumes to Talon.

Forgive me. Did she hear his silent plea? Did she realize he did not dare say the words, not while she was in Mako's hands.

Mako broke the silence of the tableau. "A good leader knows when to fight, and a great one knows when to walk away." He moved the knife, letting the tip come to rest just below Aria's ear. "I am a great leader, and I will not fight you today, brother." He moved towards the door, using Aria as a shield as he passed Talon.

Talon followed their progress with his sword. A surge of fear swept through him. He could not let them leave. If Mako escaped and took Aria with him, the next time he saw her it would be with her throat cut. He took a step towards the pair.

His brother stopped in the doorway. He pressed the knife deeper into Aria's skin. A bead of blood slid down her pale flesh.

Talon flinched.

She pressed her lips tight, but did not cry out in either pain or fear. She was as brave as a Warrior, but he had never doubted her courage, only her experience. He could not let that courage die. Not because of him.

"Fight me." Talon dropped his sword a notch. "Or do you fear failure?"

Mako's face reddened. "I fear nothing."

"You fear this." Talon flipped his sword in his hand. "Or you would not hide behind a woman. Is that the kind of leader you are?"

Mako's color deepened, and Talon knew he had drawn first blood.

But Mako's flush of shame disappeared as quickly as it had come. "We both know you are the better swordsman. You can cast doubts on my leadership, but remember it is I who have the hostage. Not you." Mako jerked Aria's head back, exposing her throat. "If it is a fight you want, I agree, but I will spill her blood before mine stains the floor."

Talon circled his sword again, drawing Mako's attention. "Leave her out of this. She is nothing to you."

"You are right. To me, she is less than nothing. A tool to be used, but..." Mako's voice trailed off, and he stared at Talon, evaluating, searching, as if seeking a revelation. Suddenly, he lessened his hold on Aria, letting her pull her head upright. Jerking her around, he searched her face, and then spun her back until she faced away from him.

Mako smiled.

What does he see? Talon wondered, apprehensive at the grin that drew his brother's lips upwards.

Mako pulled Aria closer, until his head was just over her shoulder. "But I think, my brother, that she means something to you. Something more than just a Trancer."

Were his feelings that obvious? Talon shook his head, denying the accusation.

"Do not bother to deny it. I know you care for her. Just like I knew the Tower," Mako pulled Aria's hair aside and nuzzled her neck, always keeping his eye on Talon. "*Her* Tower, was important to you, as was the child."

Talon did not doubt his brother's claim. Growing up, Mako had always sensed things about him. When he lied. What frightened him. His brother had known—not as a Trancer or a Warrior would—but with an evil malevolence, he knew everything about Talon.

It was this knowledge that drove him to destroy all Talon held dear.

But the knowledge did not make his brother invincible. He would still pay. Pay for Aria's pain. Pay for the death of the Tower.

Pay for Tarik's death.

Mako ran his tongue up Aria's cheek.

Talon's hand tightened of its own volition, aching to slay the man who dared violate Aria. "Arm yourself. I would have your blood on my blade."

"Enough." Mako raised his head. "You came for her. Let me go, and I swear I will leave her alive."

His brother would never be so generous. "Now who lies?"

"You know me too well. I will not fight you, nor will I give her up." Mako laughed. "Unless, of course, you can make me a better offer."

A better offer? He did not want to fall into Mako's web of words but there was little choice other than to play along. "Such as?"

"Drop your sword and submit to me."

Surrender? "My life for hers?"

"Yes."

"How can I trust you?"

Mako lowered the knife, letting it come to rest against Aria's breast. "Do you have a choice?"

It was true. Mako held Aria, and Talon could not risk her life. He looked at his Given's face. She showed no fear. Only resignation. Did she expect to die? He had lied to her, misled her by not revealing his past. Now that she knew, did she think less of him? Did she think that since the blood of a killer ran in his veins that he was one as well?

That he would not give his blood for hers?

He flashed back to their first night together. The night they created a child. He had bled for her then, and he would do so now. He would die for her a thousand times, and it would never be enough.

It would never be enough to prove his love.

It hit him like a fist. Love. He loved Aria. Loved her more than life. More than death.

The choice was made.

He opened his fingers. His sword clattered to the floor.

"No!" Aria cried out and struggled in her captor's arms.

Perhaps after time had passed, she would forgive him his heritage and his deception. "Be still and soon you will be free," he told her

Mako grinned in satisfaction. "Kneel before me."

Talon took a deep breath. Only Aria mattered. His life was nothing. "Let her go."

"First, kneel."

His brother was a ruthless egomaniac, and he held Aria. Talon knelt on the cold stone and prayed he had made the right choice and Mako would let Aria go in favor of a more entertaining target. *Please, Goddess, let her live.*

He raised his eyes.

Mako smiled. "You always were a fool." Pushing Aria away, he raised his knife, readying it to plunge it into her back.

Time slowed, crawled to a standstill, as Talon pulled a knife from his other boot and rose to his feet. The hilt was hot and shiny in his palm.

Mako's knife reached its arc.

Talon poised his hand to throw the blade. It never left his fingers.

Mako's knife never completed its descent.

Instead, a shout of pain rent the air as his brother arched backwards, clawing at his back like a drowning man clawed for the water's surface.

Aria ran into Talon's arms.

Mako's shouts stopped. His eyes rolled upwards, and he fell forward, face down onto the stone floor with a knife in his back.

Medea.

She stood in the doorway, her hands red with Mako's blood. Reaching down, she pulled the knife from her lover's back and wiped the red-stained blade on her dress. She smiled at Talon and Aria, her expression as virtuous. "Nobody leaves me."

Knife in hand, she walked way, padding barefoot down the hall.

Aria lifted her face to Talon. Her eyes were black, dilated. Shocked.

Talon pulled her back against him and stroked her hair. Neither spoke. It was over. Mako was dead. His brother was dead, and Aria lived.

He should be happy.

He was not. He closed his eyes as tears, unfamiliar and hot, flooded them. He remembered Mako, young and hopeful, giving him part of his bread and telling Talon that one day they would be great men. Men of stature. Men of honor.

That was what he missed. That boy. His brother.

That and Aria's love.

He kissed the top of her head. At least she lived. He could ask the Goddess for no more than that, except forgiveness.

"Talon?"

A warm hand tenderly touched his cheek. He opened his eyes. "Aria." She stood before him, her hair awry and clothes torn. She was the most beautiful woman in the world, and he had lost her.

"I am sorry."

"So am I."

The sadness in her voice tore at his soul more than a blade ever could, but he could think of nothing else to say. He wished she would scream at him, beat him. Anything, other than hate him. He could not look at her. He did not deserve to. His blood was the blood that killed. In his heart beat a clan of killers.

She touched his other cheek. "I am sorry good men died to free me. I am sorry your brother died. But most of all, I am sorry you did not trust me enough to tell me the truth about your past. Did you think I would not understand?"

The truth. It was all she had wanted, and she deserved no less. "I wanted to protect you. Protect myself."

"From what?"

He brushed her cheek with his hand, praying it would not be the last time he felt her skin against his. "From the look in your eyes when you realized that Mako and I are of the same blood. The disgust you would feel when you found out you had given your body to the enemy.

Her eyes filled with tears. He caught one with his fingertip. "From the tears you would shed when you saw how much the enemy loved you."

She caught his hand. "You are not your brother. You are not the enemy. If you were, then I would love my enemy until the day I drew last breath."

He stared at her, stunned. After all he had done. After all the lies. She still loved him. He whispered a prayer to the Goddess, thanking her for her bounty. He did not deserve Aria. He caught another tear and brought it to his lips. "I will try to be worthy of you."

"Be my mate. Be the father to my children. Be my lover. That is all I want. All I ask."

A father. It was the only hole left in his heart. As much as he wanted another child, it could never take Tarik's place. "A father? Perhaps we shall soon be blessed."

"Sooner than you think," a voice said from the back of the room, interrupting them.

It was a young girl with short black hair.

"Talon, I would like you to meet Iliana," Aria said with a smile.

Iliana? If she was alive ...

Aria took a bundle from Iliana's arms "And Tarik, your son," she said, placing the bundle in his arms.

His son? He pulled the blanket back and saw a babe with pale green eyes—the same color as Aria's when they first met. *Tarik*. It was true. His son lived!

The unfamiliar tears threatened again, then spilled. The bundle wiggled in his arms, and he drew the tiny life against his chest, terrified he would drop the child.

He looked up through his tears to see Aria grinning from ear to ear. "I told you he was alive."

Talon pulled her close. "I will never doubt you again."

He kissed her, thanking the Goddess for bringing Aria

to him. More than a Given, she had become a Giver, bringing him everything he could ever want. A son. A family.

And love.

Epilogue

"May you find peace with the Goddess and a home in her eternal garden." Aria knelt at the foot of the unmarked grave and blew out the candles she had lit earlier—a symbol of the life that had been extinguished. Gaur's request to send his friend to the afterlife with the proper rituals was done. She rose to her feet, leaving the candles behind.

They had been lit too many times, and she was tired of the smell of death.

"I see you found him."

She whirled about. Talon stood behind her with Tarik in his arms. Tenderly, he bent his head, kissing the babe's shock of black hair. When she was heavy with Tarik, she had dreamt that Talon would be a good father. The reality was far better than any dream. Since recovering his son, Talon carried him everywhere.

She gave Talon an impish grin and held out her arms. "If he is heavy, I would be more than happy to hold him."

Talon raised a dark eyebrow. "You had him already. It is my turn."

Aria laughed. "He was inside. It was not as if I could touch him."

"No, but you felt his movement. His growth as he readied to enter the world." Talon held his hand out to her, and she took it. He pulled her close, moving Tarik to one side. "Beloved, have I told you I am sorry?"

She let her arm slide up his back. "For what?"

"For missing our son's birth. For letting my brother take him? For not believing you and listening to my own hatred instead?"

She stroked Talon's face with her other hand, letting her fingertips wander over his lips until she cupped his cheek in her palm. "You told me in many ways. Every time you ached and angered for Tarik's loss. When you dropped your sword to save my life. All that you did told me what your voice could not. Your actions spoke louder. They always will."

Holding the baby with one arm, Talon cupped her cheek in his massive palm, and she leaned into the warmth. "Then I hope my actions now will please you."

"What do you mean?"

"I want to stay here, Aria. This region needs a Warrior's guild, and some of the rebels want to train. Lore and the men who followed are unhappy with the Council's actions. They would stay as well."

It was a good decision. Talon was a leader. A man of action. The Council of Seven would never accept him, and he could not accept them, either. This was the best choice.

If only her path were as clear.

Talon's voice broke her thoughts. "I want you to stay with me."

Stay? A Trancer in a Warrior's guild? It was a novel thought. Would they want her, knowing what she had almost done? "Talon, before I answer, there is something you should know."

He raised a dark brow. "This sounds grave."

"It is. When Mako had me, before you arrived, I almost did the unthinkable." She stopped, the telling too hard. Would he see her as the witch her father claimed her to be? If fear clouded his eyes, it would be unbearable.

"Which is?" Talon encouraged her.

She took a deep breath. "Before you came, I was going to kill Mako. Kill him with a thought. Let the forces within myself destroy his mind since my hand could not."

No answer. He simply stared at her, his face expressionless as he absorbed her words.

Aria turned away. It was over, her worst fears realized. She blinked, trying to stop the sudden tears.

A strong hand turned her back around. "Was it an easy decision?"

She shook her head.

"Did you do it to save yourself?"

"No," she replied, shocked that he would think such a thing. "For Tarik. For you and the men."

He smiled. "Aria, you have the honor of a Warrior. I know that, and so do my men. We would never doubt your decision. Stay with me. Stay with us."

"Will they accept me?" She stepped back from his embrace. "If I stay, they must accept me as both Trancer and woman." Talon was one of few who accepted all aspects of her. Her family had loved only the girl, and a Tower would never accept her as Talon's mate. Were these Warriors more open-minded, or would she have to fight for this as well? She wrapped her arms across her chest. She was tired of fighting.

"The men see the honor within," Talon assured her. "They would have it no other way, and neither would I."

"What of Iliana?" Her friend could not go back to her previous life. Since Mako's death, she barely spoke and preferred to stare at the wall in the makeshift infirmary. Her silence frightened Aria. Was Iliana's spirit broken or simply wounded? She could not tell, could not break past the barrier that Iliana erected in her mind. As for her friend's Trancing skills, Aria did not know if they would ever return.

"She can stay as well. The men worry for her like they would a sister or daughter. They take turns trying to make her laugh, but she ignores them."

Aria nodded in understanding. Iliana ignored her as well, doing anything to avoid eye contact. They had been so close once. Would they ever have that again?

Talon continued. "Lore tries to coax her to eat. This morning she responded by screaming at him to go away and threw the bowl at his head."

It was a step. "Give him my thanks."

"Why not tell him yourself?" Talon reached out and pulled Aria back into his arms. "You have not given me an answer, beloved. Will you stay with me? It is not a Tower, but I will do everything in my power to make you happy. All you ever have to do is—"

"Hush." Aria cut him off with a finger against his lips. She gave a small shake of her head. Make her happy? Each day alive was a blessing. Each moment in Talon's arms was a joy. Each time she saw him with his son was a reason to sing aloud.

If she were any happier, she would split in two for one person could not contain any more.

She removed her finger from his mouth and replaced it with her lips, taking a moment to savor the heat between them. "I will stay with you until my last breath, but first, I want something only you can give me."

"Anything," Talon breathed, his lips inches from hers.

"You hold my heart, my life, and my soul at your command."

She smiled. "I want a daughter."

He smiled back. "Just one?"

Don't Miss
Sharron McClellan's
Sequel to *The Given*

The Seeker

Coming in 2004
from
ImaJinn Books

Contact us at:
www.imajinnbooks.com
Toll Free: 877-625-3592